Rock is dead. Punk is dead. Everything's dead.

Hollow-eyed girls and empty-headed boys drifting through neon constellations. Hipster ghosts haunting black-light dance clubs.

Nobody knew where they'd come from, but like dragons and angels, the Witches' Carnival tapped deep into myth and appeared in every culture. They were the Council of Spirits in China and the Wandering Lords of the Hindu Vedas. Homer wrote about the Lotus-Eaters, Shakespeare about Oberon and his court, and Jung explained the trickster archetype. According to what legends you believed, they might have invented tarot cards or could turn themselves into foxes.

A band of gypsies tramped across the earth, sweeping the bonds and boundaries of the modern world away with a brush of a hand. Nobody knew where they came from. Nobody knew where they'd turn up, but the Witches' Carnival was always headed somewhere. They moved on the edge of your vision and melted away like fog the moment you turned to look.

Other Simon Pulse books you may enjoy

Tithe
Holly Black

Rx
Tracy Lynn

Street Pharm
Allison van Diepen

Uglies trilogy
Scott Westerfeld

TRIPPING to SOMEWHERE

Kristopher Reisz

Simon Pulse

New York | London | Toronto | Sydney

SIMON PULSE
An imprint of Simon & Schuster Children's Publishing Division
1230 Avenue of the Americas, New York, NY 10020
Copyright © 2006 by Kristopher Reisz
All rights reserved, including the right of
reproduction in whole or in part in any form.
SIMON PULSE and colophon
are registered trademarks of Simon & Schuster, Inc.
Designed by Steve Kennedy
The text of this book was set in Nofret.
Manufactured in the United States of America
First Simon Pulse edition October 2006
2 4 6 8 10 9 7 5 3 1
Library of Congress Control Number 2006924281
ISBN-13: 978-1-4169-4000-5
ISBN-10: 1-4169-4000-6

The crow fluttered off Meek's arm and landed on the counter. Both girls jerked back. Talons scratching across glass, the bird regarded them for a few seconds.

"You want to go home," Meek answered.

Sam smirked. "Not quite. Actually, I'm–"

"I know what you want too, honey." He turned toward Gilly.

"What's that?" She wanted him to leave. His eye, like a dead fish's, grossed her out. It made her squirm when he called her "honey."

"You'd burn the world down to become beautiful, wouldn't you?"

"What the hell?" Sam stared at him. "You're walking around telling people who's beautiful and not? You don't have any fucking teeth, crackhead."

Meek shrugged. "There's a difference between pretty and beautiful."

The comment made Gilly smile despite herself. She glimpsed someone new beneath the desperation and the tobacco-stained whiskers, someone who'd been charming once, someone poetic.

"Whatever," Sam said. "Look, if it was my store, I'd let you have the cigarettes, but it's not. So–"

"I'll pay," Gilly said.

"What?"

Pulling a five-dollar bill out of her pocket, Gilly offered it to Sam. "I'll pay for the cigarettes."

"You know that guy?" Gilly's little sister Caitlin asked after their dad came back inside.

"Oh, yeah. Meek's been a legend since before I joined the force."

"What's he a legend for?"

"Says strange stuff sometimes," he said through a mouth full of biscuit. When Caitlin pressed him on what that meant, he shook his head and shrugged. "Just strange stuff. Stuff that gets in people's heads."

Now, as Meek entered the Texaco and approached the counter, Gilly noticed the milky blue cataract eclipsing his left eyeball. He said hello in a soft mumble and asked Sam for a pack of Marlboros. She rang him up, stabbing at the cash register keys with one careful finger. Gilly kept quiet, watching the crow watch her.

"That'll be four eighty-six, please," Sam said.

The old man made a show of patting his pockets. He shook his head. "I'm sorry. I don't have any money."

"Well . . . I can't really let you have the cigarettes, then," Sam said. "Sorry."

"Suppose I gave you something better than money?"

Sam scowled at him. "Like what?"

"Well?" Meek looked down at his pet bird. "What does she want?"

Gilly glanced at Sam, then at the silent alarm button underneath the counter. Sam just tried not to laugh. "Look, man—"

talked, she straightened the rack of charm necklaces sitting on the counter, separating the pot leaves from the Grateful Dead bears.

"You did not."

"Hell, yeah, I did. That mother–"

Both girls looked up when the electronic door chime sounded. The homeless man walked into the store trailing the smell of something gone sour. His skin was burnished brown like antique wood, stretched thin across knuckles and the knots of his collarbone. A tamed crow, sleek blue-black, nestled in the crook of his arm.

His name was Meek. Gilly had seen him panhandling around Birmingham before but only once up close.

After church one Sunday, her family had stopped at McDonald's for breakfast. Meek had been there, the crow perched on top of his battered rucksack. He wanted to get some food but only had a handful of change. The manager kept telling him to go, saying he couldn't be there with the bird, anyway.

As Gilly's family walked in, the homeless man turned and smiled at her dad.

"'Morning, Officer Stahl."

"Hey, Meek."

Her dad stepped into the argument and calmed the manager down. He wound up buying Meek an Egg McMuffin and a cup of coffee while the old man waited on the sidewalk.

oNE

It was after ten on a nothing-better-to-do Thursday night. Hanging out at the gas station, Gilly sipped a Diet Coke and listened to Sam recount the three-way battle she'd gotten into with her mom and stepdad.

Sam crashed on her brother Josh's couch a lot, escaping the ground-glass angers at her own house. She had a key, but Josh's roommate was a thug-wannabe full of crude words and wormy stares. Sam didn't trust him alone, so she went to the Texaco where Josh worked and waited for him to get off at midnight. If she called, Gilly always came up to keep her company.

"Okay, so you pin it up there, and your mom sees it first, right?" Gilly asked, trying to get the details straight.

"Pinned nothing. I glued it up there." Josh had stepped out back to smoke a cigarette, leaving Sam in charge. As she

Acknowledgments

This is a story about a road so long no one can get to the end of it by themselves. There are lots of roads like this, and these are some of the people who've helped me along mine. Without their generosity and faith, I would never have made it as far as I have.

I owe more than I could ever repay to my parents, Jim and Denise Reisz, for their love and boundless support. I can't imagine who I'd be without them.

Thanks to my wonderful agent, Nancy Coffey, for her advice and encouragement; to my editor, Michelle Nagler, for her insight; and to my old boss Rebecca Pratt for her trust and kindness.

Friends are the people who believe in you even when you've stopped believing in yourself. Thank you Scott Oden, Edna Kaiser, Josh Olive, and Wayne and Tanja Miller.

Finally, I have had amazing teachers who've opened worlds to me. Thank you Linda Burns; Steve Calatrello; Dr. Randy Cross; Dr. Harry Moore, who taught me *Doctor Faustus*; Jill Chadwick; Dr. Sheila Byrd; and Leigh Ann Rhea.

For Chad, a friend when I needed one

Sam glared at her and took the money, handing Gilly fourteen cents change.

"Thank you." The cigarettes vanished into the pocket of Meek's ratty coat.

"So, now what?" Sam asked. "You read her palm or something?"

He scooped the crow off the counter, cooing to it. "Aruspicy's better," he whispered.

"Huh?"

"Reading the entrails of an animal sacrifice."

"Huh?" Sam looked at the bird in his hands, then jumped back, smashing into a rack of cigars and rolling papers. "Whoa! No!"

Hollow bones cracked and popped. The crow screeched. One free wing flapped madly. With steady, calloused hands, Meek tore the bird in two.

"You motherfucking psycho! Get the hell out. What the fuck's wrong with you?"

Kool-Aid–bright blood pattered to the floor. It ran down his wrists and stained his fingers slippery black. Intestines and tea-colored organs dangled from the crow's body. Meek dropped the halves of the bird onto the counter and began poking through its guts.

Sam's shouting brought Josh charging out of the back. "Hey, motherfucker. Hey!" Grabbing Sam, he jerked her away from Meek, putting himself between his little sister and the old man.

Meek stirred the crow's guts with his fingers, ignoring the brother-and-sister torrent raging on the other side of the counter. Gilly stood silent against the wall. She stared at the dead bird. Its polished obsidian eyes still watched her.

Meek looked up. "The Witches' Carnival is stopping in Atlanta tonight."

"Get out. Get the fuck out now!" Rounding the counter, Josh snatched Meek by the shoulder of his tattered coat as Meek snatched the torn-apart crow off the counter.

"Yeah! Take your fucking bird with you," Sam yelled after him.

Josh almost had him out the door when Meek raised the mass of feathers, bones, and guts to his lips. He kissed them. The bird cawed sharp and angry. It beat its wings. Gilly and Sam both screamed as the crow fluttered up to perch on his shoulder.

Meek turned toward Gilly. His blind eye seemed to pierce her chest. "Run fast. Leave everything behind. And you can catch them." Stepping around Josh, he shuffled off into the night.

The episode left Gilly so rattled, her hands shook for an hour. She'd been certain Josh would murder Meek. They helped Josh clean crow's blood off the counter and killed another hour until the third-shift girl showed up.

After Melissa finally arrived, Josh started his final check

of the store. Gilly and Sam told Melissa about Meek, his crow, and the Witches' Carnival.

Melissa snorted. "My cousin has sworn for twenty years that he met the Witches' Carnival down in New Orleans once."

"You think he really did?" Sam asked.

"'Course not. He just drinks too much."

Gilly started for home around twelve thirty, the only person on the highway. The image of Meek's eye, the color of a gathering storm, floated through her brain and made her skin crawl. She tried to figure out how he'd made tearing up the crow look so realistic. All three of them had been fooled. She turned up the stereo to keep from falling asleep. Her thoughts drifted toward the Witches' Carnival.

Rock is dead. Punk is dead. Everything's dead.

Hollow-eyed girls and empty-headed boys drifting through neon constellations. Hipster ghosts haunting black-light dance clubs.

They were in New York before that. There's always something ready to explode in New York. And the San Francisco thing before that, dirty feet and grotty acid rock. They skipped out before it went sour.

And before that, howling nights in Mexico City. Smoke-filled jazz clubs in Paris before that, getting drunk and stoned with black GIs who never bothered going home.

Before that, the Great War plunged Europe into darkness, lamp by lamp. But titles and peers held galas beneath twinkling chandelier light, certain the trouble would be over by Christmas.

Before that, Vienna. Before that, London and Berlin. Before that, Renaissance Italy maybe, or Beijing's Forbidden City or the music halls of the Ottoman Turks.

Nobody knew where they'd come from, but like dragons and angels, the Witches' Carnival tapped deep into myth and appeared in every culture. They were the Council of Spirits in China and the Wandering Lords of the Hindu Vedas. Homer wrote about the Lotus-Eaters, Shakespeare about Oberon and his court, and Jung explained the trickster archetype. According to what legends you believed, they might have invented tarot cards or could turn themselves into foxes.

Nobody knew where they'd come from, but they'd been everywhere, climbing the Jacob's ladder of man's history. They'd borne witness to autumn decrees and October days during the French Revolution and had a lovely picnic on a grassy knoll in Dallas.

A band of gypsies tramped across the earth, sweeping the bonds and boundaries of the modern world away with a brush of a hand. Nobody knew where they came from. Nobody knew where they'd turn up, but the Witches' Carnival was always headed somewhere. They moved on the edge of your vision and melted away like fog the moment you turned to look.

Gilly pulled into her driveway two hours past curfew. She knew she was in trouble and hardened herself to face it. Pushing open the door, she saw her dad sitting on the couch. Gilly didn't look at him. Keeping her eyes forward, she walked through the living room and down the hall.

Her dad followed her into her bedroom without a word. As Gilly flipped on the light, he held out his hand.

"Give me your keys."

Gilly handed him her key chain. It vanished into his pocket.

"When you learn to mind the rules, you can drive again," he said. "Until then, I'm keeping these."

"Fine." Gilly stared at her bed, the blanket twisted and kicked to the floor. Her dad stood behind her for several seconds. Gilly tried not to say anything else. She wanted him to think she didn't care. But as he started to leave, it snuck out. Gilly couldn't stop it.

"We weren't doing anything."

Andy Stahl turned on his heel. "I don't want to know what you were doing, Gilly. It doesn't matter. You're supposed to be home by eleven o'clock. Why can't you manage that?"

Because Sam was upset and needed someone to talk to. Because there were things she could tell Sam that her dad never heard. Because she was hanging out at a gas station, not in the projects buying crack.

"Okay, Dad."

"No, it's not okay," he said. Gilly hated when he did that. "I can't figure out how come you're the only person on Earth who doesn't have to follow the rules. I can't figure out how you got so lucky."

"I'm not." If she had kept her mouth shut, he'd be gone by now.

"That's right, you're not." He jingled the keys in his pocket. "And when you think you can be home when you're supposed to be, you can ask for these back."

Gilly still refused to look at him. "Fine. Whatever."

Her dad left, shutting the door behind him.

Afterward, Gilly couldn't lie down. She paced her room for an hour, yelling at her dad in a voice barely above a whisper. She jabbed a finger at her reflection in the mirror and said all the things she wished she'd said while he was there.

She told her dad that she'd been helping a friend. She didn't care if he punished her; she'd do it again tomorrow if she had to. She told him she was gay, and if he was going to freak out about it, fine, but at least he could admit he was freaked out. Gilly told him that she loved him, and how much she wished that could still be as simple as it had been when she'd been little. Gilly found herself standing by her window, looking at the road running in front of her house. It connected to the parkway. Take Interstate 20, and Atlanta was three hours away. If Gilly left now, she could get there by sunrise.

The Witches' Carnival was the name and shape given to every fantasy of running away and leaving it all behind. It was the fantasy of the open road, the fantasy of motion and speed until all your problems became a blur. But most importantly, it was a fantasy.

Gilly let the venetian blinds drop over the window. Undressing, she flipped off the lights and went to bed. The Witches' Carnival wasn't real. That couldn't stop dreams, glittering like sunlight across water, from closing around her as she drifted down to sleep.

The red-faced bluster of morning talk shows spilled out of the car's stereo. Gilly sat in the front seat beside her dad. As they neared the school, Gilly turned toward the student parking lot, searching for Sam.

Sam sat on the hood of her Civic. Colby was beside her, his arm around Sam's waist and one foot on the car's bumper. Alex and Dawn stood hugging belly-to-back. Everyone watched Sam. Forming her hands into a circle, she yanked them apart. Alex laughed. Dawn clapped a hand over her mouth and started walking away.

Sam wore her long-sleeved black shirt. She had on the jeans with the frayed cuffs. Through the car window, Gilly watched Sam brush strands of dark hair out of her eyes, tucking them behind her ear. She turned toward something Colby said and smiled.

Gilly felt her dad glaring at her. She dropped her gaze to her sneakers. "She's just a friend, Dad."

Andy Stahl pulled to the curb and didn't answer. "Me or your mom'll pick you up at three."

"I'll get a ride."

"Yeah. With me or your mom."

Curling her lip into a practiced sneer, Gilly climbed out and slammed the door. Pulling the hood of her sweatshirt up, adjusting the straps of her backpack, Gilly dragged her feet along the sidewalk until her dad was out of sight. Once his car had rounded the corner, she loped across the parking lot toward her friends.

". . . and Josh is just—hey, G."

"What's up?"

"Where's your car?" Dawn asked.

"Dad took it away for staying out too late."

"That sucks. How long?"

"I don't know. Until he stops being an asshole."

Sam grabbed Gilly's arm hard enough to hurt. "What the hell was that last night?"

Gilly shook her head and laughed. "Some fucked-up shit. That's all I know."

Hugging herself against the steel-gray weather, Gilly listened to Sam tell the story. Sam told stories with a dry intensity. She never edited her own embarrassing moments. If anything, she exaggerated them for comic effect. She even did decent impersonations of Josh and Meek.

Once she'd finished, Dawn said she'd seen a magician do a trick like that on TV. She figured Meek had killed one crow and had another hidden somewhere. Colby asked where a homeless guy bought crows in bulk. His guess was that Meek had trained the crow to lie limp, then splattered chicken guts around to make it look like he'd killed it.

"He didn't just kill it," Sam said. "He ripped the thing in fucking half."

"That's just what you think you saw. It's power-of-suggestion stuff."

The seven forty-five bell rang. Alex and Dawn said good-bye and hustled off for class. Sam looked at Colby, her fingers twining with his. "Hey, I need to talk to Gilly for a second, okay?"

"What about?"

"Nothing big." She kissed him. "I'll see you in Mrs. Badford's class, okay?"

"You won't even tell me what it's about?"

"Shit." Sam jumped off the hood of the car. Taking Gilly's wrist, she pulled her into the bright, chattering stream of people pouring through the school's main entrance.

Inside, students and gossip flowed down every hall. Lockers clanged. Sneakers squeaked across the green-specked tile. A cluster of boys near the Coke machines burst into thick laughter.

Sam leaned close, her warm breath brushing Gilly's cheek. "I'm going to go look for them."

"Who? The Witches' Carnival?"

"Wanna come?"

"Sam, he's just some sick fuck homeless guy. He pulled the whole thing out of his ass." They stopped at Gilly's locker. She started dialing the combination.

"Did that look like chicken guts to you?" Sam asked.

"No, but . . ." Gilly pulled her algebra book out and shut her locker. They started down the hall again. "The Witches' Carnival is a fairy tale."

"Maybe."

"C'mon. If they're real and Meek knows where they are, why's he hanging around Birmingham doing magic tricks for cigarettes?"

"I don't know. He's a sick fuck homeless guy. They march to a different drummer."

Gilly looked at Sam. "You're thinking about going. Seriously?"

"I'm not thinking, I'm going."

"When?"

"Today. Now. I only came to school to see if you wanted to come with me."

The second bell rang. The hallway clamor rose, footsteps scattering off to class. Gilly and Sam stood motionless.

"What about school?"

"Fuck school."

"What about Colby?"

"Fuck him. There's no way he'd go. Probably whine. I'm not even telling him."

"Sam, it's not real."

"I don't give a fuck." She plucked at the strand of Mardi Gras beads wrapped around her wrist. "One way or another, I'm leaving. I'm sick of living in the same house as Greg. I'm sick of spending every night at Josh's place."

Gilly chewed her lip. "Yeah." It was a sound to fill the quiet, meaning nothing.

"So come with me."

"I can't."

"Why?"

"Because . . ." Gilly didn't have an answer.

"Miss Grace, Miss Stahl, the bell's already rung."

They glanced up. The hall was nearly empty. Mrs. Schiff, Gilly's homeroom teacher, stood beside her door smiling a tight, unfriendly smile.

Sam and Gilly looked back at each other.

"You got until the end of first period," Sam said. "Then I'm outta here whether you're with me or not." With that, she started down the hall.

"Sam, c'mon."

Sam turned, walking backward and grinning a wicked,

sharp-cornered smile. "Remember, G, if you ain't pretty, start trouble." Turning back around, she hurried to class.

"Miss Stahl, do you plan on coming to class today?" Mrs. Schiff asked.

Simplify the following exponential expression. Remember to write it so each base is written one time with one positive exponent.

$$\frac{(24 \times 3)(x - 5)}{(6x - 20)}$$

Gilly stared at her textbook, the page covered with numbers and symbols. She only had hazy ideas what any of them meant. Mrs. Schiff stood by the overhead projector and went on about integer exponents. The classroom's stuffy heat made Gilly's scalp itch. She ran her fingers through her hair, dyed a violent shade of red, and wiped a damp palm on her pant leg. She glanced at the clock, then her watch, then outside at the rows of cars filling the parking lot.

Gilly knew Sam didn't believe in the Witches' Carnival. Nobody did anymore, not really. But it was too wonderful a story to let go of completely. Sam wanted to believe in somewhere she could escape to, some real home far away from the peeling-paint split-level she shared with her mom and stepdad. She wanted to believe in it so bad, she'd fooled herself into trusting a rambling, half-mad crackhead.

The bell rang. There was a clatter of voices and chairs scraping across the floor. Gilly joined the rest of the class streaming into the corridor's din. Lockers were jerked open and banged shut. Kevin Carney bolted past her with two of his friends after him.

Gilly walked with her head down, trying to figure out what to do. She had photography next period in Mr. Byrne's room on the second floor. Instead of heading up the stairs, though, she found herself walking past them. The hallway ended in a steel door with wire mesh over the window. She stood and watched the student parking lot. Sam appeared a few seconds later, cutting between the cars toward her Civic.

She was really going.

Gilly thought about her dad taking her keys away for nothing. She thought about how miserable school was going to be without Sam around. She couldn't make herself believe in the Witches' Carnival, but Gilly imagined climbing out of days like a labyrinth and breathing fresh air for a while. The door swung open. Gilly heard the soles of her sneakers beat against the asphalt. A mean October wind scoured her face.

Sam had already ducked into her car. She saw Gilly and unlocked the passenger side door.

"All right. I'm going," Gilly panted, collapsing into the seat. "What the hell, I'm going with you."

"Fucking bitch." Sam punched her in the shoulder, then

cranked the engine. "Why'd you act like that in the hall? I almost thought you really weren't coming."

"Sorry. You sprung it on me so all of a sudden, I was kind of stunned."

Steering around the wooden barrier guarding the parking lot's entrance, Sam slung out onto the street. Two wheels popped the curb, and the car's chassis jolted against the pavement.

Winter-bare trees lined the curving road leading away from school. Gilly watched them pass for a few seconds before speaking up. "Hey. Let's stop by my house on the way."

"What for?"

"Money."

"Cool. How much you got?"

"I'm broke, but you know my dad's a cop, right?"

"Yeah."

Gilly took a deep breath. She was already in trouble, she might as well enjoy it. "Did you know he's crooked?"

Two

Gilly didn't remember Operation Desert Storm ending. She'd been too young to understand the speeches or bus-loads of homecoming troops that played on the news for weeks. She didn't know about the flags and yellow ribbons that had turned a country into a family. What Gilly remem-bered, like shadows flitting along the bottom of a deep pond, was watching her dad put on his dress blues.

They stood alone in the early morning still. He talked in a happy, half-asleep voice, asking if she was excited about the parade and if she was going to wave to him when he passed. Gilly helped him button the polished gold buttons of his uniform. She remembered being very proud of that, telling her grandma that she'd helped.

Her dad had joined the Birmingham metro police after

getting out of the marines. When Gilly was nine, dressed in a church dress and white panty hose, she'd applauded as he took an oath of office and received his detective's shield. When she'd been thirteen, Gilly had walked into her parents' bedroom and found him stuffing something into a steel ammo box.

"Shit!" He slammed the lid shut, fumbling with the latch and screaming at her to get out. When Gilly stalked off, her dad came rushing after her.

"I'm sorry. I didn't mean to yell." Kneeling down, he stroked her hair. "Listen, I was hiding your mom's birthday present, okay? So you can't tell her about this, okay?"

Gilly promised she wouldn't. Her dad hugged her and whispered, "That's my girl. I'm sorry, baby."

But sweat glistened across his scalp and he smiled too much. Gilly knew he was lying.

A week later, both her parents worked late. Gilly left her little sister watching TV and crept down the hall. After ten minutes of digging through drawers and in the closet, she found the ammo box under the sink in her parents' bathroom.

Bundles lay inside wrapped in black plastic and masking tape. In true Marine Corps style, her dad had made each one neat and square with sharp corners. She knew what they were, but Gilly picked one up and peeled back the tape, anyway.

Four years later, Gilly remembered the musty scent of old bills. She could still feel the heft of that small brick of twenties resting in her hand.

Staring at it, fear had squeezed Gilly's chest. It didn't immediately connect that her dad had done something wrong, only that he might catch her. Shoving the money back into the box, Gilly fixed everything like she'd found it.

For four years, she kept her promise and never breathed a word.

Sam crunched up the gravel driveway, pulling in behind Gilly's red Tercel.

"Sure you want to do this?"

"He stole it first. How come he's the only person on Earth who doesn't have to follow the rules?" Gilly climbed out of the car. "Just relax."

Fall had turned the yard into dead grass and patches of hard dirt. The neighborhood dozed. Houses, porch swings, and cars in driveways sat motionless. Only the wind was awake, trembling through the branches with slow, chilly breaths.

Slipping her hand into her pocket, Gilly stopped dead. Her dad still had her keys. She tried the doorknob, but it was locked.

All at once, the wild adventure hit concrete. There was nowhere to go except back to school. They'd get in-school suspension for skipping class, and it'd be just another day, a little weirder than most.

Remember that time we almost ran away to Atlanta?

"Fuck it." Gilly kicked in one of the windows. Blue–white droplets of glass splashed across the living room carpet. The sound hit her like ice water, breathless shock, and then a giddy, giggling warmth swimming under her skin.

Gilly started laughing and kicked twice more, clearing out the window frame. It felt great. Grinning at Sam, she struck a bodybuilder pose, then ducked through.

Gilly ran down the hall, past her own closed bedroom door and into her parents' room. Yellow sunlight and rice–paper shadow lay across everything. She slipped into the grimy bathroom and opened the cabinet under the sink. A can of scrubbing powder hit the floor as she reached deep inside and grabbed the ammo box.

A relic from her dad's military career, or maybe just something he'd picked up at a yard sale, the box was olive drab and afflicted with rust. Gilly snapped the latch open to make sure it wasn't full of old tax returns or copies of *Playboy*. It wasn't. The nest egg had grown over the years. Gilly didn't know, but she guessed there were ten or fifteen thousand dollars inside.

Staring at crisply wrapped sheaves of money, Gilly felt the full weight of what she was doing. Her stomach twisted into a tight knot of muscle. Fumbling the lid shut, she picked up the box and turned to bolt. Suddenly she stopped. Gilly dug her cell phone out of her pocket and placed it in the bathroom cabinet where the money had been.

Gilly ran back through the house. The furniture, the pictures on the walls, all of it looked alien. She'd become an intruder. She didn't belong here anymore.

"Gilly!"

Gilly let out a startled yell at the sound of her name and whirled around.

"It's just me. Relax." Sam stood in the kitchen. She held up a bottle of Jose Cuervo she'd gotten from the cabinet over the stove. "Since you're stealing that money, anyway, it's no big deal if we take some liquor too, right?"

Gilly's heart thudded against her breastbone. "Whatever. Let's go." Heading for the front door, she heard the clink of more glass bottles being pulled out of the cabinet. "Fuck, Sam. Let's go."

"I'm coming. Hey, where's your dad keep his gun?"

Gilly had her hand on the doorknob. She snapped around again. "What? What do you need a gun for?"

Sam shrugged. "Bears?"

Without answering, Gilly unlocked the door and crossed the dead grass. Sam followed close behind. In the car, Sam dumped everything out of her backpack and hid bottles of tequila, vodka, and spiced rum inside. Gilly's eyes darted around the quiet street. She hissed, "Fuck, fuck, fuck . . . ," under her breath.

"Relax, G." Sam straightened up in her seat.

"I'm fucking relaxed. Let's go!"

Sam whipped out of the driveway, spraying gravel. She pushed the gas. The engine growled. Gilly turned to watch her home shrink away over her shoulder.

Two hours ago, she'd been joking with her friends before school like she did every morning. She was pissed at her dad for taking her car away. She had English homework that needed to get done during lunch. Now she was driving to Atlanta with ten grand in stolen cash and Sam.

Gilly couldn't get a deep breath. It was the same tangle of fear and excitement she felt creeping up that first immense hill of a roller coaster.

We can go back. Tell Sam to turn around, hide the money again, go back to school, and it'll be like nothing happened.

Then Sam turned the corner. Gilly's house vanished. She felt momentum snatch them forward. They couldn't stop now if they wanted to. Glancing at her, Sam grinned. Gilly grinned back.

"Running out of time! We're running hot. Running out of time. We're running hot."

Not bothering to keep the song's rhythm, Sam and Gilly sang as loud as they could, drowning out the stereo. "Fever's up to a hundred and one. Brain's near oblivion. Let's go have some fun. Raise hell and a back beat!"

Mack trucks lumbered under their cargo like pack animals, stirring grit and gas fumes into the cold air. SAABs, Malibus, and pickup trucks flashed orange in the morning sun.

"Running out of time! We're running hot!"

Gilly slouched in the passenger seat, beating her sneaker against the dashboard and watching the plain gray earth roll past. She glanced up at the billboards for Burger King and car dealerships that lined Interstate 20.

"Sorta, kinda feels like flying. Or maybe we're just falling. Who cares—we're hauling. Raise hell and a back beat."

Pulpy, scraped-raw guitar chords came faster and faster as the lyrics collapsed into unhinged shrieking. *We're running! We're running! We're run*–A sharp cut left nothing but the soft static hiss of the speakers.

Gilly leaned forward and began skipping through tracks. "That's like Pins and Needles's one decent song," she said.

Sam nodded. "Yeah. I saw the *Running Hot* video on TV, and it kicked ass. But then they whine through the whole rest of the CD." Her phone rang. Glancing at the number, she mumbled, "Fuck."

"Who is it?" Gilly found another okay song but turned the volume back down to a normal level.

"Mom. School must've called her."

Gilly felt a pinch in her guts. They'd call her parents too. In a few hours her dad would come home and find the money gone. She and Sam were already in Georgia, though. Fatalism dulled her fear.

Sam's phone kept ringing.

"Gonna answer it?"

Sam curled her lip. "She can go to Hell. Why should I care?"

"It was Greg's porn. Your mom didn't do anything."

"I know. She didn't do shit." Sam grabbed her cigarettes tucked above the sun visor and cracked the window. "I mean, my stepdad's a pervert. Okay. He's also an asshole and motherfucking white trash, so it's not a real big surprise. I can almost forgive him since he's probably missing a chromosome or something. But Mom didn't care. She's just, like, 'whatever.'"

"It's fucked up," Gilly said.

Yesterday, Sam had found a magazine called *Barely Legal* in her garage. Creeped out and pissed off by pictures of girls her age taking it up the ass from guys her stepdad's age, she'd glued the centerfold over the living room couch. Her mom found it and yelled at Sam for going through Greg's things.

That's how Sam wound up at the Texaco last night, and she'd told Gilly the whole story there. Gilly didn't have any more answers for her now than she'd had then.

"I mean, what the fuck am I supposed to do?" Sam

started yelling. "Just walk around the house, my mother-fucking house, and pretend like he's not jerking off thinking about shit like that?"

"He's probably sniffing your dirty underwear right now."

"Jesus, Gilly. Shit."

Gilly snorted. "Well?"

"Well? What am I supposed to do?"

"I don't know. It's fucked up."

Sam blew smoke from the corner of her mouth. "Mom's, like, 'That's what you get for snooping.' What the hell? She's my fucking mom. She's supposed to keep people like that away from me. Instead, she fucking marries him."

Gilly pounded her fist against the armrest. "And there's a Nazi goat eating your scrap metal!"

They both laughed. Sam pushed her sunglasses up to wipe her eyes and calmed down some. The story about the Nazi goat was long, confusing, and not that funny, anyway. Or at least, the chief reason it was funny was how pointless the comment seemed to everyone but them.

Their conversation switched course and turned strange, sudden angles innumerable times. They stopped at Arby's for lunch then got back on the road. Sam drove the whole way. Gilly manned the stereo, flipping through Sam's CD case.

Gilly kept playing "Running Hot." The song was a bounding, boisterous war cry. It was nihilism you could dance to.

We're running hot! These kids are losing their minds. They can't see the signs. Raise hell and a back beat! Running out of time. We're running hot!

Finally, Atlanta's glass-and-steel bulk rose up ahead of them. Sam took an exit at random, and they descended through canyons of brick, jostling with traffic past fast-food places and shopping centers.

"So what now?" Sam asked.

"Let's get a hotel room first, so we're not looking for one at two o'clock in the morning. We can figure out what to do from there."

"Sounds like a plan."

After another half-mile, Sam pulled into a Days Inn. Gilly carried the ammo box hidden inside her backpack. Full of bottles, Sam's bag clinked and rattled with every step.

The lobby had sagging green furniture and a map of Atlanta on the wall. The place was empty except for an Indian woman wearing a flowing gown and a red dot on her forehead. She sat behind the front desk watching a soap opera.

"Can I help you?" The only accent she had was a Southern twang worse than Gilly's. Surprised, Gilly lost her train of thought. Sam spoke up.

"We'd like a room, please."

"All right." The clerk began typing on her computer. "How many nights?"

"The weekend, at least. Two nights."

A few more taps at the keyboard. "Smoking or non-smoking?"

"Smoking."

"Double beds?"

"Just one."

The woman's eyes flickered from Sam to Gilly, then back to her computer. She typed and didn't say anything else.

Gilly stood stiff beside Sam. She tried catching her attention with a sideways glare, but Sam yawned and pretended not to notice.

The woman slid a carbon form across the desk. Sam filled it out and paid with her debit card. "You can pay me back," she whispered to Gilly.

The clerk handed them two magnetized key cards. "Room two twenty-eight. Back out the door, up the stairs, turn left, and it's almost at the end of the breezeway."

"Thank you."

Following Sam outside, Gilly experienced the familiar sensation of only half-understanding what was going on.

Gilly was gay. Sam was straight. It should have been that simple, but nothing ever was. They'd had sex a few times—a friendship with benefits.

The first time was during a party at Ben's house, both of them drunk, groping in the dark, quickening breaths and nervous giggles. Ben and the others had heard them upstairs and tried to break into the room. The night had become legendary among their friends. The other times had all happened while Sam was dating Colby. Nobody knew about them except her and Gilly.

Each time, everything tumbled back to normal immediately afterward. Sam pretended nothing strange had happened, and Gilly found herself following suit. Once, they'd come downstairs and eaten dinner with Sam's mom while Gilly's hair was damp with sweat and Sam's bra was gone.

The little box of a hotel room had been designed for anonymity. The air smelled blank, the ghost of every past guest scrubbed from the carpet.

Collapsing facedown onto the bed, Sam stretched her limbs and groaned. Gilly checked out the view of the construction site next door.

"So where's the Witches' Carnival?" Sam asked.

Gilly turned away from the window. "You remember Dawn talking about some neighborhood with all sorts of bars and funky stores and stuff?"

"Yeah. Little Five Points. I've been there once. It's pretty neat."

"Maybe we should start there. If the Witches' Carnival really is here, that seems like the kind of place they'd hang out at."

"Cool with me." Sam pulled the Jose Cuervo out of her book bag. She unscrewed the cap, thumped it into the corner, and took a swallow. "Oh, shit." As Sam laughed and coughed at the same time, her shirt rose up. Gilly's eyes traveled across the inch of soft pink belly and the curve of Sam's hip.

"Maybe we should get a newspaper, too," Gilly went on. "See if it mentions anything that's big enough for them to show up for."

Sam nodded. "There was a newspaper box in the lobby."

"Cool. You have any change? Dad never thought to steal a roll of quarters."

"Fuck it. We'll get one later." Another sip. Another coughing chuckle. Sam wiped her mouth and stared at Gilly. A smile spread across her face. "Why are you standing over there?"

Gilly realized she had her back pressed against the windowsill, putting as much space between herself and the bed as possible. She tried to think of a lie but couldn't.

"Because you scare me sometimes."

Sam laughed out loud. "I scare you?"

"Sometimes."

Gilly had once called Sam at two o'clock in the morning. Crying, she wouldn't let her off the phone until Sam told her if she was straight or not, if she was only goofing around or wanted to start dating or what. Sam told Gilly that she was straight, just not exactly. She promised Gilly she loved her and would never hurt her. She told her that their relationship was whatever it was and Gilly shouldn't worry so much.

"Poor baby," Sam giggled, holding out her hand. "Come here. I promise I won't scare you anymore."

There was nothing Gilly could do. Their warm fingers lacing together, Gilly climbed onto the bed and straddled Sam's hips. Neither of them moved. Then Gilly broke their gaze and took the bottle from Sam. She tilted it to her lips, an ice-cold heat spreading down through her stomach.

Sam watched her. Her fingers ran along the waist of Gilly's pants then hooked themselves into the front pocket of her hoodie. "Wanna know a secret?" she asked.

"Sure."

Sam grinned her sharp-cornered grin. "I knew you were coming with me."

Gilly's true, unguarded laugh was a rare thing. When it did come, the sound burst into the air like a flock of birds. "I almost didn't. When you told me this morning, I almost just let you go."

"No." Sam shook her head. "I knew you'd come with me, even before I told you I was leaving."

"Well . . ." Gilly took another sip. She made a face and forced the stuff down. "We're friends, right?"

Sam nodded. She tugged on the pocket of Gilly's sweatshirt, and Gilly leaned down to kiss her. The soft resistance of Sam's lips, the soap scent on her skin and tequila on her breath, Gilly's heart thumping like a rabbit's—it felt like a fly-ing dream.

Sam laughed and pulled away. She stared up at her, green eyes shimmering under dark makeup. She traced a finger down Gilly's throat to her collarbone. The touch brought a tiny gasp.

"Tell me we're going to find them," Sam said.

"We're going to find them. We're going to find the Witches' Carnival and leave everything behind us and never have to worry about it again."

"Never?"

"Never, ever. It's going to be the easiest thing in the world." And at that moment, Gilly was certain it would be.

THREE

"**G**illy."

A hand shook her shoulder. Gilly grunted and tried to burrow deeper into the covers.

"Wake up, G."

Sam yanked the blanket and rumpled sheets back. Jerking upright, Gilly felt syrup-thick drunkenness slosh inside her skull. She was in a strange bed. Her mouth was sticky and dry, and she was mostly naked. Pushing thickets of licorice-colored hair out of her eyes, she remembered they were in Atlanta.

Sam plunked down on the bed beside her, the bottle of tequila in her hand. "There's fifty-three thousand, two hundred dollars in that ammo box."

Gilly stared at her with blank, half-asleep eyes. "Huh?"

"Fifty-three thousand, two hundred dollars."

"Fifty-three . . . No. It was a lot, but . . ." She turned. The hotel room was buried under money. Stacks of twenties, fifties, and hundreds covered the floor, the bureau, and the top of the TV. "We're screwed," Gilly whispered.

Taking a sip from the bottle, Sam admired it all. "Where'd your dad get so much money?"

"Don't know. It's probably from bribes or something." Gilly started getting dressed. She had to walk across a carpet of bills to grab her black hoodie. "We are so screwed."

"Stop saying that."

"Well?" It was true. In that minute after waking, with thoughts still as vast as dreams, Gilly knew she'd taken the money to get back at her dad as much as anything else. She'd gone too far, though. Gilly had no clue how she'd talk her way out of this one.

"What are we going to do with it?"

Gilly shook her head. She was terrified but didn't want Sam to see that. "Let's throw it at each other like in a snowball fight."

"I'm serious, G."

"When are we gonna get another chance?"

Stooping down, Sam grabbed some fifties and tossed them at Gilly. The money smacked her in the face, then fluttered back to the carpet.

"There. Satisfied?"

"No." Gilly dropped to her knees. Sam dove, scooping up piles of cash in her arms. They rolled across the floor, shrieking and pelting each other with fistfuls of bills.

A sharp buzz made them freeze. Sam's cell phone vibrated on top of the bureau. Money rustled around her ankles like autumn leaves as she went to grab it.

"It's Colby. He's called twice already." Sam waited for him to leave a voice mail. As she listened to it, she kicked the bed. "Fuck, he's such an asshole."

"What'd he say?"

"He's pulling that guilt-trip shit, like he's my daddy or something. But I don't care because he's in Birmingham, and I'm gonna be in the Witches' Carnival. Gonna have boys like Colby served to me a dozen at a time. Gonna slurp their hearts down like raw oysters." Sam watched Gilly sweeping the money into one big pile. She swayed as if the hotel were a ship at sea. "It'd be so fucked up if the maid walked in right now."

Gilly laughed.

"C'mon, bitch. Let's get this picked up and go to Little Five Points."

"Cool."

"And let's get something to eat. I'm fucking starving."

They got directions from the desk clerk. Sam wasn't quite drunk, but she was feeling pretty damn good, so Gilly drove. After missing a turn, driving around for twenty minutes, stopping at a gas station and getting a totally different set of directions, they finally wound up at Little Five Points.

Warrens of old brick and sagging porches housed thrift stores, holistic medicine practices, and six-table restaurants. The neighborhood had a scruffy, sun-bleached complexion. There wasn't anything slick there except the clothes in the windows.

Gilly pulled the hood of her sweatshirt down despite the cold; she liked the wind brushing the back of her neck. She'd tucked three thousand dollars in the front pocket of her backpack and had given Sam a few grand too. They bought gyros from a mobile grill hitched to a pickup truck, eating as they threaded through the crowd.

It was the cusp of evening. Some older boys smoked cigarettes on the curb in front of a comic book store. One of them had a metal spike jutting from below his lower lip. A pack of Harley-Davidsons growled past, chrome gleaming in the purple twilight. A patrol car prowled the street like a shark.

"So did Ben keep his dick in his pants at least, or did he whip it out and come all over the seat?" Sam asked through a mouth full of pita bread and steak.

"Goddamn. I'm eating." Gilly tossed her empty Coke can into a construction Dumpster before adding, "You're so sick."

Ben had started dating Tracye two weeks ago. Gilly had heard from Alex that the relationship bloomed after Tracye gave Ben a hand-job at the movie theater.

Ben was cool, but he could act retarded sometimes. Neither Gilly nor Sam liked Tracye much, except Tracye was best friends with Dawn, who dated Alex, who'd been Gilly's friend for years and had dated Sam before she broke up with him and started going out with Colby. Colby's best friend was Chad, who dated Stephanie Penn, who Gilly liked, but her cousin Jessica Penn was a bitch.

Everybody was everybody's business at Folsom High School, and the shifting sands of hook–ups, breakups, fights, and make–ups always provided something worth talking about.

"Look, I don't want to go to the movies and sit in Ben's crusty spooge, okay?"

Gilly tipped her head back and laughed. "Next time you go, and the floor's sticky, right? And you think it's just Coke . . ."

"Fuck, G. You're the sick one. I'm never going to the movies again. We're burning that place down."

All the time they walked along, discussing the particulars of Tracye and Ben's relationship, a second, more desperate conversation raced through Gilly's head. They'd had sex a few hours ago. That didn't necessarily mean a thing, but Sam wasn't talking to Colby now and maybe that did.

They watched some kids practice skateboard tricks on a bus stop bench. Two girls plastered the brickwork hulk of a club with band flyers, each one heralding MERRICAT! FRI & SAT. Gilly's hand swung by her side. She let her fingers brush

Sam's skin so gently, it might have been accidental. "So you're never talking to Colby again?" she asked.

"Not if we really find the Witches' Carnival."

"Yeah, but if we don't. I mean, have you like officially broken up with him?"

"He'll be so pissed off, I don't know what the fuck he'll say. Or Mom. Mom'll probably lock me out of the house for pulling this shit."

"It won't be that bad."

Sam deflected the question twice with a flick of her wrist. Asking a third time would sound pathetic, so Gilly gave up.

Sam talked about her mom and Greg. Gilly listened to the melody of her voice shot through with obscenities. She liked the way Sam jabbed fingers in the air whenever she spoke.

"It's nice out tonight," Gilly announced.

Sam glanced around. "Yeah. This is a pretty cool place."

Gilly grabbed Sam's hand. Warm palms touched. "I'm glad we did this," she said, desperate to fill the sudden silence between them.

"Yeah."

Gilly felt Sam's pulse. One beat. Two. Then Sam squeezed Gilly's hand gently and pulled hers free.

Once, Sam had promised Gilly that she loved her and would never hurt her. What Sam didn't understand was, mean to or not, she could hurt Gilly easier than anyone. She could tear Gilly to pieces without a cruel thought against her.

Stupid bitch. Gilly's inner voice laughed at her. All at once, she didn't want to be here. She wanted to be home, alone, in her room.

"So how do we find the Witches' Carnival?" Sam asked.

"Fuck. How should I know?" Gilly pulled her hood up and sunk her hands into the front pocket of her sweatshirt.

Always fucking up. Always lying to yourself until you believe it, then making an ass out of yourself. Goddamn fat fucking stupid bitch.

"Gilly."

"What?"

"Come on. Don't be like this, all right?"

Gilly scowled. "I'm not being like anything."

"Please? Don't be like this."

Gilly wished she could make it Sam's fault, but it wasn't. She hadn't done anything Gilly hadn't hoped for all the way to Atlanta. Now, after Gilly had tried forcing things to go where they weren't allowed to go, Sam wouldn't hold it against her. She would speak softly and wait for Gilly to get over it too.

Gilly sighed. "Yeah, okay."

"We cool?"

"We cool like Elvis. We cool like four Elvises stapled together." Gilly left a hundred things unsaid, but for the most part she told the truth.

"So seriously, what do we do now?"

"I guess we just keep our eyes open."

"That's it?" Sam asked.

"Yeah, but the Witches' Carnival isn't exactly real, so reality kind of warps around them. Like, they come into town and it'll rain flowers or frogs. Or all the cats start dancing on their hind legs. Weird stuff like that."

"So all we can do is wander around and hope something fucked up happens."

Gilly shrugged. "Pretty much."

"How do you know all this?"

"I read some books about them."

"When?"

Gilly's mind touched on the cheap paperbacks about the Witches' Carnival, Wicca, and vampires that she'd binged on through middle school and the first years of high school. It was embarrassing, remembering how she'd carried those books hidden in the bottom of her backpack like protective amulets, praying they could make her someone magical and beautiful, someone else. Finally, she shrugged. "I don't know. Long time ago."

They kept walking in no particular direction, letting the street scenes flicker around them. The last, branding–iron–bright sliver of sun vanished behind the buildings leaving the sky seared red and gold.

"Wish I'd brought my coat." Sam rubbed her arms. "It's getting cold."

"Buy a new one. We've got plenty of cash."

"Yeah." Sam's pace slowed. "But it's really your money, G."

"Actually, it belongs to the Birmingham Police Department. But my dad stole it, see? And then I stole it fro–"

"Gilly. Fuck." Sam punched her in the arm, then waved her hands around the busy street. "Inside voice when you're talking about stolen money."

"Ow. That actually hurt."

"Sorry. But it's really cool? You don't care?"

"No. I mean, it's not like–like I'd hold it over your head or anything. If you want anything, get it."

"Well, hell. Let's go buy stuff."

"Buy stuff! Buy stuff!" Gilly and Sam jumped up and down, yelling in unison. They dashed across the street toward a store called The Junkman's Daughter. Stepping through the door, Gilly blinked against the harsh fluorescents. The musty-sweet smell of incense made her nose itch.

They wandered past racks of vintage rock shirts, got lost among leather and vinyl, looked at displays of body jewelry and CDs and 78s heaped into bins, and explored shelves stuffed with weird toys, candles, bongs sold as "water pipes," funny stickers, perverted refrigerator magnets and more clothes.

"Damn," Gilly said, staring at a row of *Texas Chainsaw Massacre* lunch boxes. "It's kind of like Wal-Mart except everything's got a skull on it."

Sam fell in love with an army jacket bearing the German federal eagle on its sleeve. Gilly picked up a pair of earrings. Stepping back onto the now-dark street, they felt like they owned the night.

Drifting through boutiques and thrift stores, Gilly and Sam laid down cash for anything that caught their eye. A hundred and fifty dollars went to CDs. They stopped at RiteAid pharmacy for toothbrushes and other essentials. At another store, Sam bought a set of adult-size Underoos, bright blue with Superman's scarlet "S" on the front.

They paced around the door of Exxxcite Video and Novelties, peering at the mannequins in the window dressed in lingerie and bondage gear. A sign read: NO ONE UNDER 21 MAY ENTER! ID REQUIRED!! Sam wanted to go in. Gilly chewed her lip and dragged her heels.

"Sam, you're here because Greg had one magazine. Now you want to check out a whole store full of porn?"

"I'm not going to buy anything. I just want to look around. C'mon, G."

A man came out while they argued on the sidewalk. As he pushed the door open, Gilly glimpsed the concrete floor inside and shelves of videos. Women stared out from posters on the walls, Asian girls and tanned, gasping blondes.

She chickened out. Sam groaned but dropped it. They wandered down Euclid Avenue and into a clothing store called Lunar.

"Sam, I need your help." Gilly walked sideways down the cramped aisle, two different-colored sneakers in her hands.

"What's the matter?" Sam stood in front of a mirror, holding up silk print skirts with wrap-around images of Vishnu and the Lady of Guadalupe.

"New shoes. Now everybody expects me to wear black, right? So the obvious choice is pink. The problem is everyone expects me to expect them to expect black. Therefore, they expect pink, so the obvious choice is black. Except everyone expects black, see?"

"Poor baby. It's hard being ironic these days, isn't it?"

"It is," Gilly wailed. "It really, really is, and nobody understands."

"Get them in blue."

A second of thought and Gilly's face lit up. "You see?" she squealed, hopping up and down like an excited five-year-old. "This is why I love you. This is it. Right here. Nobody'll see blue coming." She darted back down the aisle.

The spree lasted for hours. By the time the stores closed, Sam and Gilly had managed to spend a thousand dollars on everything from jewelry to a stuffed octopus.

The crowds of people had dwindled, leaving a few laughing silhouettes propped against cinder-block walls. Bars switched on their neon signs. Music seemed to spill from every other door. Stray chords of garage rock, blues, and honky tonk stumbled arm in arm into the night.

Not swept up in the speed and noise of the neighborhood anymore, Sam and Gilly could hear the scuff-slap rhythm of their shoes on the cold pavement. Sam lit a cigarette and started playing with the box, turning it over in her fingers. Whenever she got some cigarettes, Sam took them out of their package and put them into a box Josh had bought at a tobacco store. From a specialty brand called Coffin Nails, it was matte black with a grinning silver skull on the front. Sam had loved it the moment she saw it and begged Josh until he gave it to her.

"Let me bum one," Gilly said.

Sam pulled out another cigarette, lighting it with the one already smoldering in her hand. Waiting, Gilly breathed warm air into her fist. October's damp chill had soaked down into her muscles and bones. She was tired, her feet hurt, but Gilly didn't care. Her skin was electric. Her senses felt vulture-acute. The night was mysterious and filled with music.

It'd been stupid to get upset a few hours ago. Sam wasn't in love with her. She would never slip letters gooey with frosting-sweet words into Gilly's locker the way Colby did for her. Gilly would never get roses on Valentine's Day or little teddy bears holding satin hearts for no occasion at all. But she would get a few nights like this, and that was good enough.

"This was one of your best bad ideas," she said, taking the cigarette from Sam.

"Yeah. Still haven't found the Witches' Carnival, though."

"Well, you get your information from a crazy bird guy, you take your chances."

"I'm supposed to be at work right now."

"Domino's can probably manage without you."

"Hey, bitch, I put the toppings on the pizzas. That's a very important job. I had to watch a video and everything."

Gilly laughed. "You did not."

"Bullshit, I didn't. And there's a test–" Sam's phone started vibrating. "There's a test afterward," she finished, checking the number.

"Colby again?"

Sam shook her head. "Josh," she said, pushing the talk button.

"Hey, big brother."

. . .

"Don't cuss at me. I'm fine."

. . .

"I'm out."

. . .

"Just out."

. . .

Sam sighed. "Atlanta, all right? Don't you fucking dare tell Mom."

. . .

"Why do you think?"

. . .

"Yeah, well, I decided to go, anyway. Who knows?"

. . .

"I don't give a shit. I'm not going back to that house as long as Greg's there."

. . .

"Because he's a retarded crackbaby. Why do you think?"

. . .

"No."

. . .

"No. I've got a place to stay. I'm fine."

. . .

"No, it's not with a guy. Chill out, okay?"

. . .

"I know."

. . .

"Josh, there aren't any guys anywhere in the fucking pic-ture. Not even Colby. Relax, okay?"

Gilly walked along, listening to Sam's conversation. Her parents were probably panicking about her, too. By now they'd know she'd taken the money, and they'd murder her the moment she stepped through the door. Gilly tried not to think about it. She tried not to think about what might hap-pen between her and Sam, either. The moment felt too perfect. Whatever happened would happen if she fretted about it or not.

"No. But I got some shopping done at least."

. . .

"I don't know. If we find the Witches' Carnival, then never."

. . .

"I don't know. I need a couple days to think about stuff, all right?"

. . .

"C'mon, Josh. I wouldn't–"

"What the–" Gilly stopped dead and spun around.

The quick motion made Sam jump. She flashed startled glances up and down the empty street. "What? What is it?"

Gilly stared at a lamppost molting layer after layer of pictures of lost pets, advertisements for palm readers, and offers to make twelve thousand dollars a week from her own home. With a shaking hand she ripped a band flyer off and showed it to Sam. "That's us."

"Huh?" The flyer looked like every other band poster Sam had ever seen. Printed on bloodred paper, a collage of disparate pictures had been forced into a pseudo-coherence. Across the top was written: MERRICAT! FRI & SAT in Magic Marker, two opening acts listed underneath. The same flyer hung on walls and lampposts all around Little Five Points.

"What are you talking about?"

"Goddamn, Sam. Look." Gilly pointed at two small photos bookending Merricat's name. Smiling into the camera, they were Sam's and Gilly's class photos from last year's yearbook.

"What the fuck?" Sam squinted at herself. The pink blouse she wore in the picture still hung in her closet back home. Her hair was pulled back because she'd tried to highlight it the day before picture day, and it didn't come out right.

From the distant end of the phone call, Josh continued to lecture her.

"Uh, Josh? I'm . . . I have to go now. Something weird just happened."

. . .

"I'm not sure. I think we just found the Witches' Carnival. Bye."

FouR

Taking their bags to the car, the girls continued up Moreland Avenue. Fifteen minutes ago, these streets, this night, had been theirs. Then, a flyer for a band they'd never heard of materialized with their photos on it.

Suddenly, Meek transformed in Gilly's mind from a homeless lunatic to a soothsayer. Suddenly, finding the Witches' Carnival became more than a lark. Suddenly, Gilly felt herself crossing the borderland between awake and dreaming. Her footsteps didn't falter or slow, but they didn't hurry, either.

"I think it was over here," Sam whispered, hopping down an embankment onto the sidewalk.

Half a block up, the club where Merricat was playing glowered over the street. The building had been a grain warehouse long ago, back when Atlanta was a different city. Now it was Conspiracy, the club's name sculpted in blue neon across the roof.

Light from the sign formed a tide pool around the entrance. Sparkling creatures flit and played within it, dressed in brilliant colors and shimmering black. Plastered across the club's haggard visage were posters identical to the one in Gilly's hand. She and Sam stopped across the street, lingering in the shadows. As they stared at the building, a legion of their own Xeroxed faces stared back.

Pretty boys and heartbreaker girls crowded the sidewalk. An L-shaped tunnel made of plywood guarded the club's entrance. The wood had been painted bright red and covered in skater tags. From inside, they could hear the opening act thumping across the sound system.

"How do we get in?" Gilly whispered.

"Just act like you own the place." Sam stepped off the curb. Holding out her hand to stop a car, she hurried to the other side. "Come on, G." The racket of voices and music drowned out Sam's shout, but Gilly saw her mouth move and knew what she'd said.

Crossing the street and plunging into the glare of blue neon, Gilly felt nervous-sick. Tropical fish swam around her. They were all older than Gilly; they were all gorgeous. She watched them lean against the wall and against one another, smoke cigarettes, and talk about things she wouldn't understand. She didn't belong here. A girl's lips spread into a grin. Her eyes flickered in Gilly's direction, and Gilly knew the girl was laughing at her.

Keeping close to Sam, Gilly waded through the crowd and into the tunnel. The air turned sweltering hot, ripe with sweat and sex. The claustrophobic space brought whitecaps of sound crashing down on them. Strings of Christmas lights shuddered from the primal-scream beat. Through open doors at the end, Gilly glimpsed an ocean of bodies roiling beneath swinging blades of light.

Then the bouncer appeared. He held his thick arms folded across his chest. Dreadlocks tumbled down his shoulders like a lion's mane. "I need some ID."

A familiar, clammy fist clutched Gilly's heart. Thoughts hurled themselves forward jumbled and half-formed. She couldn't think. She couldn't breathe. Everything moved too fast. He was huge. They should bribe him. She didn't know how. She was afraid to look him in the eye, so she stared at his chest. The bouncer's yellow T-shirt read SECURITY. Gilly had to say something.

"No, we–" Her voice seized in her throat. Gilly couldn't remember the Witches' Carnival or anything except the bouncer's concrete bulk. She turned to Sam, hoping for rescue.

Smiling up at the bouncer, Sam motioned with her hands and shouted something Gilly couldn't hear. The bouncer didn't bother listening. Shaking his head, he pointed to the exit behind them.

"Go. Now." The words rumbled over the music.

Sam pulled folded bills out of her pocket. The bouncer grabbed her wrist. Reaching around, he grabbed Gilly by her backpack. Gilly hated him touching her, but she didn't fight.

He pushed them past a knot of club hoppers, down the tunnel, and back outside. Conversations stopped. People turned to stare. The man let go of them and said, "Smile big, now."

Without thinking, Gilly glanced over her shoulder. The bouncer snapped their picture with a digital camera. "Try to get in here again, I call the cops. Understand?"

"Fuck you," Sam said.

The bouncer disappeared without bothering to answer.

Gilly and Sam were left to maneuver and sidestep back through the crowd. People weren't sure what had happened but snickered, anyway. Pretending not to notice, Gilly felt them watching her. She wished they'd die.

Sam swore under her breath. Gilly kept silent.

She could have explained, or better yet, shown him the poster with their pictures on it. She could have told him her brother was the drummer; how the hell else did her photo get on the poster? All the ways she could have gotten them inside suddenly came to mind. But the bouncer had glared at her, said a few hard words, and Gilly became a trembling little mute.

At her core, Gilly was a coward. Shy, terrified of being yelled at or embarrassed, eager to please—she hated herself for it. Layers of black clothes, hair dye, and sneers only hid her cringing spirit. They'd never been enough to change it.

"How do we get in now?" Sam asked. Pissed off, she held her arms across her chest in an odd imitation of the bouncer.

"I don't think we can," Gilly said. "If that guy calls the police, we're fucked."

Sam waved her off. "That's crap. He doesn't want the cops to show up any more than we do."

Gilly couldn't convince herself that was true. She was afraid of the police and afraid of being laughed at again. Still, her eyes drifted across the old husk of a building. Maybe there was a side entrance or fire escape they could sneak through.

A coterie of beautiful demons had ventured onto the roof. Washed in the light of the neon sign, their forms seemed sculpted from turquoise and ivory. One man perched on the very edge of the roof, the steel-capped toes of his cowboy boots jutting out into the night. He smoked a cigarette and gazed at the hipster children below.

Others stood behind him, sipping drinks and joking with one another. Gilly watched them. Calm, poised, untouched by the wind or cold, they held themselves like immortals. They were lords of three a.m. empires and pulse-beat kingdoms.

A woman in the group half-turned, eyes sweeping toward the shadows where Gilly and Sam hid. Gilly stared up at her, fascinated and jealous. Something inside Gilly's brain clicked into place. She'd seen the woman earlier that evening, putting up flyers for Merricat.

"Sam." Gilly's throat felt like chalk. "That's them. That's the Witches' Carnival."

"Where?" Sam followed Gilly's gaze up to the roof. "How do you figure?"

"Just look, Sam."

Sam looked at the three women and two men perched over the night like succubi. "Jesus fuck." She walked toward the bright glow of the club again, yelling, "Hey. Hey!"

The witches glanced down. They watched Sam cross the street with Gilly hustling after her. The man wearing cowboy boots blew a jet of cigarette smoke from the side of his mouth. A girl in wire-framed glasses knelt at the roof's edge, watching them approach the way she'd watch ants crawl across the pavement.

"Hey. Get us in!" Music and shouted conversations swallowed up Sam's lone voice. Cowboy motioned to his ear and shook his head.

"Get us in! Come on." Sam pointed at the door. The witches all smiled vaguely and shrugged.

"Fucking hell." The moment slipping away, Sam tore one of the band flyers off the wall. Holding it up, she jabbed a finger at her and Gilly's photos. "That's us," she screamed. "Get us in, all right?"

The witches still couldn't hear. Watching Sam point to the poster, Cowboy nodded and gestured toward Conspiracy's front door, suggesting they catch the show.

Sam hollered and waved her arms, but it was useless. Standing beside her, Gilly didn't make a whisper.

Cowboy, the girl with glasses, and an Asian woman stood along the roof's edge. Another man lurked behind them, dark tangles of hair twisting in gusts of wind. Off to the side stood the woman who'd first found Gilly in the shadows. Her eyes glittered. Her face was serene. As her friends motioned back and forth with Sam, she kept still, watching Gilly. The witch tilted her head to one side. Her mouth bowed into an amused smile that trilled through Gilly's chest. Gilly felt lost and floating, a little high.

Sam couldn't make them understand. The Asian woman said something to Cowboy. He nodded and stepped back from the roof's ledge. Grinning and waving good-bye, they went inside. The wild-haired man followed them. Then the woman holding Gilly captured in her gaze blew her a kiss and fell in behind her friends.

Gilly's voice burst out, "Wait. Wait!" But they were gone, all except the girl with glasses. Still kneeling by the roof's edge, curiosity narrowed her eyes and drew her mouth into a fine line.

Sam tried one last time. "We are on. The fucking. Poster!"

The girl scrounged through the courier's bag slung across her shoulder and pulled out a pen and some paper. Jotting something down, she crumpled the paper into a ball and tossed it. Gilly snatched it out of the air.

It was two pages torn from their yearbook. Friends and enemies, people Gilly had known her whole life, stared up at her. Each page had a square hole where Sam's and Gilly's pictures had been cut out. Across the top of one, the girl had written, *Want it? Cool. Now grab it. (Can't do everything for you, you know.)* Her signature was a smiley face with X'ed out eyes.

The girl grinned, held her hand up in a pair of devil's horns, and started to follow the others. Their cries couldn't draw her back.

Gilly stared at the empty roof. "Sam, we've got to get in there."

"I know." Sam wadded the flyer up and bounced it against the brick wall.

"Think of something, okay?"

"Me think of something. You're the smart . . ." Sam stared at Conspiracy's front entrance for several seconds. When she spoke again, her voice came out in a strange, wicked tittle. "All right." She started walking backward, still looking at the door. "All right. We're going back to the hotel. C'mon."

• • •

They parked by the hotel entrance and rode the elevator up to the second floor. Back in their room, Gilly pulled the ammo box out from under the bed. Sifting through the bills, they separated twenties from fifties and hundreds.

"Fuck. This is taking too long. C'mon. We'll do it on the way." Sam jumped up. She was edgy, her whole body tightened down like a spring. As Gilly gathered the money back together, Sam dug a little SpongeBob SquarePants out of her purse. The plastic figure used to hold candy inside. Thumbing open the lid in the top of SpongeBob's head, Sam shook out a Xanax. Then she opened the mini-fridge where they'd stashed the liquor.

As Sam twisted off the cap of a bottle of Captain Morgan's Spiced Rum, Gilly said, "Should you really be taking that with alcohol?"

Sam popped the pill in her mouth and took a swig. "Makes it kick in faster."

They drove back to Little Five Points with Slipknot on the stereo. Gilly sat in the passenger seat sorting money. She glanced at the clock: 11:20. A little more than twenty-four hours ago, a broken-down street preacher had told them where to find the Witches' Carnival. Since that moment, Gilly had tumbled forward, everything speeding past, fanciful and prophetic at once, with no time to think about any of it.

Gilly tried to get a handhold. She made herself feel the slick bills between her fingers and the jerking motion of the Civic as Sam darted through traffic. This was a bad idea. Someone could get hurt. Seriously motherfucking hurt. But the Witches' Carnival was real, and Gilly had to catch the girl with eyes like chips of mica. She had to catch her and never go home.

Sam prowled past Conspiracy. The crowd on the sidewalk had doubled. Inside, the opening acts were through their sets and Merricat had come onstage. Sam parked in the alley behind a clothing boutique next door to the club.

Gilly had collected six grand in twenty-dollar bills, a few hundreds mixed in for fun. She gave Sam half. Gilly's hands fluttered around like moths, one way then another, unable to land. She tried to tug the hood of her sweatshirt up, stuff money into her pocket, and close the ammo box all at once.

"Calm down. It's gonna be cool," Sam said.

"I'm calm." Gilly turned to look at her, and the metal box slid from between her knees, hitting the floorboard. "Shit." She started snatching up the money. Sam leaned over to help.

"Hey, G."

"What?"

"Are you pretty?" Sam asked, cramming money into the box.

"What?"

"Are you pretty? I want to know. Are you pretty?"

"No." Gilly shut the ammo box and hid it under her seat. The whispered word tasted like ash. It was easy for Sam to say it because, really, Sam was gorgeous and knew it.

"Well, if you ain't pretty, how do you expect to get what you want?"

Gilly rolled her eyes but grinned, anyway. "Start trouble."

"Fuck yeah, start some trouble." Climbing out of the car, Sam stalked toward the club's bright light and manic noise.

"You think that bastard kicked us out because we didn't have ID? Bullshit. Some Paris Hilton bitch comes walking into there, fifteen-year-old with fake tits, motherfucker wouldn't have looked twice at her except to feel her up, cocksucker bastard."

Trailing a stream of half-connected obscenities, she pushed through the crowd. "Get out of my way. Get out of my way! I'm on a mission from God, goddamnit! Think you've got the world on a string? Fuck you. Gonna tie that string around your fucking neck. Nothing but trash. Goddamn nothing!"

Sam stopped dead at the center of the crowd. Every eye turned toward her. Nobody spoke. Picking some mop-headed boy at random, Sam snarled, "So fuck you," and tossed a fistful of bills into his face.

The boy yelped before realizing what Sam had thrown.

By the time he'd caught a twenty in his hand, Sam was already whipping money at the girl beside him.

"And fuck you," she spit.

"And you."

"And you."

"You too, you little hump."

"And you."

"You too."

"And you."

Money whirled around like snow. One girl took a step forward, grabbing at the bills. A second girl bumped into her from behind. A boy shouldered them both aside, and a moment later the sidewalk had exploded into a riot. They weren't fighting exactly, just pushing and shoving, shouting and climbing over one another to get at the money.

"Fuck you."

"And you."

Tossing money from the thick stack, Sam hurried backward, a mass of kids and clutching hands rolling toward her.

"And you—go! Fucking go!"

She and Gilly bolted down the square black throat of the tunnel. People trickled out, coming to see what the commotion was. Gilly and Sam rammed past, flinging money behind them.

The same bouncer barred their way. He caught Sam by the arm. "Hey. I already—"

Money burst into the air like paper sparrows. It fluttered, swiveled, and spun through the cramped tunnel. All at once and all together, the mob crashed into the bouncer. He let go of Sam and threw his weight against the human cascade, trying to keep it contained. Gilly was slammed hard against the wall. Through waving arms and thudding bodies, she watched the bouncer stagger and go under.

Gilly and Sam clung to each other to keep from getting trampled. Sections of plywood collapsed behind them. Pitched forward and back, somehow they managed to claw their way into the club.

Once inside, they kept throwing money in the air. It littered the concrete floor and twisted in the swinging shafts of light. A raw sound exploded from Gilly's belly, too wild to be a laugh, just a joyful howl, as she watched chaos spread around them.

Two more bouncers in yellow shirts headed their way. Sam grabbed Gilly's sleeve and pulled her in an opposite direction, dissolving into the crowd.

The singer called for everyone to calm down, and nobody listened. The house lights came on, *cha-clung, cha-clung, cha-clung*. Their hard glare burned away the club's mystique, leaving kids in designer clothes shoving one another and screaming for friends inside a derelict warehouse. Some still fought for the money, most just tried to get out.

Sweat-shining bodies pushed in from every side. Gilly couldn't see where she was going. Then a hand emerged from the mob and took her shoulder. Gilly's head snapped around. It was Cowboy.

"Come on." Three feet away, he had to shout to be heard.

Sam saw him too. They snaked through the crowd, following the top of his head.

A voice rang out, "Chris! Chris Marlowe!"

Gilly loved the idea of someone yelling out Elizabethan playwrights during a riot. She wanted to shout back, "Shakespeare! John Donne!" Then Cowboy switched direction and began following the voice.

"Chris Marlowe!"

The crowd parted, and Gilly saw them. The Witches' Carnival stood on top of the oak slab bar. Staring at them, the cacophony around her quieted to the rustle of wind blowing through tall grass. The woman who'd spotted Gilly in the darkness held out a hand to help her up. Climbing onto the bar, Gilly's limbs were as light as dandelion fluff. Her head swam.

"Hi," the woman said.

Drunk on momentum, Gilly kissed her. For a moment the world was the moisture of the witch's lips and the smell of her skin, like fresh-cut grass. Startled, the woman jerked back. Gilly stared at her, mouth open, amazed that she'd ruined everything in under a second.

Why are you always so stupid? Her inner voice demanded. *She's not gay. Even if she is, why—*

Surprise blossomed into a widening grin and bright laugh. The woman beamed such an open, effortless smile that Gilly couldn't imagine what she'd done to earn it.

"Hey, there," she said. "I'm Maggie."

"Um, hey." Gilly didn't realize that she was beaming back, relishing her undeserved bounty.

The girl who'd tossed them the pages from their yearbook stood behind the bar, filling glasses from the tap.

"Grabbed it," Sam shouted to her.

The girl—somewhere Gilly would learn her name was Tonja—grinned, said nothing, and handed them glasses of beer.

"So do you start a lot of riots?" Maggie asked, her breath tickling the downy hairs by Gilly's temple.

Gilly shook her head. Sweeping a hand over the chaos, she said, "First one."

The club promoter ushered the band backstage, leaving cables and tipped-over mike stands. People stormed the stage. Some punks smashed apart Merricat's drum kit. The security guys tried to menace everyone outside. An alarm shrieked as a fire door was thrown open. Pin spots in the rafters continued swinging translucent shafts of blue light back and forth.

The tangle-haired man surfaced from the crowd. Older than the kids around him, in his hard-earned thirties, he strolled through the panic. As he approached the bar, the Asian girl handed him a beer. Gilly glimpsed an eagle and trident navy tattoo on his forearm.

"Looks like the show's over," he said. "What about it, Qi?"

The Asian girl nodded. "Seems that way."

One by one, the witches hopped off the bar. Marlowe helped Sam down with genteel grace. "You wouldn't happen to have a car, would you?" he asked.

Sam nodded. Seven people folded inside the Civic would be a tight fit, but when the Witches' Carnival asked for a ride, you said yes.

Walking along the wall, they slipped out through the fire exit beside the captured stage. Club hoppers spilled out the doors and clogged the street. In the moth-flickered beams of headlights, flushed faces laughed at whatever the hell had just happened. Devotees to the aesthetic of not giving a shit bounced around like children. They ran up and down and ninja-kicked one another.

Sam heard the wail of sirens nearby. Wanting to get away before the police showed up, she jogged toward her car.

"How about you let me drive?" the ex-navy man asked, reading the worry on Sam's face.

When Sam hesitated, Maggie reassured her. "Don't worry. Jack'll get us out of here."

Jack climbed behind the wheel. Qi and Tonja shared the bucket seat, and the rest of them squeezed into the back.

KRISTOPHER REISZ

Shifting into gear and pulling farther up the alley, Jack swung around the boutique. Maggie was still armed with her glass of beer. It sloshed out as Jack whipped back onto the street, cutting off a white Mustang. "Told you," Maggie laughed to Sam.

They slipped into the night. Gilly twisted around to watch two squad cars pull up in front of Conspiracy. "So where are we going?" she asked.

"Don't worry"—Maggie took a sip of beer—"we'll find somewhere. Did you catch any of the show?"

"Not really. Maybe a couple seconds."

"They any good?" Sam asked.

"One of the best rock bands in history," Qi answered from the front. She flipped through Sam's CDs and didn't look up.

"Think so?"

She shrugged. "If they weren't, we wouldn't have turned up."

Merricat was a guitar, bass, and drums outfit that had stomped through Atlanta for several years, playing slick, hardworking rock and making it look easy. Chords lifted from old blues 78s, lyrics as jagged as shattered glass, there wasn't anything special about their music except they played it better than anyone else.

Their first full-length CD, *Cup of Tea*, had come out three months ago. It had gotten a gushing write-up in *Creative*

Loafing and four stars from *Blender*. Their label had a couple of national acts interested in Merricat opening for them on upcoming tours. When Merricat stepped onto Conspiracy's stage Friday night, a feeling crackled through the audience that the band was months away from outgrowing local venues.

Then things got weird. Halfway through the first set, a riot broke out. Club staff cut the sound system and got them off stage until things calmed down.

Zack, the guitarist, searched for the friends they'd met the day before, the two men and three girls he'd corralled into playing roadies, helping the band set up in exchange for a free show and free beer. His T-shirt damp and his hair limp with sweat, Zack poked through the dark passageways and grimy dressing rooms backstage. Getting worried, he clanged up the metal stairs to the balcony overlooking the dance floor. He found his newlywed wife with Merricat's singer. As the chaos below ebbed to an echoing still, he watched them kiss and laugh in the shadows.

By daybreak, Zack had loaded up his van and headed to his parents' house in Augusta. Posters announcing Merricat's last show hung on lampposts and cinder-block walls around Little Five Points for weeks after. Rain smeared the ink, and one by one, they sloughed away or were covered over.

The Witches' Carnival didn't create Merricat and didn't

break them apart. The Carnival blew into town to catch a good band while they could. A handful of history's most thrilling hours are pinned into books, arranged in neat columns like butterflies. Most come and go, squandered by the people who were there, never known by the ones who weren't. And in the quiet that follows, the Witches' Carnival moves on.

FIVE

ndy Stahl sat on the couch. Even with cardboard covering the window Gilly had broken out, the chill in the room raised gooseflesh along his arms. He was exhausted but refused to go to bed. The porch light burned, but Gilly wasn't coming home.

A snapshot of Gilly and Caitlin stood on top of the entertainment center. Andy had taken it during a vacation to Gulf Shores maybe ten years ago. Caitlin, just a toddler, dug at the sand with a plastic shovel. Gilly knelt beside her, mugging for the camera and holding up a dappled yellow shell she'd found.

Tugging his gaze away from the picture, Andy retreated into detached cop-think, trying to reconstruct the chain of events.

At eleven o'clock that morning, the school had called Karen, his wife, and told her Gilly had cut class. After work, she'd picked Caitlin up and come home to find the window smashed. Her house broken into and her daughter missing, Karen had gotten scared. She called Gilly's cell phone and heard it ringing inside the bathroom cabinet.

By the time Andy came home, Karen had crushed her fear down into a diamond-hard anger.

"You swore she didn't know about the money," she hissed at him, low so Caitlin wouldn't overhear.

Andy tried calming her down. "This is nothing to worry about, okay? she'll come back."

"She took the money, Andy. Exactly how far is your head shoved up your ass? Do you really think she just went to the mall?"

"I don't know where she went. Just don't panic. She's going to come back. She's just pissed because I took her keys away. That's all this is, okay?"

"You need to talk to Family Services."

The Family Services Unit handled all missing-person cases across Jefferson County. Andy shook his head. "You know we can't do that."

"Why not?"

"You know why not! She'll come back. There's no reason to fuck up our lives over this."

Karen turned away and didn't answer.

"Honey, look. Gilly's my daughter. You think I'd just . . . She'll come back, okay?"

"I never wanted that money in the house in the first place." Karen walked out of the bedroom. She hadn't spoken a word to Andy since.

Now it was past midnight. Andy studied the picture of Gilly at the beach and grit his teeth until his jaw ached.

The truth was, he wanted to call Family Services. He wanted the sheriff's department, the Birmingham metro police, and the state troopers out looking for Gilly. He wanted sniffer dogs and helicopters. But when they found her, they'd find the money—a cop's kid running around with fifty grand in cash. It wouldn't matter if Gilly tried covering for him. They'd call Internal Affairs before they'd call Andy to pick up his daughter.

Terrified that Gilly was missing and terrified of what would happen if she was found, Andy was trapped.

Squeezing his eyes shut, he pulled himself together. Gilly was seventeen. She hadn't had a plan. Hell, it might turn out she really had gone to the mall. Andy was a detective. He hunted people down for a living. His partner Malik had another stash of money in his house. They were in this together, and they could track Gilly down themselves.

Bowing his head, Andy clasped his hands together.

God in Heaven, please let me make this right. Give me three days. If she doesn't come back by then and I can't find her, I swear I'll go to

71

Family Services. I'll tell them everything. I won't care. Just watch over her. Just let me make this right and not destroy my family.

He bargained. He wouldn't punish Gilly. He'd get rid of the money. If only God would protect his daughter and let Andy find her. No great peace washed over Andy as he opened his eyes, but he felt a little better.

He had seventy-two hours. He went back to the chain of events, piecing together what had happened before Gilly's school had called Karen.

Gilly's car sat in the driveway where it'd been since Thursday night. That meant someone else had driven her from school to the house, then from the house to wherever. At least one other person was involved. What else did he know? He was a detective. This was the one thing he did better than anything else.

"It's not parenting, that's for sure," Andy mumbled.

He should let Malik sleep, but Andy couldn't deal with this alone in the dead-still house anymore. Going to the kitchen, he dialed Malik's number. After four rings, Malik's machine picked up and told him to leave a message. Andy hung up and dialed again. Then again. Finally, Malik answered, his voice husky from sleep.

"What the hell, Moonpie? It's one o'clock."

Andy took a deep breath. "We've got a problem, man."

six

From the garden, a lone violin sang in a trembling soprano.

"Can you dance?" Maggie asked.

"No." Gilly shook her head. The jade gown shimmered across her body.

"Don't be silly." Maggie's voice came from behind still lips of lacquered papier-mâché. "All you have to do is look at me. Nothing else, just me." Slipping a sequined mask over Gilly's eyes, she let her fingers travel down the girl's bare arms. "Understand?"

Gilly nodded. Hand in hand they stepped through French doors and into the garden. Fairy lights twinkled in the branches of trees and among the knife-sharp leaves of yucca plants. They were near the sea. Even a few days before Halloween, the salt-scented air felt warm against Gilly's skin.

Masked dancers swirled through the evening like the planets, men in black tuxes, women bright as stars. A sonata played on a stereo. Someone had dressed the speakers up with collars and bow ties.

"Just look at me," Maggie whispered.

Gilly and Maggie held each other like already–fading memories. One by one, other instruments joined the violin's song, and somehow Gilly found herself dancing.

"This is strange." She felt like a bird flying, nothing but air all around them. "I think I'm scared."

Maggie laughed. "Don't be scared. Why are you scared?"

"How is this happening?" She couldn't help it. Gilly turned to look out for the other dancers and started to stumble.

Maggie whispered, "Look at me."

Meeting the witch's blinking–alive eyes behind the glassy mask, Gilly felt herself sailing on the sonata's voice again.

"It's happening because you wanted it to," Maggie said. "You came looking for us."

"Yeah, but–our pictures were on that poster. You let us find you."

"Tonja helped Merricat make the poster for their show. She found a yearbook who knows where and cut two pictures from it." Maggie shook her head. "But she didn't know those pictures were of two people who were looking for us."

"But it couldn't have just been chance."

"It wasn't chance at all, Gilly. People are yearning creatures. They imagine and strive and hope. Stories about an enchanted band of vagabonds existed before the Carnival itself. But those fairy tales became the focal point of billions of daydreams, and eventually those daydreams condensed like vapor into something real." They swept and turned through the garden as Maggie spoke, ribboning past strange creatures in jeweled scales and peacock feathers. "The Carnival only exists because you want it to, you and everyone else. So why's it peculiar that, when you wanted to find it, a path came into existence too?"

"But . . ."

"But, but, but." Maggie laughed. "Gilly, please don't divine the ultimate nature of reality before you're at least eighteen. It'll make old ladies like myself feel bad."

"Okay, but—"

"Shh . . . here's all you need to know. I am here and you are here, and the night is beautiful." Her hand drifted up Gilly's back, resting between her bare shoulders. "There's nothing to be scared of. Everything is wonderful."

As the masquerade ball went on, Sam and Qi fell in with a circle of college students. Sitting in a cluttered office, they took hits off a pipe made from a mini-stapler.

Two of the office's walls were floor-to-ceiling bookcases. Surrounded by crack-spined paperbacks of Chaucer, Milton, and Frost, Sam found herself the center of attention. In her typewriter-quick patter, never bothering to lie, she talked about ditching school and stealing the money. She laughed and told everyone she'd crashed their party. Invited guests, young men and women on the cusp of great things, sopped up every word.

"So why'd you run away?" a girl asked. She held her mask in her lap, absently snapping the elastic band.

"We wanted to find the Witches' Carnival."

"Seriously? You think they're real?"

On the edge of her vision, Sam saw Qi touch a finger to her lips. Sam shrugged. "They might be. It's worth a shot, I guess."

A scattering of smirks and giggles filled the office. Sam laughed with them and let the conversation drift to other things. The designer of the pipe showed off how it could still work as a stapler. After a while, Sam stepped onto the iron-railed balcony. Qi followed her.

In the sparkling garden below, they spotted Jack in a tuxedo, his ragged hair pulled into a ponytail. Chris talked to a man wearing a devil mask. But Sam's eyes followed her best friend as she danced with Maggie.

"It's kind of weird," she told Qi. "Gilly doesn't run up and kiss people. She doesn't dance. She's usually so quiet. I mean, it's cool as hell, but for Gilly, it's weird."

"Part of it is Maggie," Qi said. "She has an talent for making people fall in love with her."

Sam started to nod, then she remembered she was talk-ing to a witch. "So is Gilly like . . . under like . . .

"A spell?" A hint of a smile crossed Qi's face. "Don't worry. Maggie just loves everybody, finds something good in everybody. And when people see the way she sees them, they tend to fall in love right back."

Sam stared down at the two waltzing figures. "How the fuck do you love everybody?"

"Insane, isn't it?"

Sam studied Qi from the corner of her eye. She under-stood why Qi didn't want people to know she was part of the Witches' Carnival. What she didn't get was how any-body couldn't figure it out. Qi's features suggested she was Sam's age, maybe a year or two older. The way she carried herself, though, it was impossible not to see that she'd watched empires come and go. When Qi spoke, even the other witches fell silent.

"Here you are! I've been looking everywhere for you guys."

Sam and Qi glanced over their shoulders. A middle-aged woman swept into the office. Tonja followed carrying a tray of chocolate chip cookies.

"I was scared you'd all left. I didn't want everyone to leave before—Hey, Andrew. You made it. Oh, I'm so glad."

The college kids had startled Sam when they began jok-ing about searching the office for their papers and changing

77

their grades. They were smoking pot in a teacher's house, an English professor named Dr. Whiting.

The way the students started talking all at once and hugging her, Sam guessed this was she. Dr. Whiting was shorter than every one of her students, and mannish, with broad shoulders and thick tendons running down either side of her neck. She complimented one girl on her dress, an electric violet matching the streaks in her hair, and wanted to make sure everybody had danced some. When a few of her students laughed and shook their heads, she scolded them.

"Why not? Don't worry, just get out there and make something up. Nobody here's a championship ballroom dancer. They'll never know. All right, Lindsey and David, you have to dance one dance together. One dance. You don't get any cookies until you promise."

Sam followed Qi back inside. As Dr. Whiting haggled, students hovered around the tray Tonja had set on the desk. Tonja picked up a cookie and took a bite. Then she took two more and handed them to Qi and Sam, saying, "They have mescaline."

Sam knew mescaline was something like LSD, but she'd never tried it. She bit into the cookie. It was warm and soft from the oven. It had a bitter, almost metallic, undertaste. She took a bigger bite.

"Now listen, guys," Dr. Whiting clapped her hands to quiet her clamoring students. "Nobody has to take any mescaline if they don't want to. I want everybody to have fun tonight and still like themselves tomorrow, got it?"

Everyone nodded. Nobody set down their snack.

Sam gobbled the rest of her cookie. Licking chocolate off her fingers, she wondered what was about to happen.

When the mescaline hit, it hit hard. The others had enough pot in their systems to cushion the blow, but Sam was riding without shocks. Before long she felt nauseated. A film of sweat covered her face. The light was too bright, making Sam dizzy.

Sitting in a corner of the office, Sam closed her eyes, gulping air like a fish and trying to not puke all over herself. The students, Dr. Whiting, and the witches jabbered about whether they felt high yet or not. Sam wanted them to shut up. She wanted Gilly to be there and got angry at her because she wasn't.

Then, alone in the dark behind her eyelids, sick, scared, and pissed off, Sam noticed how pretty their voices sounded, crystal girls and boys laughing like church bells. Sam sat and listened, and it calmed her down some. Dr. Whiting's words hummingbird-fluttered around Qi's soft, certain tones. It wasn't random chatter. The closer Sam listened, the more she realized their voices rose and fell in harmony like a choir.

"How're you doing?" Dr. Whiting's dress rustled as she sat down beside Sam. It gave Sam a jab of fear. She'd crashed this woman's party. She had to explain herself quick, or she'd be in deep shit. Sam opened her eyes and opened her mouth to lie.

"Oh."

She saw the woman, the shape of her face and chin and eyes and every eyelash. She saw the delicate wrinkles around her mouth and the softness of the skin at her throat. She saw her breathing.

"Honey?" Dr. Whiting rubbed Sam's back. "Do you feel sick?"

Sam nodded. "Little bit."

"That's okay. That's normal. Just relax and let your body adjust, okay? I'm Kathy, by the way."

"I'm Sam."

"Hi, Sam." Reaching out, Kathy stroked her hair with a tender, protective hand. Sam wondered how long it'd been since anyone had touched her like that.

"I crashed your party."

Kathy smiled. "Yeah, I guessed that."

"I'm sorry."

"Shhh . . . don't be sorry. Nobody's mad at you. Maybe it'd help if you lay down for a few minutes."

Sam shook her head. "I think I'm okay."

"Good. Mescaline can be a little rough going at first, but hang in there. The fun part's coming."

Sam saw how muscles, tendons, and bone shaped, reshaped the woman's body with each motion she made.

She saw each body in the room in constant, subtle motion. They swayed like pine boughs. "I think it's here."

At the other end of the hall, trembling-eager hands tugged at clothes and revealed hot skin. Mouths explored curves unseen in the dark.

"Can I wear the mask?" Gilly asked.

Maggie had a laugh like bloodred wine. "Sure, sweetie. You can do whatever you like."

Muffled voices drifted in from other rooms. Music as delicate as blown glass played in the garden below. Gilly's head swam with Maggie's scent and the salty taste of sweat on her throat and between her breasts.

On the untucked bed, Gilly kissed hard and pawed, excitement scattering in every direction. "Having fun up there?" Maggie asked, lying beneath her.

Gilly froze. Chuckling, Maggie took her wrist and shoulder. "Roll over."

Gilly's back sank against the quilt. She felt Maggie's gentle weight. Legs tangled together.

Maggie let Gilly stroke and cup her breasts while her own fingers traced the girl's ribs and navel like holy relics. She barely touched her, but that was enough. With patient, practiced skill, Maggie steered Gilly's frenzy toward a single, ascending path. "There you go." She smiled and gave Gilly's thigh a pinch. "Open your legs."

People in the hall started into a drug-slurred rendition of a familiar song, their voices jostling together. "Sorta, kinda feels like flying. Or maybe we're just falling. Who cares— we're hauling. Raise hell and a back beat!"

Lips against skin, Maggie sang along as she nibbled her way down Gilly's body. "We're running . . . hot. The kids are . . . losing their minds. They . . . can't see . . . the signs . . ." She went lazily along, relishing her morsel's unsteady breaths, the soft gasps, the arching hips.

There was a sharp rap on the door. "Sorry to interrupt, but is Gilly in there?" It was Sam.

Panting, it took Gilly several seconds to find her voice. "Go away, Sam."

"Listen, G. I really want you to—"

"Go the fuck away, Sam!"

Rolling off the bed, Maggie crossed the room.

"Okay, but listen," Sam rambled on. "There's mescaline out here, and it's really great, and I—"

Maggie opened the door a few inches and stood behind it. Gilly heard Sam's voice along with the chattering of several new friends. She covered herself with a pillow.

"Everything okay, Sam?" Maggie asked.

"Everything's great. There's mescaline, and it's amazing, and everyone's amazing, and I know you and Gilly are— yeah. But I didn't want you missing out."

Maggie turned toward Gilly. "There's mescaline downstairs."

"Maybe later."

"Okay. That's cool. I'm so sorry. It's just . . ." Pushing her head through the doorway, Sam whispered in Maggie's ear, making Maggie laugh.

"I do my best. But we could use some privacy right now."

"Sure. I'm sorry." Leaning through the doorway, Sam looked over Maggie's shoulder at Gilly. "Bye, G."

Flashing a sarcastic grin, Gilly waved. "Bye."

Maggie shut the door and locked it. As she walked back to the bed, Gilly asked, "What'd she say?"

"She said she was glad I'm here because I make you so happy, and you're her best friend and a really great person, but you're always so sad and she worries about you."

That embarrassed Gilly more than Sam pounding on the door. "God. She's such a crackbaby."

"She loves you, Gilly. She couldn't enjoy herself because she was worried you weren't having fun too."

"But I was having fun! She barged in and ruined my fun!"

Maggie laughed. "Want to know something fascinating about the Witches' Carnival?"

"What's that?"

"We never sleep."

"Really?"

Maggie shook her head. "Don't even get tired. Which means you and I have hours to have fun." She ran her fingernails down Gilly's stomach. "We have days, weeks. Months. Years."

"Bo–be–do–da–dum–da–dum . . ."

Sam discovered that if she sang part of a bar, the notes went on by themselves to the finish. It wasn't imagination. The music was crystal clear, coming from somewhere outside her own skull.

As time passed, her nausea receded to a slight stomachache. Kathy had left the office after Sam started feeling better. Qi and a few other friends had followed her. Tonja stayed, Jack had shown up, and they'd all ventured down to the kitchen for more cookies.

They wanted to watch the sunrise. Crossing the garden, Sam waved to Kathy and stopped to take pictures with her cell phone. Kathy suggested they climb onto the roof. From there, they could see the sun coming up over the ocean.

Wooden shingles pressing into her back, Sam watched. The infinite black nothing became a smoldering indigo. Clouds emerged. Houses around them swelled with blues, greens, and reds. The sea turned a glistening non–color.

Sam breathed in. The waves rolled up onto the beach, which was the edge of all creation. She exhaled, and the murmuring void swept back out.

Then a thread of celestial white traced the horizon. Blade–

thin, it cut the sky from the sea. Evelyn, the girl lying beside Sam, sniffed back tears. Sam reached out and squeezed her hand. A sense of togetherness filled her. Sam had more in common with these people, one sunrise, than she had with any of her friends back home or any of the boys she'd slept with.

Sam knew it was the mescaline, but the drug hadn't tricked her. It hadn't made her stupid like pot or beer did. The mescaline had peeled a dead skin away and exposed living nerves underneath. It had been scary at first, but now Sam thanked God for giving her the chance to be completely alive.

"Do-be-dum-da-dum . . ."

Maggie padded across the room humming. Lifting the blinds, she cracked open the window. A morning-crisp breeze carried bird songs into the room.

Gilly lay curled under the blanket, drifting through the gauzy place between awake and asleep.

"You know what? I think I'm going to keep you as a pet."

Without opening her eyes, Gilly smiled. "Yeah?"

"Mm-hm. You have the prettiest ears I've ever seen."

Smirking, Gilly clapped a hand over the side of her head.

"Don't you laugh at me." Maggie pried Gilly's hand back. She ran a finger around the outer curve of the girl's ear. "I appreciate a finely crafted ear."

The stereo in the garden had been turned off an hour

ago, but Gilly still heard muffled conversations going on through the house. "You don't have to stay," she said. "You can go downstairs if you want."

"Maybe in a little bit." Maggie settled onto the bed. She sat naked, one foot on the floor, the other resting on her thigh, scraping at flecks of week-old toenail polish. Gilly's gaze traveled across the witch's body, the round belly she wanted to rub and the thatch of glossy curls between her legs.

Maggie sang under her breath. "Sorta, kinda feels like flying. Or maybe we're just falling."

"Okay." Gilly propped her head in her hand. "Chris Marlowe. Is he like . . . *that* Christopher Marlowe?"

"Playwright, poet, libertine of distinction, that Christopher Marlowe." Maggie inspected a mosquito bite on her shin as she talked. "He was also a spy for France. When the queen found out, he faked his death, jumped on a ship bound for Portugal, and eventually wound up in the Carnival."

"Wow."

"Oh, you ever hear that story about Shakespeare poaching the king's deer?"

"Maybe. Kinda."

"Don't believe it. Chris started it a while back. He's got something of a jealous streak."

"So once you're in the Witches' Carnival, you live forever?"

"You live a bit longer than most. Nobody gets to lives for-ever."

"Still . . . Wow." Already, Gilly could barely grasp the won-der that she was in the Witches' Carnival, that she could go anywhere and do anything she could imagine. Now that was dwarfed by the idea that, in four centuries, she'd be going places and doing things her imagination couldn't even guess at today.

"So what about you?" Gilly asked. "How old are you?"

Maggie brushed strands of hair away from Gilly's face and smiled. "A bit older than most."

"No. Come on. How old are you?"

Sighing, Maggie stretched out in bed. "Let me see. I was born November 4, 1869. In Chicago."

"So you're–"

She held a finger against Gilly's lips. "I'm very bad at math, sweetie. And I prefer it that way."

"Fine. Next question. There's only five of you. Five people isn't really a carnival. You're more like the Witches' Coffee Klatch."

Maggie laughed. Her breasts shook. "Well, I didn't make up the name. I hope you're not too disappointed."

"No, but still, if everybody fantasizes about running away and joining the Witches' Carnival, you'd think more than five people in history would have found it."

"Everybody fantasizes about running away at one time or another, but almost nobody does it. Most people are either too scared or not scared enough to turn their backs on everything they know. And dozens of witches have joined the Carnival for a while and then left."

"What? If you're in the Witches' Carnival, why the hell would you ever leave?"

"Oh, love, duty, honor. The same silly reasons anybody does anything. Plus, lots more have been killed while they were in the Carnival."

"Really?"

Maggie nodded and turned away. "I told you, sweetie. Nobody lives forever. Especially the ones like Jack. He's too wild. His luck will run out before too long."

Gilly didn't know what to say. When Maggie looked back at her, she was smiling again. "So what about you? Why did you want on this ship of fools so badly?"

"Honestly, I didn't. I didn't really think the Witches' Carnival was real."

"You're lying."

"No. I mean, we sorta—"

"No. You're lying," Maggie said. "Maybe you told yourself you'd go to Atlanta for a couple days, blow through your father's money, then go back home. I'll even believe that you halfway convinced yourself of that. But down deep, you wanted to leave everything behind and never look back. Otherwise, you never would have found us. So why?"

Gilly tugged at a loose thread on the quilt. She realized

what Maggie said was true, but she didn't know why. She'd never been beaten or raped. Neither of her parents was a drug addict. Finally, she whispered, "The game."

"What game?"

Gilly's stomach cramped. She could hear their voices and smell the ammonia-sting of the hallway. She heard lockers clang and sneakers squeak. She shook her head. "It doesn't have a name."

"*. . . So are you really a lesbian?*"

Ashley and her friends had Gilly cornered. Gilly kept her back to them, rearranging the books in her locker, yanking out months-old wads of paper, anything so she wouldn't have to look them in the eyes.

"Yes." She tried to sound like she didn't care about them. Her voice betrayed her, coming out hoarse and trembling.

"Aren't you afraid you're going to Hell?" Ashley didn't give a damn about Gilly's eternal soul. Her voice was cheerful and full of ground glass.

"No."

Every game has rules. If Gilly pushed past them and ran away, Ashley and her friends would know they'd gotten to her, and they'd win. If she cussed them out, showed any anger at all, they'd know they'd gotten to her, and they'd win. If Gilly ignored them, pretended they weren't standing a foot away talking to her, that was a reaction, too. They'd win.

"Well, it's in the Bible that people like that go to Hell."

Gilly couldn't win. The only way to keep from losing was to stand there and let them pick and pick, doing everything she could not to flinch. Sometimes they gouged holes in her skin before getting bored.

"Don't you believe in the Bible?"

A round of play began when Ashley decided it did. It ended when Ashley decided. She could come back and start playing again whenever she liked.

Gilly tried explaining the game to Maggie, but the harder she tried to strip back the adolescent drama and reveal the violence underneath, the stupider it sounded.

"You know what they're saying, even if they never say it. Everybody knows, but nobody'll do shit."

Words were flimsy and cheap. Gilly couldn't pile adjectives high enough to equal being alone in a school full of people, being peered at and prodded. Being a thing.

"It's fucking fun for them. Proving they can make you twitch and squirm or whatever." Gilly was near tears. Just talking about Ashley brought the mouse-like rage back. "I shouldn't care about that bitch, but–I don't really, but–fuck it. I don't know. Fuck it."

Gilly was right: Maggie didn't understand the words. But she heard the hurting edge in Gilly's voice as she said them. Maggie watched the girl draw into herself. Knees pulling toward her belly, arms tightening across her chest, she looked like a flower closing against the dark.

Maggie laid her head next to Gilly's, so close that they shared one breath. In the dull light of morning, she took Gilly's hand and kissed her fingertips.

"Okay. This one!" Sam shouted.

Standing in the prickling-cold sea, her gown billowing around her waist like a jellyfish, Sam watched the wave hurl toward her. She let it snatch her off her feet and rocket her forward. Her body tumbled through boiling foam and swirling occult greens for hours. Not once did she feel frightened or hungry for breath. Finally, her arms and chest hit sand. Sam broke the surface of the sea laughing. Another wave washed over her. She got to her feet and ran to David as he got to his.

"See? I told you it was fun."

David's tuxedo jacket lay on the beach. Sam could see his chest through his soaked shirt, nipples and the dark shadow of his belly button. His body shook. His mouth opened to scream, but the water had snatched away his breath.

"'T's fucking cold," he croaked.

"It's not that bad." Tonja pushed damp hair like seaweed out of her eyes. "At first it's cold, but after a few seconds you start feeling really warm."

"That's you going into shock. It means you're dying."

They both laughed at him. "Come on. Let's go again."

"No way. I'm so cold, my balls hurt." David splashed up to

the beach where Jack and Evelyn stood bone dry, sharing a cigarette.

Sam and Tonja body surfed one more time before the others managed to coax them out of the water. They started back to Kathy and Jerrod's house, four blocks from the silver strand of beach. Sam was aware of every pebble, each fragment of shell and pale green shoot of grass. She loved the cool, salt-crusted sand crumbling between her toes. Brass-colored creatures had followed her out of the ocean. Sam couldn't see them clearly, only streaks of metallic movement, but they resembled salamanders. They darted over the sand and across her bare feet. She giggled when they snuck under her dress and up her legs.

Sam and the others slipped through the back gate in the limestone wall. The garden lay still, strewn with crumpled napkins and paper cups. The white Christmas lights draped through the trees shined pale against the glory of morning. A lone couple Sam didn't know danced to music only they heard.

Kathy's kitchen was cluttered-happy. A blue picnic table dominated the room. Pots, pans, and mismatched coffee mugs lined a shelf over the sink. Family snapshots and crayon drawings covered the refrigerator.

Stepping through the door, Sam hugged Qi.

"You're soaked."

Sam told her about the ocean and bodysurfing and the salamanders, making Qi laugh.

The man in the devil mask–his name was Peter–dropped spoonfuls of batter onto a cookie sheet. He, Marlowe, and Qi had been speaking in low, business-like voices when Sam and her friends had walked in.

Glancing up, Marlowe asked, "Take a dip, Hijack?"

Jack shook his head. "They're braver than me."

Grinning, Marlowe motioned for Jack to follow him. The witches and the horned man stepped out of the kitchen. Sam wanted Qi to stay, but Qi promised she'd be back in a minute.

Kathy fixed Sam, David, and Evelyn bowls of Trix, then went back to preparing the next batch of mescaline. They ate and talked. Sam had found that she could talk about anything and not feel ashamed or scared. Words came out of her mouth that she didn't expect to say, but once she heard them, she knew they were the truth. Each dose of mescaline let her peek a little deeper into her soul.

Sam jumped. There was a mutt dog under the picnic table. The lower half of its body was gone, nothing but scar tissue. It whimpered and tried dragging itself along by its front legs.

"You okay?" Evelyn asked.

Kathy turned and looked. "Sam, honey, what's the matter?"

Sam stared at the dog. She knew it was a hallucination. "Shoo." The dog vanished, sinking down into the floorboards.

"Sam?" Kathy asked again.

"I'm fine. Hi." She told them what had happened in between bites of cereal.

"I'm sorry, sweetie," Maggie said.

Gilly found the green-sequined mask tangled in the bed-sheets. She played with it, shrugged, and didn't have anything to say.

Maggie went on. "I wish people didn't have to leave everything behind to be happy. I wish there were more cool people in the world."

"Fuck that. There're too many cool people in the world already. They're like fucking dandelions."

Maggie laughed.

"Well. I mean, so you buy your clothes at Hot Topic and get your belly button pierced? So what? It doesn't mean shit."

"Know what? You sound a tiny bit bitter."

"No. You can do whatever you want, just—okay, I had this friend named Tracye."

"Who was cool."

"She spelled 'Tracye' with an 'e.' When someone has a useless vowel at the end of their name, you know they're cool. Anyway, we sat together at lunch, and maybe I had a little crush on her, but mostly she was just fun to hang out with. We had some art classes together, and we liked the same music, and . . . you know."

"She was cool."

"Right. Cool. Anyway, Tracye's one of the first people I told I was gay, even before my parents. And she's all 'Whatever. I don't care.' Because she's cool, right? That extra 'e' stands for 'everybody gettin' along.' So one day at lunch the little Abercrombie and Fitch skanks start playing their game. Whispering real loud, making stupid jokes." Gilly slipped the mask over her eyes. "So I already want to fucking kill myself. Then they turn on Tracye. They ask her why she hangs out with me. If we're dating. Shit like that. Finally, Tracye goes, 'No,' then she grins and says, 'I don't like fish that much.'"

"Was she trying to be funny?"

Gilly shook her head. "I don't know. I mean, it's not the worst I've ever heard. But she's my friend, y'know?"

"Yes, but why did she—"

"Because she's cool! That's my point!" Gilly spit out the words. "She liked me, but it didn't matter. If she let them pick on her too, she wouldn't be cool. Can't have that! What's fucked up is she hated Ashley as much as I do. She still wanted to be my friend. She'd still talk to me in class and everything. Just when the shit started, she'd sell me out. That's all."

"Toss the little hussy," Maggie snapped. "Who cares how many art classes you had together? Toss her and piss on her."

"Then what?" Gilly yanked the mask off again. Staring at

her reflection in the jade sequins, she watched hundreds of pinhole mouths move as she spoke. "I have to go to that fucking school every day. I have to go to that fucking lunchroom every day. Who do I sit with? Ashley and them?"

Maggie lay silent for a few seconds. "Oh, sweetie."

Gilly sneered. "Yeah. I remember that day. I remember sitting there choking down my lunch and everything tasting like mud and sitting there and just trying not to start sobbing like a . . ." She flung the mask, sending it spinning across the room. "Point is, I can go to the Galleria and buy cool; doesn't mean I get the guts that come with it."

Maggie squeezed Gilly's arm. "You're pretty smart, kid. I hate that you had to get smart the hard way."

"Fuck it. I'd rather hang out with losers."

"Yeah?"

Memories flickered in Gilly's eyes. She chuckled. "Any day of the week."

"*. . . I just think it's nasty.*"

Ashley and her clique pressed close, pinning Gilly to the wall without laying a hand on her. Gilly worried with the books in her locker, pretending that the words didn't hurt, never doubting that Ashley and Tracye and all the others knew how much they did.

"Isn't it gross? Doing stuff like that?"

Gilly couldn't answer. If she opened her mouth, her voice would crack. Mute and beyond redemption, she hated them.

"I mean–"

Bodies crashed together. A hollow metal *clang*. Papers and books scattered to the floor. Gilly snapped around to see Ashley bounce against the lockers and yelp, "Hey!"

"Hey!" Samantha Grace stood in front of her, twisting her voice into a shrill whine.

"Watch where you're going."

"I did. I slammed into you on purpose." Two inches shorter than Ashley, Samantha glared at her like a pissed cat.

Ashley stared back for a second, then glanced around the crowded hall.

"Looking for a teacher?" Samantha asked. "Go get one. I'll wait. Go. I'll tell them what I did. Go get one. Go."

Neither Ashley nor her friends moved. Gilly stood frozen too. She barely knew this girl. Samantha dated Alex Oden, the three of them had biology together, and that was all. Swooping into Ashley's game from nowhere, she started changing the rules mid–round.

"What's your problem?" Ashley sneered, glancing down at the girl's dirty sneakers and slightly–too–tight babydoll shirt.

"You're a crackwhore bitch and you're messing with my friend."

Ashley fake–stifled a fake laugh. "She's your friend?" The last word became obscene. If Samantha took it, she'd be tainted. It didn't matter who made up the rules; the game was fixed.

"Hell yeah, Gilly's my friend. Gilly kicks ass. And nobody cares what you think. They're just mad your mom could only afford half an abortion."

"Whatev–"

Samantha shouldered Ashley aside and continued down the hall. Shutting her locker, Gilly followed after her.

"So Ashley and her friends start whispering and snickering," Gilly said, telling Maggie about the day she and Sam became friends. "But Sam never turns around. Just grumbles 'fucking bitch' and keeps walking."

"I knew I liked Sam." Maggie beamed. "I didn't know why, but I knew I liked her."

"Yeah." Gilly laughed. "'Go get a teacher. I'll wait. Go.'"

"See? You can win the game. It takes a little pluck, but you can win."

Lying with her arm tucked under her head, Gilly let the laughter seep away. "No. You can never win."

"Sam did."

"How? They still pick on me. The same shit every day, the giggles and rumors and shit. They pick on Sam now too. She's always hanging out with me, so half the school thinks she's gay too." Gilly didn't mention their friendship had benefits. She was pretty sure you weren't supposed to talk about stuff like that with someone you'd just had sex with, and it was beside the point, anyway. The rumors would have sprung up whether Sam was totally straight or not.

Maggie traced her fingers along Gilly's ribs. The bedroom was built under the eaves of the house. Gilly stared up at the slanting roof, barely noticing Maggie's touch.

"But she takes it," Gilly said. "Whatever I go through, Sam catches it too. She knows she'll catch it. But she just takes it and takes it and doesn't slink away and doesn't turn her back and just takes it."

Gilly had kept from crying the whole time. Now, tears stung the corners of her eyes and made her vision swim. "It's just–they still pick on me, y'know? And it still hurts. But at least I don't have to handle it alone."

She wiped the tears away and braved a weak laugh. "That day she shoved Ashley, we go to biology and Sam doesn't say one word to me the whole class. But the moment the bell rings, she's standing over me, going, 'And why do you sit with those artsy bitches at lunch? Don't you fucking know they're making fun of you?' And I say something like I'm used to it, Tracye's really okay, and that gets Sam pissed at me, going, 'You're such a pussy. Kick their asses. Sit with me and Alex. Whatever. Don't just sit there eating their shit. Jesus fuck.'"

"So you sat with her after that?"

"I was afraid not to. It took me a while to figure out that calling you a pussy is just Sam making polite conversation."

Maggie grinned. "She sounds like a good person to have beside you."

"Yeah. I mean, Sam can drive you crazy sometimes and act like a complete–But I'd do anything for her." Pulling the quilt over her shoulder, Gilly curled against Maggie. She spread her fingers along the warmth of the witch's belly. "You know what sucks, though? I never thanked her. I'm such a bitch. That first time she stuck up for me, I knew I should have said thanks, but I was so embarrassed at having to be rescued, I couldn't make myself do it."

Maggie was quiet for a long time, stroking Gilly's hair. "Why don't you thank her later today?" she whispered.

"It was, like, two years ago. It'd be weird."

"Yes, but it'll make you feel better. So thank her later today, okay?"

Gilly yawned and nodded. "All right."

"Promise?"

"I promise."

"Good girl." Maggie's fingertips trailed up the back of Gilly's neck and along the edge of her ear. Gilly lay quiet under her touch.

She'd confessed her cowardice out loud. Gilly had told her story and decided she would never tell it again. It wasn't her story anymore; she was in the Witches' Carnival.

Gilly had decided that this was a dream. The Witches' Carnival didn't exist in the real world. And the Gilly who existed in the real world was not brave or cunning enough to have done everything that she'd done in the past day. The real Gilly was not beautiful enough to be lying in bed beside a woman like Maggie. Gilly had decided this was a dream, and also that she'd let that real Gilly, deep asleep somewhere in the outskirts of Birmingham, wither away and never wake up.

Already, Gilly could see herself arcing across the earth bright as a comet, moving too fast for the Ashleys and Tracyes, the thousand tiny insults and humiliations of the waking world, to ever catch.

Making the dog vanish had given Sam a rush. She felt invincible. She tried bringing the salamanders back; she wanted Kathy to see them. That was harder, though.

"Don't you guys want to change into something dry?" Kathy asked, pulling the cookie sheet out of the oven. "You must be freezing."

Sam nodded. "In a little bit."

Kathy noticed her staring at the mescaline cookies. "Think you can handle another dose, Sam?"

"Sure."

Kathy made a nervous, tight-lipped noise. "How many have you had so far?"

A single salamander skittered up the wall. Sam loved Kathy and didn't want her to worry. "Just the one."

"And how do you feel?"

"Like I'm home."

That made Kathy smile. "Okay, but stay close by. No more bodysurfing, got it?"

"Okay."

After letting them cool a few minutes, Kathy handed Sam and David cookies on paper napkins. Sam took a bite. She felt herself slip deeper, deeper down.

sEvEN

The parking garage's slab walls deadened the clamor of downtown Birmingham. Sipping cups of coffee, Andy and Malik sat in their unmarked Cavalier, piecing together as much as they could.

Andy had searched Gilly's room earlier that morning. Her clothes were still there, and she'd left her overnight bag wedged in the corner of the closet. She hadn't taken anything except the money.

"It was a smash-and-grab thing," he said. "She didn't know she was going to leave until after she got to school."

"All right. So Gilly's pissed at you. She goes to school. Cries on this other kid's shoulder. But it's the other kid's idea to run away."

"Sounds like it."

"What about a boyfriend?" Malik asked.

"No." Andy didn't want to get into Gilly's sexual preferences.

"You sure? Any boy she's mentioned lately?"

"It's not a boy, okay? That's not it."

"All right, all right. Calm down. Whoever it is, they're the closest thing we've got to a lead."

Andy nodded. "We need to get the attendance records from her school. Find out who else skipped yesterday." He was exhausted. The coffee couldn't wake him up anymore, only make him as twitchy as a meth addict. He drank it, anyway.

It was Saturday, so the school was closed. Malik got in touch with Gilly's vice principal, a man named Billy Irby, who had agreed to meet them at the school.

Pulling out of the garage, they headed for the county. Abandoned rock quarries cratered the redneck towns around Birmingham. As years passed, the mile-wide pits filled with stagnant water. They became convenient dumping grounds for old refrigerators, stolen cars, and dead bodies. If your drug deal went bad, you barely had to leave the interstate anymore to get rid of the evidence.

Andy drove up Falcon Drive and into the school parking lot. Climbing out of his car to meet them, Mr. Irby had the heavy sway of a retired boxer. Andy had met him two years ago, during a parent-teacher conference after Gilly cut gym

for a straight week. When Andy shook his hand and introduced himself as Steve Hammond, another detective in the
robbery unit, it was obvious the vice principal didn't
remember him. Afraid to push his luck, Andy stayed behind
to call the station while Malik and Irby went inside.

Andy called Lieutenant Swopes and fed him a story about
hunting down witnesses for the UAB Hospital robberies.
While they talked, Andy watched the football team go
through blocking drills on the field beside the school. He
wondered if any of them were Gilly's friends, if they had
classes with her or talked to her in the halls.

Andy tried thinking like a cop, but Gilly was his daughter, not some name typed on a boilerplate warrant. She was
touchy, able to string a room with trip-wire looks. But her
nose wrinkled when she laughed. She liked sweet tea and
chewed the ice cubes the same way Karen did. She always
helped him in the garage.

Malik and Mr. Irby reappeared, shoulders hunched
against the cold. Andy shook the guilty thoughts out of his
head.

"Shit, it's nasty out." Malik climbed into the car and
slammed the door. He dropped a folded printout in Andy's
lap. "All the students who were absent or skipped class
yesterday."

Andy scanned the names. "There's two dozen kids here."

"But only two of them disappeared between their

first- and second-period classes. One was Gilly." Malik waved good-bye to Mr. Irby. "The other was Samantha Grace. Name sound familiar at all?"

"Samantha . . . shit. Sam. She's been over to the house a couple times."

"All right. We know where to look." Pulling out of the parking lot, Malik started thinking out loud. "First, we talk to Grace's folks and keep them from calling Family Services. If they already have, we're still okay. We tell Family we're looking at Grace for another case and take over the investigation."

Andy took a deep breath. He hadn't told Malik about their seventy-two-hour time limit yet. "Listen, man. I hope to God we can find Gilly ourselves. But Family Services has a lot more resources than we do. They can put out a bulletin, coordinate with other departments. And they don't have to sneak around to do it."

"I don't give a fuck if they can fly and talk to dolphins," Malik snapped. "We're in major shit here, Moonpie. Your kid's running around with fifty kay that's gonna put both our asses in jail if anybody but us finds her. Do you get that?"

"She's still my kid, Malik."

The silence between them stretched as taut as piano wire. When Malik answered, he wouldn't look Andy in the eye. "We've been partners a long time, so I'll lay it out for you. I know you love Gilly. I know you want her found more than anything. But I've got kids of my own. And they need their daddy at home, not rotting in Kilby Penitentiary. I'm not going down for this, Andy. Whatever I've got to do, I'll do it, but I'm not going down because your kid fucked up. You hear what I'm saying?"

Andy heard. Malik had stashed his share of the money somewhere investigators wouldn't look. When it came down to brass tacks, he'd flip on Andy, make a confession, make up a story, do what it took to stay out of jail. There was no seventy-two-hour time limit. Either they found Gilly or nobody did.

"I got you," he said.

"Good." Malik slapped Andy in the chest and grinned. "Relax, man. Sooner or later, Gilly's gonna come back. Our job's to keep the police out of it until she does."

EIGHT

"Are you Gilly?" The bedroom door banged open, ripping Gilly out of a dead sleep. She yelled, sitting bolt upright and clutching the patchwork quilt across her breasts. Bleary eyes focused on a middle-aged man in the doorway.

His voice was rushed and nervous. "Sorry. Didn't mean to startle you, but are you Gilly?"

"Y-yeah." Maggie was gone. Gilly glanced around, trying to get her bearings. Somebody was crying down the hall.

"It's Sam. She's a little worked up."

Gilly forgot Maggie and turned toward the crying. Getting to her feet, she wrapped the quilt around herself. "Oh, God. What happened?"

"No one's sure. She might have taken too much mescaline."

Gilly shoved past him and into the hall. The sobs came from the open bathroom door. The man followed her. "She was okay an hour ago," he said.

People shuffled around the doorway and inside the bathroom. Sam sat trembling in the tub. Shrinking away from the gawkers, she pressed her face against the mildewed tile, protecting her head behind her arm.

A short, broad-shouldered woman knelt beside the tub. "Sam, look. Your friend's here."

Sam didn't turn to look. In between sniffling sobs, she mumbled to herself. ". . . ugly-ass purple fucking furniture. And that fucking bitch just—that fucking—"

"Sam? What's wrong, Sam?" Gilly took a careful step forward. Sam's purse lay beside the sink. Gilly noticed the SpongeBob SquarePants candy box sitting beside it.

"Sam, look. It's Gilly. Everything'll be okay. Don't be scared." The woman touched Sam's hair. Sam flinched.

"I'm rotting, rotting." She shook her head. "It's not my fault."

Sam wasn't in the sunny bathroom anymore with its wrinkled magazines and tree-frog shower curtain. She'd fallen through the floor, as if the frozen surface of a pond had cracked underneath her. They all stood by, watching her slide into the cold, green-black water.

"Calm down, okay?" Gilly begged. The way Sam babbled terrified her. She wanted Sam to stop shaking. She wanted her to say something that made sense. "Fuck, Sam. Open your eyes."

"Shhh . . . don't yell," the woman whispered. "Just keep telling her it'll be okay."

"It'll be okay," Gilly parroted. "It'll be okay."

"Gilly?" Sam choked her name out. She still wouldn't look up.

"It'll be okay, Sam. Just tell me what's wrong."

"Gilly," she whispered so nobody else could hear. "I'm really fucking high."

"It's okay, S–"

"No, it's not! I can't get it to stop. It keeps happening, and I can't make it fucking stop!" Her face crumpled.

"Sam." The woman stroked Sam's wet hair. "You're hallu-cinating, honey. But none of it can hurt you. Even if it looks scary, none of it's real, I prom–"

"It is!" Sam lurched forward, splashing water over the edge of the tub. "I was there! I can hear them fucking! And I can't turn up the TV because of the stupid fucking remote."

Everyone stood and stared, but none of them did a thing. When Gilly spoke, her tongue felt thick. "Are you talking about Danny and your mom?"

Sam turned toward her for a moment, then scrunched back against the wall. "It's happening. I'm rotting. I can hear them, and I'm rotting."

"You're not rotting, Sam." With no thought except Sam

was scared and sick, Gilly stepped into the tub with her. Ignoring the soap-murky water that soaked through the quilt, ignoring the silent eyes watching them, Gilly pressed her temple against the wall so Sam could see her face. "You're not rotting, baby. That was a million years ago. You're not rotting."

Sam cried, her lips peeled back in a repulsive grin. Bubbles of spit formed in the corners of her mouth. "In the middle of the house. You don't know it's there, but the room's there, but there aren't any doors, and I can't get out. Qi could get in, but she left. She left me like this." She showed Gilly her hands. Whatever Sam thought was wrong with her, Gilly couldn't see it.

Gilly squeezed Sam's hands. "You're okay, Sam. Danny was a long time ago, remember?"

"Listen! They're in the fucking–" She punched the tile wall and split her knuckle. Gilly grabbed her, clutching Sam to her chest to keep her from hurting herself.

"It's okay. It's okay. Please just calm down, okay?"

"No, no. Go look downstairs," Sam begged. "There's no TV playing *The Animaniacs*. It's playing in the room. *The Animaniacs* aren't even on TV anymore."

"You're hearing things, Sam. You took a lot of drugs and your ears are playing tricks on you."

Sam pressed her forehead against Gilly's shoulder, her eyes squeezed shut. "I can't tell anymore," she sniveled.

"I'm not lying to you. You're my best friend. Danny was a long time ago. Nothing's happening downstairs. It's just the drugs, Sam. I swear."

It's all right. You're okay. There's no hidden room. Nobody's having sex inside the walls. Gilly held Sam and recited the words over and over. Somehow, they reached down into the icy darkness that only Sam could feel. Sam still trembled, but her crying slowed to soft, hiccupy sobs.

Gilly glanced up at the strangers watching them. She didn't like them seeing Sam naked, and her country grammar rose to the surface. "How about y'all get the fuck outta here?" she snapped, meeting their eyes dead-on.

They filed out of the bathroom tossing bits of encouragement behind them. Everyone left except the short woman and the man who'd woken Gilly up. She guessed they owned the house.

"How much did she take?" Gilly asked. Her legs prickled with pins and needles from sitting crooked in the tub so long.

"Two cookies. About four hundred milligrams. That's a little heavy for a first trip, but she seemed to be doing so well."

Gilly chewed her lip. "You're sure it was two, or she just told you two?"

"Uh . . ."

"Sam, how much mescaline did you take?"

"I'm sorry."

"I know. It's okay. But how many cookies did you take? Two?"

Sam gave an exhausted shake of her head. Eyes still closed, she whispered, "Four."

The woman and man looked at each other, then stared at Gilly. "I tried to look out for her," the woman said. "There was so much going on, and she didn't . . . oh, Sam, honey . . ."

Gilly glanced at SpongeBob lying beside the sink. "Did you take Xanax on top of that?"

Sam choked and babbled. "I couldn't control things anymore. I didn't want to rot, but I couldn't make it stop."

"So you took a Xanax and a bath, hoping the hallucinations would stop?"

Sam nodded. She was crying again. "It's going on inside me, Gilly."

After another ten minutes, they got her calmed back down. The woman sent her husband, Jerrod, to find a bathrobe. Then she and Gilly eased Sam out of the tub, handling her as carefully as a cup filled to the brim.

They took Sam to the room where Gilly had been asleep. Still wrapped in the sopping quilt, Gilly left a trail of bath-water down the hall floor. She remembered the Witches' Carnival and felt a twitch of anger that they were downstairs enjoying a late breakfast during all of this. But Maggie's warm, wild scent still lingered in the bedroom under the eaves. As she stepped through the door, Gilly's anger faded quickly.

They got Sam to the bed. She lay crumpled and still, damp tendrils of hair across her face.

"Jesus, Sam." Gilly sat down next to her. She tried to laugh, her heart pounding hard enough to hurt. "Don't scare me like that."

Sam sniffled and didn't answer.

The woman knelt beside the bed. "Sam? Do you remember me?"

"Kathy."

"That's right. I know everything's scary right now, but it'll be over soon. I'm here and Gilly's here, and we're going to stay with you. Just try to relax. Everything'll be all right."

"I'm really sorry about this," Gilly mumbled.

"No. I should have watched her closer. I just . . . I'm sorry."

"Well, we'll get out from underfoot in a little bit, okay?"

"You're not underfoot. Let's let Sam rest some."

"Well . . . thanks, but we–"

"We already know you ran away from home and crashed the party," Jerrod spoke up. "Don't worry. Nobody's going to call the police. Let Sam rest, and we'll figure out what to do after that, okay?"

Gilly nodded. "Thanks."

"No problem." Kathy smiled. "You think you could get her

to eat a candy bar or something? The sugar might help."

"I'll try. Listen, though. Have you seen another girl around here? Her name's Maggie. She's older, has dark hair?"

Both Kathy and Jerrod shook their heads. "Don't think so."

"How about a guy named Chris Marlowe? Or a girl named Qi? I think she's Chi–"

"Are they friends of yours?" Kathy's face brightened. "I could have talked to either of them for hours."

"Do you know where they are?"

"I think they left."

Gilly stared at her. "What?"

"I think they left with, uh, well I think they left awhile ago."

"There's a note for you here, by the way," Jerrod said.

Someone had folded Gilly's clothes and laid them on the dresser. A square of paper sat on top with her name written across it. Jerrod handed it to her. Gilly opened it.

I'm sorry, Gilly;
We couldn't take you along. I know you wanted to come,
but please don't think we left you just to be cruel. We have
to leave everyone behind. I hate it sometimes. You're
beautiful & funny & have a lot to stick around for.

Sincerely,
Maggie

Gilly stared at Maggie's graceful script, reading the words over and over, trying to understand what they meant.

"Why don't you stay with her, and I'll go find something for you two to eat," Kathy said.

Gilly nodded. "Okay."

"Sam should be all right. If we keep her calm, she'll be all right."

"Okay."

"Are you going to be all right, honey?"

Gilly folded the note and held it in her lap. "Yeah."

. . . And the Earth is a ball full of oceans and some mountains which is out there spinning silently in space. And living on that Earth are the plants and the animals and also the entire human race. . . .

Sam had been killed. She could smell the shit and rotting meat stink of her burst bowels. As her skin turned black and muscle underneath liquefied, Sam heard the Animaniacs singing *Yakko's Universe* on the TV in Danny's living room, which was downstairs even if it wasn't. She heard her mom groaning. Danny grunted like an animal.

It'll be over soon. Everything'll be all right.

Her body wasn't decaying. There were no noises in the walls. The harder she tried to ignore them, though, the more certain they became.

NINE

As the airport bustled around him, Peter Spiegelman realized his new friends were insane.

He should have backed out the moment they waved off a cut of the profits, considering the fun of drug smuggling payment enough. He'd been desperate, though. His original transport crew had gone chickenshit on him at the last moment, and the whole deal was teetering toward collapse. Marlowe and his friends appeared in Jerrod's kitchen like manna from heaven. Peter decided to trust in providence and bought a plane ticket.

The others didn't bother with tickets. Peter hadn't noticed, at first, working hard at acting normal and even harder at not "acting normal."

Then, standing in line at the security checkpoint, he

watched Tonja rip pages out of the book she'd swiped from Kathy's office. She tore the pages into halves and passed them around. Peter watched Tonja write *Ticket to London* and *U.S. Passport Tonja Lewis* across the scraps. Pulling pens from pockets and bags, the others did the same thing.

Peter stood frozen, waiting for the punch line. There wasn't one. Holding their homemade tickets, they chatted about London and the party.

Memories of Peter's three-year bit in Stillwater State Penitentiary rushed through his head. They felt, sounded, and smelled so vivid, he might have gotten out yesterday. It had been a lot longer than that, twenty-six years. Peter was older, and prison was rougher, a pit full of animals. He wouldn't survive another stint.

Suddenly, Qi was handing her pieces of paper to the security guard. She dropped one of the bags Peter had jerry-rigged–two kilos of mescaline under a false bottom–onto the x-ray machine's conveyor belt.

Peter fought the urge to turn and run. He'd never make it to the doors, and it'd only tag him as a coconspirator. He had to stay in line, act normal, and pray security wouldn't connect him to the lunatics holding his drugs.

"Oh, my goodness," the guard said, glancing at Qi's ticket. "I always wanted to go to London. London or Paris. You're lucky." She wished Qi a good flight and waved her through.

One by one, Peter's new partners slid bags full of drugs

into the machine, flashed their Dadaist identification, and gathered on the other side of the checkpoint. Nobody noticed anything strange except Peter. The guards, the machines, the barriers—millions of dollars' worth of security apparatus—parted for them like the Red Sea.

Peter showed his ticket. No trap sprung. No other shoe dropped. As the others swept through the crowded terminal, he had to hustle to keep up, pushing arthritic knees into a half-jog.

Peter stared at a fairy tale as it dodged businessmen carrying laptops and talked about getting something to eat before the flight. They stepped onto a moving sidewalk. Maggie hopped onto the handrail, riding it toward Gate G7. She kicked Peter playfully in the leg.

He looked up at her. "You're the Witches' Carnival, aren't you?"

Maggie smiled and nodded.

"I didn't think you were real," Peter confessed.

"Surprise."

It went on for hours. Before Kathy and Jerrod left to attend to other things, they got Sam to eat some cream puffs left over from the party. The sugar didn't help much. She'd pass through black doldrums for a while, curled up on the edge of catatonia. Then some phantom would flicker behind Sam's eyelids, and it'd start again.

She'd whimper and shake. She'd slap Gilly's hand away if Gilly tried to touch her. Watching Sam go mad over and over, Gilly felt her own sanity crack.

A TV sat on the dresser. With the sound turned down low, it seemed to blunt the storms inside Sam's brain. She stared at old episodes of *Matlock* and *ER*, still crying for no reason. She picked at a zit on her chin until her fingernails were crusted with dried blood.

Gilly found another note while getting dressed. Tucked in the pocket of her hoodie, it was wrapped around a Baggie full of what looked like dingy yellow salt.

A good-bye present. Yummy mescaline! Makes about ten cookies. Eat one every few hours until the world stops sucking. Have fun! Be careful! Share!

The signature was a smiley face with X'ed out eyes, the same as on the yearbook pages Tonja had tossed them the first time Gilly and Sam saw the Carnival.

Gilly stuffed the mescaline and both notes into her pocket. She didn't want to think about them. The green-sequined mask lay next to her clothes. She dropped it behind the dresser. She didn't want to think about that, either.

Gilly gazed out the window at a black-and-white-striped lighthouse pricking the blue air. She paced the room and listened to the soft voices beyond the door. Gilly didn't like strangers. As much as any reason, she wanted Sam feeling better so she could laugh and chat with these people as if she'd known them her whole life. In the meantime, Gilly stayed hidden in the room, trying to keep as quiet as possible.

Noon came and went. Then one o'clock. Then two. Then three. All the other guests had left. Gilly heard Kathy talking with a little girl downstairs. A kid seemed weirdly blasphemous in this house of masquerade balls and hallucinogens.

Gilly stared at the lighthouse some more. Something didn't fit. Suddenly, she realized that Atlanta wasn't on the coast.

She'd noticed the warm salt breeze the night before. She'd known they were near the ocean but had never stopped to wonder how or even which ocean. Gilly tried thinking back through the swirl of last night. She remembered sitting in the backseat with Maggie, Jack behind the wheel. She remembered driving fast, hurling down a dark interstate, dodging between eighteen-wheelers, so fast that it scared and thrilled her at once.

Bedsprings squeaked. Gilly turned to watch Sam push herself up on one elbow.

"You okay?"

Sam moved in torpid shudders. Her hair was a bird's nest. Dried tears streaked her face. "I need a cigarette."

They went outside to smoke. Sam took small steps and kept one hand on the wall, as if the floors all sloped down.

Slipping out the front door, they sat on the stoop. All the houses on Kathy's block whispered history and wealth. Two and three stories tall, every one was draped with balconies, wrap-around porches, and walled gardens. Ancient trees shaded the lawns.

Sam smoked her cigarette down to the filter without a word. Flipping the butt into the gutter, she shook another one out of the pack.

Gilly asked again. "So you okay?"

Sam nodded.

"You were really fucked up."

"Yeah. I thought . . ." She stared at her hand and flexed her fingers. "I don't know what I thought. It was fucking twisted."

Taking the Winston Light from Sam, Gilly took a puff. "You started talking about Danny and your mom."

Sam nodded again. "Yeah." She still wore Kathy's bathrobe. Staring at her toes poking out from beneath the green chenille, she cleared her throat and changed the subject. "So . . . the Witches' Carnival?"

"They were real."

"Seriously? You're not shitting me?"

"Jack, Chris, Qi. They were all real."

"Fuck." Sam took her cigarette back.

Gilly considered telling her about the lighthouse off the Atlanta coast but decided it could wait until Sam was steadier on her feet.

"They left, didn't they?"

Gilly pulled Maggie's note out of her pocket and handed it to Sam. Sam read it, then handed it back to Gilly. "Bunch of motherfuckers."

"So what do we do now?"

"Hell, I don't know."

"Well, what do you think we should do?"

"Jesus, Gilly. What the fuck are you looking at me for? I almost fucking killed myself a couple hours ago."

"Sorry. Shit." Gilly looked down.

Sam coughed and took a drag. "You didn't see them leave or anything?"

Gilly shook her head. "I fell asleep, and Maggie was there. I woke up, and she was gone."

"Sorry, G. I know you liked her."

"Yeah, well . . . fuck it. What else did we have to do this weekend?"

Sam snorted, flashing her sharp-cornered grin.

"Sam? How're you doing?" They both looked up. Kathy appeared in the doorway. A little Asian girl hung on to her arm.

"A lot better," Sam said.

"Guys, this is Emily," Kathy said, stroking the girl's head. "She just got back from Grandma's house."

"Did you?" Sam beamed. "Oh. That sounds like fun."

Emily gave a solemn nod of her head. When Kathy sat down, the preschooler climbed into her lap.

"Sam, are you sure you're okay?" Kathy asked, acting like Sam was anyone except a runaway who'd crashed her party, taken too many drugs, and collapsed into a sobbing wreck in her bathtub.

Sam's Civic was parked by the curb, covered in a thin layer of road dust. While Sam and Kathy talked, Gilly got up and found the ammo box in the trunk. Still full of money, someone had hidden it under the bags from her and Sam's shopping spree through Little Five Points. It didn't matter; fifty thousand dollars couldn't buy the one thing Gilly really wanted. She slammed the trunk and walked back to the stoop. Kathy looked up.

"Gilly, are you hungry or anything?"

"No, thanks. But would it be okay if I took a shower?"

"Sure. You remember where the bathroom is? Just make yourself at home."

"Thanks." She hesitated a moment. "By the way. Who brought the cookies to the party last night?"

"Peter. An old friend of ours. How come?"

"Just curious. Do you know how to get in touch with him?"

Kathy smiled. "Actually, he was just passing through town."

"Do you know where he's headed?" Gilly asked.

"Sure don't. Sorry."

Gilly thought she was lying, either protecting them from

Peter or protecting her friend from being chased by two half-wild high school kids. She nodded, anyway. "All right. Thanks." Gilly reached for the brass door handle. Sam grabbed her hand.

"Maggie's trash for doing you like that, G."

Gilly shrugged and went inside.

Water from Sam's bath still sat in the tub. Gilly let it drain out, then turned the faucet handle. Hot water whistled up the pipes. Sitting on the toilet, she kicked off her shoes, pulled her sweatshirt over her head, and started to cry.

Biting down on the fabric of her hoodie, she tried not to make a sound. Curling into herself, Gilly hugged her belly, forehead almost touching her knees.

The bathroom filled with steam. Minutes passed until she gathered herself enough to finish undressing. Stepping into the shower, Gilly lifted her face, letting hot needles of water sluice away the tears and spit and snot.

Gilly tried to hate Maggie, but the sex had been wonderful and a promise of nothing. She remembered Maggie kissing her stomach, warm lips, and the cool tip of her nose against soft skin. She could almost feel her hands, one tucked under the small of Gilly's back, the other sliding across her thigh. Trying to drive the memory away, Gilly beat her palm against her temple.

And afterward, Maggie stayed with her. Gilly only knew sex as furtive gropes and screws, as being shoved away as often as being pulled close. Sam wouldn't go down on Gilly, but she'd let Gilly go down on her. She loved Gilly, but not the way she loved Colby.

Maggie had offered her everything, and afterward they'd lain together, talking in quiet tones as the clean colors of morning filled the room. It had made Gilly feel luminescent.

Maggie traveled across the earth. Every city threw open its gates for her. Every head bowed. There wasn't a prince, pirate, or gutter punk she couldn't charm. And for a few hours, she'd stopped and listened to stories from Gilly's tiny life.

But Gilly and Sam were just a pair of pot-smoking, white-trash fuckups. No matter how much money they stole or how fast they ran, they could never keep pace with the Witches' Carnival.

We have to leave everyone behind. I hate it sometimes. You're beautiful & funny & have a lot to stick around for. It was head-patting bullshit, the kind of honeyed lie people told to make themselves feel better.

Gilly stood under the shower spray. Wiping her eyes, she stared down at her body. She was fat. Pimples sprung up across her chin and forehead so often, Gilly worried they'd scar. One cruel word could short-circuit her brain with hissing fear and hurt.

Her parents loved her, but she disappointed them. It came through in all the things they never said. Bad attitude, bad skin, gay—she wasn't whatever it was they wanted her to be.

At school, Gilly neither excelled nor caused trouble, so to the teachers she didn't exist. The people who did notice her were usually hunting for weak prey. She followed Sam like a puppy because she was the only person who'd ever stuck up for her.

After a lifetime spent falling short, it was easy to get suckered into the myth of the Witches' Carnival. Jumping into Sam's car and flying toward Atlanta, Gilly had told herself it wasn't real. But she couldn't help imagining: *What if the Witches' Carnival existed? What if we found them? What if they saw something in me, some hidden beauty that nobody else had ever been smart enough to see?*

Meek hadn't made it up; the Carnival was real. In the end, though, they saw the same thing in Gilly that everyone else did: nothing in particular.

"So, six kilos of high-grade mescaline. What's the wholesale price on that?"

"I've got four locals waiting to buy a key apiece, three for fourteen thousand pounds, and one for eleven thousand. The lowball price is because he promised to bring in some small-timers who'll buy up the last two keys."

"So that's it?" Marlowe asked. "You spend a year and a half putting this supply together; now you get in, grab the money, and get out?"

"Yep," Peter said. "By this time next week, I'm going to be

in Zurich drinking Bordeaux straight from the bottle."

Whatever Jedi Mind Trick the Witches' Carnival pulled in America, it worked on British airport security too. They'd moved through customs like quicksilver and now followed overhead signs toward the exit.

"I've mentioned this before." Marlowe glanced at the other witches, but Peter didn't doubt that he was talking to him. "Do you know what the problem with hedonism is these days? It's all for profit. Nobody's interested in sin as fun anymore, sin as art."

Qi nodded. "Perdition is often its own reward."

"Look, guys. I can't thank you enough for helping me. Really. But I've got big plans and zero time to . . ."

They stepped through the sliding-glass doors. Peter stopped dead, staring past the long queue of taxis. It was raining flowers.

Blossoms and the odd leaf cartwheeled down from the sky, making the air smell sweet. People crowded the departure court, faces craned up. Some laughed like children. Others stood silent in open-mouthed wonder.

Petals brushed Peter's skin as they fell. They landed across taxis and asphalt with the softest *hush* he could imagine. Purple specks covered the concrete all around him.

"Peter! Coming?"

The witches climbed into two dusty black cabs. Peter walked toward them still staring up.

"What is–? It's–"

"Foxgloves," Marlowe said, brushing flowers out of his hair.

"Pretty, aren't they?" Maggie hooked her arm around Peter's. "London scatters flowers whenever we come to town. Come on, sweetie." She tugged him into the cab.

"So where're you guys from?" Kathy asked. She'd convinced Sam to eat something, and they'd moved into the kitchen. Sam hunched over a bowl of chicken and vegetable soup. Kathy sipped tea from a coffee mug with FLAGLER COLLEGE written across its side. Emily lay on the floor coloring.

"Alabama."

"How long have you been on the road?"

"Couple days."

Kathy looked at the beat–down figure across from her. "Plan on going back?"

"I don't know. But don't worry about it, okay? We'll get out of here in a little bit."

"I'm going to worry about it, Sam. I like you. I'd like to know that you're somewhere where people are going to look out for you. You and Gilly both."

"Yeah, well . . ." Even though Sam's armor was battered and cracked, if Kathy had yelled, she would've still been hunched and ready to tell her to fuck off. But the genuine concern, softly spoken, slipped through her defenses. "Me too," she confessed.

"So what do you think about going home then?"

"I don't know."

"What's holding you back?"

Sam remembered Danny's purple furniture. Even when she'd been six, she'd known it was ugly. She remembered his entire apartment smelled like cooking oil. She shook her head. "I don't know."

"What if you called your parents? Just to tell them you're okay."

Sam snickered. "You think that if I call Mom I'll get homesick and decide to go back, right?"

Kathy squirmed in her seat. "My Psychology 101 seems to be failing here."

Sam laughed again. She didn't mind Kathy trying to trick her, but it wouldn't work.

"Do you know why I want you to go home?"

"Why?"

"Because I think you want to go home. Something's going on, though, that makes you think you can't."

Sam stirred her soup, poking at carrots and bits of chicken.

"Sam." Kathy sighed. "You can keep running, if you want. But you're not going to find anyplace on earth where you'll stop thinking about home."

"I can give it a shot."

"Sam."

Sam sniffed and wiped her eyes. Reaching across the

table, Kathy touched her hand. "Why don't you call your mom? Just see what happens. Take it from there."

"Now?"

"Why not now?"

Picking up her purse, Sam dug for her cell phone. "You didn't mention any of this last night when I was having fun. You wait until I feel like hell, then pounce on me."

In the bathroom, Gilly finally pulled herself together. She stepped out of the shower, her eyes raw from crying. She got dressed, combed her hair back with her fingers, and went looking for Sam.

It was getting dark outside, and the house felt evening-muffled. Gilly followed Sam's voice downstairs.

"Hey, Mom. It's me."

. . .

"In Atlanta."

Gilly stopped just outside the kitchen archway and eavesdropped. She heard Kathy whisper. Then Sam again.

"What? Jesus f–Mom? Actually, I'm in Florida. Saint Augustine, Florida."

. . .

"I don't know. I got confused. Don't worry about it. I just wanted to tell you I'm okay."

. . .

"No. I just told you."

. . .

"I have no clue. They actually came to the house?"

. . .

"Well, I don't know what that's about, I swear. Did they say anything?"

. . .

"Mom, I'm not involved in anything."

. . .

"You know why."

. . .

"Yes. The magazine."

. . .

"It's a big deal to me. Why don't you get that?"

. . .

"Mom, just listen."

. . .

"Listen!"

Gilly heard it in Sam's voice: She was going home. She'd beg her mom to say, "Come back. I miss you," but whether she did or not didn't matter. Sam was exhausted, defeated, and would take whatever her mom offered her.

. . .

"It's not just that. It's a lot of things."

. . .

"No, it's not."

Gilly slipped back up the curving staircase. In the guest bedroom, she pulled the sequined mask out from behind the dresser.

They were headed back to where they belonged. But one night long ago, Gilly had run away with her best friend. She'd met the Witches' Carnival and danced in the shimmering dark with the most beautiful woman she'd ever met. She wanted proof it had happened, even if the memory tortured her.

The TV was still on. Gilly glanced up and saw a shot of Big Ben. For a moment, she thought it was snowing around the tower, but the swirls filling the air were lavender and pink.

Gilly turned up the volume.

"Britain's capital got a surprise today as wildflowers fell on the city. The unique blizzard lasted about ten minutes and covered the southern part of London. Obviously, events like these are rare, but scientists have documented similar flower-falls in the past, and even ones involving sheaves of corn and live frogs. No one knows exactly what causes them, but one theory is . . ."

As the reporter rattled on, Gilly touched the TV screen.

The city and pinwheeling blossoms lay beneath the cool glass. The Witches' Carnival moved unseen just past her fingertips and an ocean away.

Tomorrow, she and Sam would go back home. Nothing would change. People would ignore her, people would hurt her. Someday Ashley and all the others would bleed her to death, and Gilly wouldn't be able to stop them because she was weak and ugly and a coward.

Wildflowers continued falling across London. Gilly saw her sealed fate. She gave up all hope. The world was going to kill her. It was the most euphoric moment of her life.

Fuck Ashley. Fuck Tracye. Fuck her disappointed parents and idiot teachers. Fuck everything. Gilly didn't care anymore and wasn't afraid anymore. If she was going to die, she'd kill herself before giving anybody else the pleasure. What's more, she'd do it with some style.

"Sam! Sam!"

Footsteps pounded up the stairs, not just Sam but Kathy and Jerrod, too. "What? What is it?"

"The Carnival went to London," Gilly said. "I'm going after them."

All three of them stared at her. "What?"

"That's where Peter went, right?" she asked Kathy.

"Well . . . yes."

Gilly tugged the bag of dirty yellow salt out of her pocket. "Tonja left us some raw mescaline as a good-bye present.

Now it's raining flowers in London. See? They've hooked up with Peter. We find him, we find the Witches' Carnival."

"But how are you getting to London?" Sam asked.

"I don't know yet, but I'm going."

"Wait, wait," Jerrod spoke up. "The Witches' Carnival?"

Gilly and Sam both ignored him. "Come on, G." Sam shook her head. "I know you liked her, but she dumped you. It's over. It sucks, but it's over."

"Remember Atlanta? Remember we had to figure out our own way into that club? It's like that. They don't think we're fast enough or clever enough to be part of the Witches' Carnival. Fuck them. They're gonna learn real quick."

Sam sighed. "You're gonna get arrested, G. Either arrested or dead."

"I'm not going back. I'll hunt them across London and the next place and the next place if I have to. I'll hunt them across Hell if I have to. But I'm never going back home."

Kathy waved her hands in the air. "Whoa. Hold on a minute. You're talking about the actual Witches' Carnival?"

"Yes. Now tell me how to find Peter," Gilly said.

"I already told you, honey. We don't have any way to get in touch with him."

"Bullshit. You don't have a cell phone number? Nothing?"

"No. Now, Gilly, calm down," Kathy took her arms. "I know it gets hard sometimes. I know sometimes–"

"Fuck you! You don't know shit about me." Gilly shook her off. "You don't know about my life. You don't know the crap I go through. Tell me where Peter is."

Kathy shook her head. "It's time to go home, Gilly."

Gilly clenched her hands into fists. "Tell me!"

"No."

"You teach English at Flagler College, right?" Sam asked, stabbing buttons on her cell phone.

Everyone turned. Caught off guard by the question, Kathy stuttered, "Uh, yes, but–"

"If you don't tell us how to find Peter, I'll make sure your boss knows you've been passing out drugs to your students." Sam flipped her phone around. On the screen was a photo of Kathy and David, both of them glassy eyed, holding half-eaten cookies. "I'll e-mail some pictures along too."

"Sam." Kathy's face showed deep hurt.

"Sorry. Gilly's my best friend. Maybe I could deal with going back with her, but . . ."

Gilly looked at her. "So, you're in?"

"If you ain't pretty . . ." Sam shrugged.

"Start trouble."

"Look. Girls." Kathy stared at them, trying to think of something to say.

Jerrod spoke up. "Get me a pen. I'll give you Peter's number."

"Jerrod!" Kathy spun around.

"If they're determined to go, let them. It's not worth losing your job over." Without looking at Sam or Gilly, he turned and walked out of the room. "You can't save everyone, Kath."

Betrayed on all sides, Kathy couldn't make herself surrender yet. "Girls. Please. Think about this. Even if you find these people, do you honestly think you've met the Witches' Carnival?"

"Speaking of that, actually I need another favor," Gilly said.

"What now?"

"You're really an English teacher?"

"Yes."

Gilly smiled as pleasantly as she could. "Do you have any of Christopher Marlowe's plays I could borrow?"

A few minutes later, Gilly walked out to the Civic carrying *The Norton Anthology of Elizabethan Literature*, a textbook the size of a cinder block. Tucked inside was Peter's cell phone number written on one of Jerrod's business cards.

Sam had gone back upstairs to return her and Gilly's ball gowns. She dragged her feet saying good-bye. "Don't be mad," she told Kathy. "I'm sorry, and thank you for everything. I just have to do this, okay?"

"Sam, I don't know who these people were, but the Witches' Carnival isn't real."

Sam hugged the gowns to her chest. "I know you don't believe it, but I swear it's true."

137

"Sam." Kathy sighed.

"Please don't be mad, okay?"

"I'm not mad. It's just…what about everything we talked about? You said you wanted to go home."

Sam nodded and dropped her eyes to the floor. "I do."

"Even if you have problems with your mom, wouldn't it be better to try to work them out?"

Sam didn't answer. Kathy reached out and stroked her hair. "Well?"

"When—when I was six, and my mom and dad were still together, Mom started seeing this guy from work, guy named Danny. I didn't really know what was going on, but she'd take me over to his apartment. And, uh, they'd leave me watching cartoons while they went and fucked in the bedroom."

"That's awful, Sam."

"And after they were finished, we'd be driving home and she'd always go, 'Now you can't tell Daddy about Danny. If you tell Daddy, he'll get mad and leave us.'" Sam felt her face burn. "But I was six. I didn't know how serious shit like that was. So one time I got mad at her, and I told Dad, and they screamed back and forth, and—sure enough. And he's heading out, still screaming, and I'm crying and my brother Josh is crying. And Mom looks at me and says, 'What did I tell you?'"

Kathy tried to think of something worth saying. "I'm sorry, honey."

Sam shook her head. "I love her, and I know she loves me. It's just, she's got problems. She should've never had kids."

"Sam."

"Everything you said was right, though. This guy told me once that I want to go home more than anything. But I realized last night that that back there isn't it. If I want to go home, I've got to find it first."

"Sam. I . . ."

"Listen, here are your dresses back." Sam shoved the ball gowns into Kathy's arms. "Sorry I went into the ocean in mine. Maybe after you dry-clean it, it'll be okay."

"Wait. These aren't mine."

"Yeah, they are. We kinda borrowed them from your closet. Sorry."

"Which closet?"

Sam walked into the hall and opened the door to the closet. "This one."

"What—"

Sam gave Kathy a sudden, rough hug, cutting off her thought. "Good-bye. Thank you for everything. You're so cool." She laughed. "I kind of wish I could just stay here with you forever. But don't worry, okay? As long as I've got Gilly with me, we'll find our way home somehow."

Turning, Sam rushed down the stairs, out the front door, and jumped behind the wheel of her Civic.

"Ready?" Gilly asked, setting the textbook down between her feet.

Sam wiped her eyes and nodded. As she cranked the ignition the stereo came on.

"We're running hot! These kids are losing their minds. They can't see the signs. Raise hell and a back beat! Running out of time! We're running hot."

They pulled away from the warmly lit house and down the street.

Inside, Kathy stared into the hall closet. Several tuxedos and ball gowns already hung on the bar. They were the ones Sam's friends had worn to the party. Everything was in perfect order, except Kathy had lived in this house for twelve years and had never noticed the closet before Sam pulled it open.

For the first time since she was a child, Kathy believed in the Witches' Carnival.

TEN

Everything was crumbling. Andy told his wife that they'd tracked down the girl Gilly had run away with. They'd kept Samantha Grace's mom from filing a missing-person's report. He promised Karen that he and Malik would bring both girls home soon.

"So now it's not just your own daughter you're putting in danger, it's somebody else's kid, too."

"I'd never put Gilly in danger. You know that. Look, Family Services has a hundred cases to work. You don't think I'll look for my daughter better than they will?"

They stood in Caitlin's bedroom. Karen picked clothes up off the floor and didn't say a word.

"Do you know what 'accessory' is?" Andy hissed, glaring at the back of her head. "Do you think those Internal Affairs rats are going to believe there was fifty grand sitting under the bathroom sink and you just never noticed? This entire family is fucked if Gilly gets found with that money. You. Me. Her. I don't know where Caitlin'll wind up. Everybody fucked. So maybe you can help me try to save it instead of shitting on me every time I open my mouth."

Karen dropped a blouse into the laundry basket. "Or maybe I should go to the station right now and cut a deal. I'd get amnesty. They'd start looking for Gilly. Maybe that'd be the best thing."

Her voice quivered as she spoke. Andy knew she wouldn't do it, but she'd thought about it. He left the room, banging the door shut. Grabbing his jacket off the couch, Andy got in his car.

He spent hours driving around Birmingham. What if he turned back now, and Gilly was walking down the next street? Or the street after that? Long after any real hope had gone, Andy kept moving out of desperation.

He hated himself. If he'd never brought that money into the house, none of this would have happened.

When a dirty cop confesses on TV, he always says, "I got sick of struggling to pay my mortgage and watching gang-bangers drive around in sixty-thousand-dollar Cadillacs."

The truth was the exact opposite. The higher-ups, the real sharks, had money and power, but they also had enough sense to keep a low profile and enjoy them. The kids selling down by the railyard or hustling stolen goods from a van usually lived in public housing and rode the bus.

They took in a lot of money but passed most of it up to the sharks. It was the image they loved, getting to play the gangsta. In the end, they'd be arrested or killed for a fake gold chain and less money than they could have made at McDonald's.

Four years ago, eighteen Xbox games had disappeared from the Hackworth Road Wal-Mart. No violence had been involved, and the net loss for the store was a couple hundred dollars. City Hall always wanted to seem friendly toward the big corporations, though. That meant the mayor would personally shine their shoes, sing *arias* to them, and send two detectives to fetch their video games.

Andy and Malik tracked down the stock boy who'd vanished along with the games, but he'd already traded them to a dealer named "the Don" for decks of heroin.

The Don lived with his mom and two brothers. When one of the younger kids let Andy and Malik through the door, the Don made a dash for his bedroom. They grabbed him, handcuffed him, and sat him on the couch. Malik spent ten minutes trying to sort the stolen games from the ones belonging to the younger kids.

"What about this one?"

"Yeah. That's one he had."

"What about this one?"

"No, that's mine."

"This one?"

"Don't take that one. I'm almost done playing it."

The Don's mom yelled the whole time. "You can't take my boy. You know he didn't do anything. I'll sue your ass. I'll sue the whole police department's ass. You can't take him."

Andy went to search the boy's room for the rest of the missing games. Momma followed him. "My boy goes to church. You don't care about that, do you? He's just another nigger to you, ain't he?"

Tucked under the Don's mattress, its grip sticking out for a quick grab, was an M9 pistol. Andy pulled the automatic out. He hadn't seen an M9 since leaving the marines. Shoving Momma aside, he walked back into the living room.

"Hey, moron. This what you were running for when we came in?"

The Don looked up, saw the gun, and turned away, refusing to say anything. Momma didn't have the same stoicism. "He needs that for protection. There's gangbangers everywhere in this neighborhood, and the police don't do shit."

What could they do? Scare them? Mentor them? Line them up against a wall? How many urban outreach programs would it take to stop human de-evolution? A generation was selling crack for minimum wage, and Andy had almost been murdered trying to get back a bunch of video games. What other options did he have except to grab what he could, make sure his family was provided for, and let the rest of the species sink back into the primordial swamp?

"Look at me, you little shit." He cracked the pistol's butt against the Don's skull. The boy yelped. Momma screamed. Malik jumped to his feet, shouting, "Whoa! Andy!"

"I'm gonna sue you, motherfucker. Hit my boy when he hasn't done anything. Why don't you try hitting me? Hit me, motherfucker."

"Where's he keep his stash?" Andy answered.

"My boy hasn't got any stash, motherfucker. Your ass has got a lawsuit."

"You want this to go away, lady? Tell me where he keeps his stash."

In a Tupperware bowl in the kitchen cupboard were ten decks of heroin and a roll of greasy bills. Andy pocketed the money and the gun, flushed the drugs, and smashed the game disks under his heel. They uncuffed the Don and left.

Back in the car, he counted the money—a little over three hundred dollars—and dropped half in Malik's lap.

"Going renegade on me, Moonpie?"

"Thinking about it. Gonna try it for a while and see how it feels."

After that, they worked out some rules. They didn't take drugs or merchandise, only cash. They never took money that belonged to anyone who'd miss it. Wal-Mart had insurance, the guy running the corner store probably didn't. After that first time with the Don, they didn't take the money if it was less than two grand. If they were going to risk jail time, it had to be worth it.

They never got greedy, which meant they couldn't be touched. After four years, Andy had fifty thousand dollars and slept just fine at night.

Now, driving around Birmingham, Andy worked hard to convince himself he was still a good cop. He'd do everything to help the people who actually deserved help. In fact, if he thought about the money as an under-the-table incentive program, giving him a reason to get up every morning and deal with trash like the Don and the Don's momma, it probably made him a better cop than he would have been otherwise.

A tattered figure stepped in front of his car. Jamming the breaks, Andy's body snapped forward, seat belt digging into his belly and shoulder. The car shuddered and threatened to fishtail, but he managed to stop.

It was that street preacher, Meek. Andy was screaming before he got the window rolled down. "Goddamnit, get the hell off the street!"

Meek stood in the glare of Andy's headlights unconcerned. His eyes searched the sky.

Andy was about to climb out when a solid black *whomp* struck the hood of the car. Meek's crow beat its wings against the streaked windshield. It clawed and pecked at the glass, fighting to get at him.

Somehow, the bird terrified Andy. He rolled up the window and wanted to lock the door. Meek had been a legend before Andy joined the force. Cops talked about how he said things, knew secrets no matter how deep they lay buried. They always laughed when they told stories about Meek, but everyone cut the old man a wide berth, anyway.

An SUV behind Andy began honking its horn, but he sat frozen. Exhausted and scared, the black bird became an omen in Andy's mind. He stared at Meek, and the man's emaciated frame seemed to hold the weight and fury of a biblical prophet. All at once, Andy became certain that God was punishing him.

He'd stolen the money. He thought he'd gotten away with it. But now his daughter was missing, and he didn't know if she was okay, and he couldn't get her back.

I'm sorry, he begged. *It's my fault, and I'm sorry. Just give her back to me. I've learned.*

The crow screeched. God stayed silent, leaving Andy twisting on his own sword.

Gilly and Sam ate dinner at Captain D's, comparing notes on everything that had happened last night and trying to remember exactly how they'd ended up in Florida. After a few bites of fish and some fries, Sam pushed her plate aside and laid her head in her folded arms.

"You okay?"

"Just tired." Sam's voice was a hoarse whisper. Suddenly, she snapped her eyes open and stared at Gilly. "Your dad came to my house today."

"What?"

"When I called Mom. She said two cops came to the house. I bet it was your dad." Sam's face was buried in her arms again.

"Did he tell her what's going on?"

Sam's head rocked back and forth. "Lied through his ass. Mom thinks I'm hooked up with drug dealers now."

Gilly turned this over in her mind. He was lying, covering his tracks and making sure nobody knew about the stolen money. Still, he was out searching for her, and the thought carried a slender stab of guilt.

After dinner, they bought a laptop at Best Buy, and then got a room at the Ponce de León Hotel. Sam collapsed into bed. Sitting cross-legged on the floor, Gilly logged into her AOL account and began searching for a way to London.

Her first stop was the State Department's website. To get legal passports, she and Sam needed to be over eighteen and have fixed addresses. Plus, the process would take a minimum of two weeks. Gilly dug through Google for stories about identification fraud. She skimmed dozens of articles about organized crime and professional forgers before finding one headlined: GRINNELL STUDENTS ARRESTED FOR MANUFACTURING FAKE DRIVER'S LICENSES.

The article was about a pair of graphic–design majors who'd sold fake driver's licenses made with the high–end printers and scanners in their school's graphic–arts lab. Their business only came to light after a client of theirs was busted for drug possession. The cops found both his real license and the fake in his wallet.

The story quoted the arresting officer saying, "The bogus IDs were almost perfect. If Marshall hadn't confessed, I don't know how we would have caught these guys."

Two years ago, Vic Handler, a boy Gilly knew from art class, had gotten a scholarship to the Rhode Island School of Design. Gilly hadn't seen Vic since he'd left Alabama. From what she remembered, though, he was an okay guy and just seedy enough to help them for the right price.

Typing with two careful fingers, Gilly searched for exactly what made up a passport, trying to figure out if Vic could forge a pair for her and Sam. But it turned into another dead end.

Before 2006, a passport was just a little book. Theoretically, anyone with the right equipment could reproduce the watermarks and microprinting that had been the only security features for years. Then 9/11 happened. Then five hundred blank passports vanished from a warehouse.

Spooked by terrorists and bad press, the State Department began implanting microchips into each passport. Called RFID tags—short for Radio Frequency Identification—the chips could communicate your personal data and a digital photo to a radio scanner across the room.

The music videos on TV gave way to late-night infomercials. Gilly hunted for everything she could find on RFID tags, hoping to glean some way to trick them. Each webpage she clicked on made her more certain there wasn't one. She was frustrated and near tears. All her tough talk about chasing the Carnival couldn't get her across the ocean. She and Sam would be arrested the minute they tried to board a plane, tripped up by a thirty-cent microchip.

She didn't give up. She kept searching. But Gilly couldn't stop the thoughts from coming. *This is pathetic. Let's see, a fat girl afraid of everything and a burnout trying to give herself a chemical lobotomy. Not exactly a pair of supervillains, are you?*

Gilly listened to Kathy's words over and over. *It's time to go home. It's time to go home.* Each time, the voice sounded less like Kathy's and more like her own.

Sam jerked awake, sputtering syllables and staring terrified around the unfamiliar room.

"Sam? You okay?"

Sam glared at Gilly for a full second before recognizing her. "Did Kathy have a dog? Like one without any hind legs?"

"I don't think so. Why?"

Sam's face crumpled. She started crying, burying her clammy face in her hands.

"Sam? What's the matter."

Sam didn't answer. She wiped her nose and reached for her jeans. "I'm going to go walk around, find a snack machine or something."

"I'll come with you." Gilly stood up, wincing at the pins and needles prickling her legs.

Not bothering to put on their shoes, they padded down the corridor. The hotel felt like a derelict ocean liner. It was all brass, light, and vaulting space, but they never saw or heard another guest.

A breakfast room stood off of the lobby, chairs stacked on top of tables and vending machines humming against one wall. They bought candy bars and Diet Cokes. A revolving glass door led to an empty patio overlooking the beach. Gilly realized they were probably going home tomorrow and she hadn't seen the ocean yet. "Let's go out here," she said.

The breeze brushed their faces, salty and a little too cold for comfort. Pulling off their socks, they walked across the sand to a playground area. Sam slumped in a swing. Eyes closed, mouth open, she looked like some broken thing tossed onto the beach by the waves.

"Seriously, are you okay?" Gilly asked again.

"Yeah." Sam unwrapped her Milky Way with shaking fingers. "So how are we getting to London?"

Gilly stared across the dark ocean and imagined the Witches' Carnival, somewhere on the other side. "I don't know," she said.

Sam nodded and didn't say anything. Waves swelled and crashed against the wet sand. A long silence passed before Gilly added, "I have one idea, sorta. But I don't think it's going to work."

Gilly told Sam about the Iowa students, Vic Handler, and finally the RFID tags. She was glad to have someone to share the weight of the problem, never hoping Sam could come up with a solution. Even at the top of her game, Sam knew less about computers and microchips than Gilly did. Now, she seemed barely aware, never saying a word, staring at the sand with eyes puffy from crying.

"I've looked and looked and looked, but . . . I'll keep trying, but . . . I don't know."

"Leave the microchips out," Sam said without glancing up.

Gilly turned. Figuring Sam was too sick to think clearly, she started explaining everything again. Sam cut her off.

"Look, G. Take the best, most high-tech security system in the world and put a guy making eight-fifty an hour in charge of it. Know what you get?"

"What?"

"A security system worth eight-fifty an hour."

Gilly snickered.

"Fuck the RF–whatever chips. You're a white kid in a heavy metal T–shirt. Nobody's going to look at you and think, *I bet she's a terrorist and this passport's fake.* They're gonna think the chip's broken and wave you through. Nobody'll suspect shit. They'll just want to get rid of us as fast as they can."

"Yeah, but if they do suspect something, we're going to be right there at the airport. There's no way we'll be able to talk our way out of it."

"So what?" Sam snapped, more exhausted than angry. "You're going to chase the Carnival through hell and all that, but you didn't think it'd take any guts?"

Gilly started swinging on the swing, pumping her legs. She'd talked tough at Kathy's house, but that didn't amount to shit. Now she'd had a few hours to think about it, and she was afraid. But even after her scorching declarations had gone cold in her belly, Gilly discovered something hard and quiet inside her. It was another kind of bravery, as different from the first as stone was from fire.

Their lives were behind them. There wasn't anything left to hold them back and no one left to blame. She and Sam could have whatever they wanted, but only if they were smart enough and fast enough to grab it.

Gilly rolled the plan over in her head. They could soak the passports in water and say they'd left them in the rain;

that's why the chips must have shorted out. They could travel at the busiest time of day and take separate flights. "If this doesn't work and we go to jail," Gilly finally said, "I'm pimping you out for cigarettes."

"Whatever, bitch. Let's go inside. I'm fucking freezing."

They went back to the room, but Sam was afraid to go to sleep. Drunk or high, she'd gone through nasty stretches before, but they wore off as soon as the drugs did. Mescaline didn't provide any boundary between truth and delirium. Sam had clear memories of her body decomposing, how it'd felt and smelled. She remembered the flies laying eggs under her skin. She remembered Danny's living room in the center of Kathy's house. Her only proof that none of it had happened was that everyone kept telling her it hadn't.

While Sam smoked cigarettes and strained to hear noises that weren't there, Gilly tapped at her computer and scratched notes on a hotel notepad. Her eyes burning from staring at the computer screen, she worked with a renewed determination. She searched for everything she could find on microprinting, holographic imaging, airport security, and the Rhode Island School of Design. She did more research into RFID and fine-tuned their plan.

The data on a RFID tag was encrypted so it could only be read by certain receivers. Instead of leaving the chips out all together, they'd attach working tags the State Department hadn't programmed. Tags from packages of Gillette razors would be the easiest to get. Then, when airport security scanned them, the receiver would recognize something was there, but the screen would only show garbled nonsense.

Just after two, Gilly shut off her laptop. She'd culled everything she could from the Internet. There was still plenty she didn't know, but from here on out, they'd have to wing it. Still, pretty good for a fat girl and a burnout.

Gilly filled Sam in. Sam didn't add much except grunts and nods, her eyes fixed on the flickering light of the TV. As she brushed her teeth and got ready for bed, a small, wicked smile spread across Gilly's face.

Since she'd started hanging out with Sam, Gilly had found herself scaling the stone facade of the Galleria, splashing beneath a waterfall in Hurricane Creek State Park in her Minnie Mouse bra, and on one vaguely remembered night, wandering around town with a bottle of Boone's Farm wine and a flare gun. If they actually got to London, though, it would top all the lunatic misadventures Sam had ever dragged her on. And for once, Sam had wanted to give up and Gilly was the one who'd dragged her along.

Picking up *The Norton Anthology of Elizabethan Literature*, Gilly lay down. The textbook weighed five or six pounds with onionskin pages. Its table of contents listed several plays and poems by Christopher Marlowe. Gilly decided to start with *Doctor Faustus* since she'd at least heard of that play before, knowing it was about a man selling his soul to the devil.

> *Not marching now in the fields of Trasimene*
> *Where Mars did mate the Cathagens.*
> *Nor sporting in the dalliance of love*
> *In courts of kings where state is overturn'd,*
> *Nor in the pomp of proud audacious deeds*
> *Intends our Muse to vaunt his heavenly verse:*
> *Only this (gentlemen) we must now perform,*
> *The form of Faustus' fourtunes, good or bad.*
> *To patient judgments we appeal our plaud,*
> *And speak for Faustus in his infancy.*
> *Now is he born, of parents base of stock,*
> *In Germany, within a town call'd Rhodes.*
> *Of riper years to Wittenberg he went,*
> *Whereas his kinsmen chiefly brought him up.*
> *So soon he profits in divinity,*
> *The fruitful plot of scholarism grac'd,*
> *That shortly he was grac'd with doctor's name,*
> *Excelling all, whose sweet delight disputes*
> *In heavenly matters of theology;*
> *Till, swollen with cunning, of a self-conceit,*
> *His waxen wings did mount above his reach,*
> *And melting, heavens conspir'd his overthrow;*

For, falling to a devilish exercise,
And glutted now with learning's golden gifts,
He surfeits upon cursed necromancy;
Nothing so sweet as magic—

"What the hell?" Gilly had to read the passage twice to understand half. Maybe it would make more sense if she hadn't been up for hours. Now, the archaic words squirmed around the page.

Gilly shut the book and settled onto her back, an arm thrown over her eyes to block out the light from the TV. She let memories of Maggie play through the dark. Gilly imagined her face. She relished the way Maggie had touched her, the way she'd smelled. After a few minutes, Gilly was fast asleep.

ELEVEN

"**H**ow can you eat that without puking?" Sam made a gagging face, watching Gilly down black coffee and Pixy Stix.

"This is the breakfast of champions. Cereal and waffles, they just sit in your stomach waiting to be digested. This stuff fights back. Gets chemical reactions going. Gets you ready to face the day."

"Pixy Stix aren't even candy. They're just sugar in a tube."

"Candy is sugar."

"No. Candy is sugar made into something. Like chocolate or something."

"They make it something. They make it blue." Gilly stuck out her brightly stained tongue. "Thee? Bwoo."

"Jesus fuck." While Gilly had slept soundly, Sam spent the

night nodding off, then jerking awake. When a hard blade of sunlight cut through the gap in the curtains, she gave up on sleep, took a shower, and woke Gilly.

Their first errand was to deposit the money in Sam's debit card account, keeping ten thousand in reserve, hidden in the battery compartment of Gilly's laptop. Then they found a store called The Gift Tree on a touristy corner downtown. They bought a basket full of raspberry-scented soaps, candles, and bath salts. Emptying the jar of bath salts, they filled it with mescaline. By ten thirty, they were in sight of Daytona Beach International Airport.

Sam had never flown before. On the plane, she let out a gasp as roads, buildings, then the whole city, then the squiggling white coastline dropped out from under them. The plane banked east. Forgetting how exhausted she was from her sleepless night, Sam gazed down, mesmerized by miles of lapis lazuli waves.

"By the way." Sam turned to Gilly after the flight attendant had come by with their drinks. "I didn't mention this yesterday because you were all brokenhearted, but you're a filthy slut, Gillian Stahl."

Gilly looked up from *Doctor Faustus*. "What?"

"You jump in bed with a girl the first night you meet her? You're a slut."

"Maggie's different. There's an exception to the slut rule if they're a member of the Witches' Carnival."

"Bull. Did you see me knocking boots with Jack or Chris? No. Know why? 'Cause I'm not a filthy, dirty, nasty slut like you."

"Probably tried. They just didn't want your sloppy cooter."

"No, no, we ain't talking about my sloppy cooter, we talking about yours. I thought so much better of you. I thought you had more respect for yourself, G."

"Quiet. I'm reading."

"Uh-huh." Sam turned back toward the window. "So what'd you and Maggie do all night? I know you didn't screw for nine hours straight."

"We talked a lot."

"What about?"

Gilly shrugged. "I told her about Tracye."

"You told her about Tracye giving Ben a hand-job at the movies?"

"No. Jesus. I told her about how we used to be friends, but how Tracye always has to make sure everybody knows how cool she is all the time."

"Tracye's a dumb bitch. How long does that take to say?"

"Well, we screwed for the other eight and a half hours."

"Slut."

Gilly grinned and went back to her book. She thought about the day Sam had defended her from Ashley's clique. Maggie had made her promise to thank Sam, but it'd sound stupid two years later. "We talked about other stuff," she said. "But it wasn't anything important."

Sam lowered her voice to a conspiratorial whisper. "So you think Vic'll help us?"

"Hopefully."

"Yeah, but his family's real religious, aren't they?"

Gilly looked up again. "Not that I know of."

"Keith is."

"Since when?"

"Since always. He's always so nice and everything. And he always dresses like a pussy."

Vic's brother Keith dressed well but never flashy, with a small silver hoop in each ear. He didn't smoke. Gilly had never heard him cuss. And he had a beaming forthrightness that was disconcerting until you realized he was actually being sincere.

Gilly bit down on a laugh. "Sam, I think he's gay."

"No. They're like Mormons or something."

"No, Sam. I'm pretty sure they're not."

Sam sneered. "Whatever. You think everybody's gay."

When Gilly didn't answer, Sam went on. "See that guy up there? He's gay. And that guy? Gay. Oh, Gilly, check out the guy and girl kissing. They are both so gay."

When they landed, the sun was blood red, hanging low in the sky. Stepping outside, their breath trailed behind them in tattered streamers of vapor. It felt supernatural, getting plucked up from coastal Florida and dropped into the brooding New England cold two hours later.

A taxi carried them through downtown and across a river. From the air, Providence looked like any other city. Gilly had seen office towers and streams of headlights flowing along the highways. But its modernity was camouflage. Underneath, Providence was old brick and thick-trunked maples. Courtly homes lined narrow streets. They passed churches that had been historic a century ago.

At the Rhode Island School of Design, a campus rent-a-cop looked up Vic's address on his laptop and gave them directions to Congdon House, a three-story colonial house a couple blocks away. Climbing the steep front steps, Gilly knocked, then pushed the front door open.

The electric rattle of a sewing machine spilled out of the lounge. A girl was hard at work turning lengths of rough silk into a skirt. Another girl stood on the battered coffee table wearing an ash gray frock coat draped over her T-shirt and jeans. A boy knelt beside her, pinning the coat's hem.

The girl on the table noticed them first. Gilly gave her a weak smile. "Um, hi."

"Hello." The girl smiled back.

"Um." Gilly stared back and didn't know what to say. The other girl shut off her sewing machine. Then the boy looked over. Gilly's palms sweat. She became anxious that she hadn't washed her face since that morning, that her skin was oily and her hair was probably awful.

Finally, Sam spoke up. "How do we find Room Twenty-Five?"

"Twenty-Five? Take the stairs right behind you. Second floor. Turn left. It should be the second door," the boy said.

"Thanks."

"No problem."

They headed up the staircase and rounded the landing just as a couple came down, their arms around each other. Glancing at Gilly and Sam, they nodded, then went back to their conversation about Michelangelo.

Gilly hadn't realized how childish she'd feel surrounded by college students. Suddenly, the entire plan seemed stupid. Approaching Vic's room, she squeezed Sam's arm.

"You do the talking, okay?"

"What? This was your fucking idea. I barely know him."

"I didn't know him all that well either."

"You knew him better than I did."

"But you're the one who's good with people. I'll fuck it up. If you want the passports, you've got to do the talking."

Sam rolled her eyes. "Just get us inside. I'll take over from there."

Gilly knocked. She hadn't seen Vic in two years. Back then, he'd been pudgy, with apple-red cheeks that made him look like an overgrown twelve-year-old. She recognized him when he opened the door, but the fat was gone and replaced by a scraggly beard.

Vic stood silent, narrowing his eyes, trying to place a name with the face. "Gilly?"

"Hey, Vic."

"Hi." Vic stared at her for another second. "What are you doing here?"

"We, um, well–"

"We came to bring you this lovely gift basket," Sam said, handing him the raspberry gift basket.

"Gee, thanks. You're Josh Grace's little sister, aren't you?"

"Sam."

"Yeah. How're you doing?"

Sam smiled. "Great. Care if we come in?"

"Hell, why not?"

The scent of pot lingered in the room, covered with a flowery layer of air freshener. Clothes lay scattered across the floor. Art books filled the windowsills. One wall was covered with framed silk-screened prints of the Cheshire Cat. The others had been left blank.

"So what's going on?" Vic asked.

Vic's roommate sat on one of the twin beds, reading a textbook and tapping a highlighter against his leg. Sam said, "Hey, man. I know this is your place, but could you give us, like, ten minutes with Vic?"

The roommate glanced at the three of them, chuckled

something, and left. Sam thanked him profusely, locking the door after he was gone.

"Okay, seriously. What's going on here?" Vic still had the gift basket in his hands.

Taking the laptop from Gilly, Sam pulled out the ten grand they'd kept. She dropped it on Vic's drafting table without a word.

Vic stared at the stack of hundreds. "Is that real?"

"Yep."

Vic looked dizzy. "Gilly, what's going on?"

"Okay. We need your help with something, but it's sort of illegal, so if you want us to just leave, it's cool."

"What? You want me to kill somebody?"

"No," Sam said. "We've got other people for that. We need you to make some fake passports."

Vic stared at them. "All right, that's not 'sort of' illegal." Tossing the gift basket on the bed, he made quotation marks in the air. "That's more 'really, really motherfucking' illegal."

"But you're a graphic-design major, right?"

"Yeah."

"So you could do it if you wanted to."

"Maybe. I've never thought about it."

"You'd need microprinting capability, an intaglio press, six-cell holographic printing, and something to make water-marks," Gilly counted the requirements off on her fingers.

"Well, maybe. I'd have to look at one to know for sure. But–"

"Okay, Vic," Sam said. "There's ten thousand dollars sitting there. We'll get you another five thousand if you help us out. Now, you know we're not terrorists or undercover agents or anything. Nothing bad is gonna to happen if you do this. You'd just really be helping us out."

"Why do you need passports, anyway?"

Sam and Gilly glanced at each other and shrugged. "The Witches' Carnival is in England. We need to catch them."

Vic opened his mouth, then closed it. Then opened it again. Then closed it again. "You guys are serious."

"Sorry for springing it on you like this. The whole Witches' Carnival thing is a mindfuck. Trust us, we know. But if you can do it, we'll hand you fifteen thousand cash and you never hear from us again."

"Where the hell did you get this kind of money?"

"You remember my dad's a cop?" Gilly asked.

"Kind of."

"He's crooked."

Vic nodded. "In the middle of any other conversation, that would be shocking."

"I'll tell you what. You don't want to get involved? Fine. No hard feelings. But we'll pay you a thousand bucks to introduce us to someone who will do it."

"No, no, wait. Fifteen thousand dollars?"

"Fifteen thousand dollars. But we need them by tomorrow."

"Tomorrow!"

Sam shrugged. "Gotta keep on your toes if you want to catch the Witches' Carnival."

"The Witches' Carnival . . . fifteen grand . . . tomorrow . . . five-to-ten years in federal prison." As Vic thought out loud, his eyes flickered toward the stack of hundred-dollar bills. "Here's the thing. Maybe I could get them by tomorrow, but I'd need to bring in at least two other people. Which means I'd only get a third of the money. And five K just isn't worth the risk."

"Well, how much would the risk be worth?"

"I don't know. Maybe thirty thousand all together?"

"Fuck you." Sam laughed. "You aren't even a real graphic designer—you're just a student. Twenty thousand all together."

"Twenty-five. If that's too steep, maybe one of your friends who's a real graphic designer will do it for less."

"All right. Twenty-five. We'll get you the rest of the money when you give us the passports."

As they shook hands, Vic warned, "I haven't said yes yet. Let me make some calls." He found his cell phone under a pile of papers. "Can't believe I'm even thinking about this."

Vic made two short calls, telling both people to meet him on the beach and not say anything to anyone. Walking across campus, he didn't chat or ask about old friends back home. He kept his hands in his pockets and his head down. "This is crazy. This is so motherfucking crazy."

The beach was a wide knoll in the middle of campus. Park benches sat empty in the cold evening. Vic waved to two figures leaning against the rear wall of a residence building. Frost-crisp grass crunching under their feet, the five of them met in the center of the quad beneath an abstract sculpture of knotted stone.

Vic introduced Erin, his girlfriend, and Paul, a boy with long hair and a Dora the Explorer wristwatch.

"All right, here's the deal," Vic said. "Want to make eighty-three hundred bucks in one day?"

"How?" Erin asked, glancing sideways at Gilly and Sam.

"Make a pair of fake passports."

"What? Fuck no, Vic. Who the hell–"

"Erin, Erin, calm down." Vic took her hand and explained everything: how he knew Gilly and Sam, Gilly's dad and the ten thousand dollars sitting in his room. When he told her why they needed the passports, Erin glared at Gilly. "You want to find the Witches' Carnival?"

"Yeah."

"Okay, so when you're wearing your tinfoil hat, does the shiny side go on the inside or outside?"

"We're not–"

"No, listen. Half the people around here are completely nuts. Not judging. But you're not going to find the Witches' Carnival in England or anywhere else. They aren't real."

Erin had steel-framed glasses and wore her curly hair tied

back. Gilly took a nervous step away from the snap in her voice. Sam held her ground.

"If they aren't real, that's our problem."

"Yeah? It'll be my problem when you two get busted and they ask you where the passports came from."

"The only way we get caught is if you can't make the passports right, and if you can't, we don't want them, anyway."

Erin turned to Vic. "You're actually thinking about this?"

"I'm sorry. But you know I could use the money. You know I've been thinking about dropping out of school. The main reason I'm doing this is so we can stay together."

"You could get a job. You could hit your parents up for the money."

"I know. We've been through all this. I'm sorry. I wouldn't have dragged you into this, but I need to look at a real passport and you're the only person I can trust who has one."

A cold, foot-shuffling silence settled over the group.

"I'll let you borrow my passport," Erin finally said. "But I'm staying out of this. And if anybody catches you with it, you goddamn better say you stole it."

"Thank you. Thank you." Vic kissed her cheek. Erin stared straight ahead.

"You still want a cut of the money?"

"No."

"Okay. That's what, then? Twelve thousand, five hundred split two ways. What about it, Paul? Easy money."

Paul hadn't spoken since Vic told them about the plan. Tucking his hair behind one ear, he looked at Sam and asked, "Why do you think the Witches' Carnival's in England?"

"Well, it's kind of a long story, but–"

"Have you ever met them?"

Sam nodded. "Two nights ago. We lost them yesterday."

"Oh, Jesus Christ," Erin groaned. "Come on, Vic. This is crazy."

"There's a girl named Maggie, isn't there?" Paul whispered.

Erin said something nobody heard.

"You've met them?" Gilly asked.

A beautiful, naked smile broke the surface. "A few years back. When me, my brother, and my granddad protested at the Republican Convention. They really were the Witches' Carnival, weren't they?"

"You're full of shit," Erin said.

"No. I did." Hunched against the bitter autumn, the memories tasted apple-sweet on Paul's tongue. New York's streets–his streets–bristled with cops in riot gear, but a river of college kids and housewives passed through dauntless. Chants rose and fell. Paul remembered bongo players beating out the rhythm and a contingent of Hasidic rabbis all black cassocks and dignity.

They were close to Herald Square when things turned

bad. The cops erected barricades, and the flow of people bottlenecked. Suddenly, Paul couldn't move at will. Like a riptide, the pushing, shoving crowd swept him away from his brother and grandfather. The police threw up orange plastic netting, corralling the protesters and arresting every-one inside. Paul got crushed up against the netting. It cut into his forearms.

Above the shouting, he heard glass shatter. A rock whizzed overhead. The cops lobbed teargas. Trapped, Paul watched plumes of yellow smoke coil and crawl toward him. When it touched him, it was like cigarettes being ground out against his eyes. The pain made him gasp. He inhaled more smoke and felt it sear living tissue inside him.

Paul was on his knees, rubbing his eyes, which only made the pain worse. More rocks and bottles arced toward the police line. The crowd surged backward. Paul knew he'd get trampled. A riot shield smashed him to the ground. The pavement scraped open the side of his face.

"Get down! Get down and don't move. Give me your hands!" There were two cops. As one forced him down, the other yanked Paul's arms back and looped plastic restraints over his wrists. Alone and terrified, Paul let out a broken whine. The cop told him to shut the hell up. He cinched the restraints tight, digging into Paul's skin.

"Christ. He's just a kid."

The hard, leather-gloved hands vanished. Gentler ones

came down, sliding under his arms and pulling Paul to his feet. He could barely make out two figures dressed head to toe in black. He thought they were more cops.

One of them cut the restraints. Blotting tears and teargas away with his sleeve, Paul saw they wore military–surplus gas masks and heavy denim jackets. They were members of a black bloc cell, militant anarchists he'd been warned to stay away from.

"Are you all right, sweetie?" A woman's soft lilt came from behind the mask.

"Let's get him out of here." The other bloc soldier, hair spilling around the edges of his mask, had cut through the netting with tin snips. Flanking Paul on either side, the pair escorted him through the chaos. Two cops charged toward them. Paul tried to stumble back, but the woman held his arm and kept walking forward.

"Get down! Get on the damn ground!"

The man on Paul's left opened one side of his jacket. Paul watched it happen but didn't understand. Both the cops stopped. One of them apologized as they passed by. They crossed the bright yellow barriers. Riot police stood ranged like samurai. The man kept his jacket open, and the cops waved them through.

Squeezing between some squad cars, they came out in the parking lot of an Amoco. With help, Paul sat down on the curb. The woman crouched beside him and pulled off her gas mask. A black bandanna covered her face. "Poor baby," she whispered, looking him over.

The man handed her a bottle of vinegar. Untying her bandanna, she soaked it, then pressed the dripping cloth against Paul's eyes. "Nice little bit of adventure, huh?"

He tried to smile. Blood slammed in his ears.

She talked to him. Later, Paul couldn't remember what they'd said, only that her voice was like piano music and that she held his hand the whole time. After a few minutes, the woman pulled the bandanna away. "How's that? Any better?"

"Yeah." Paul nodded. His eyes still burned, but he could open them most of the way. "What's your name?"

"Maggie."

"You're gorgeous."

He said "gorgeous" knowing it wasn't even close. As Maggie removed the cloth, Paul's first thought was that he was gazing at a religious icon, a plain figure through which the believer glimpsed something ethereal and infinite.

Standing on the cold beach with Vic and the others, Paul became a believer all over again. He struggled to describe Maggie to his friends. "She was . . . I don't know. It wasn't her eyes or her smile, but they were part of it. I don't know. She was the most alive person I've ever met."

Erin groaned. "Oh, my God."

"Listen. So I'm sitting there staring at Maggie. I could have stared at her for hours, but then I remembered Trent and Granddad."

Paul remembered scrambling to his feet, scared all over again, stammering, "I lost them in the crowd. They won't arrest Granddad, will they? He's sixty-six."

"You best go look for them." Maggie opened her jacket. Underneath, she wore a hand-drawn badge with the word *Police* written across it. Pulling it off, she taped it to Paul's T-shirt. "Trust me, it'll work. Good luck."

She and her friend turned to leave.

"Wait," Paul said.

"What?"

"I-I don't know."

Maggie kissed his cheek. Paul's skin burned from the teargas. The kiss hurt like hell, but he loved it. When she pulled away, it just hurt like hell.

"Go find your family, sweetie," Maggie said, tugging her gas mask back on. The pair vanished down an alley toward the sound of more breaking glass.

Paul stumbled back the way they'd come, between the cruisers and through the barricades. It was impossible to avoid the police, but it didn't matter. The moment they saw his badge, cut from blue-lined notebook paper, the cops left him alone. One asked if he had any more Flex-Cuffs.

Paul found his brother and grandfather half a block away from where he'd almost been arrested. They sat along a storefront with a group of protesters, their hands cuffed behind their backs. His grandfather had gotten some of the gas. Tears and snot covered his face. He grit his teeth against the urge to scream.

Using the knife on his grandfather's key chain, Paul cut through the plastic restraints and got them away from there.

"I tried to go back and look for her, but Granddad was hurt bad, Trent could barely see himself, so I had to get them to a cab and everything. After we got Granddad to the hospital, I went back to Herald Square, but the whole thing was over. I never saw her again."

Paul told Vic and the others a bare skeleton of the most amazing day of his life. He didn't tell them that since then, he'd filled sketchbooks with pastels, watercolors, and charcoal drawings of Maggie, but nothing flat and motionless could capture her. He didn't tell them that it haunted him, the moment she stood between staying and going and all the things he could have said besides, "I don't know."

When Paul first whispered Maggie's name, Gilly had been stunned. They'd bumped into someone else who'd met the Witches' Carnival. But then again, the witches hadn't exactly been hiding out at the party or at the dance club in Atlanta. As she listened to Paul's story, it slowly dawned on Gilly that that night, all across the world, there were hundreds of thousands of people who'd met the Witches' Carnival, maybe even suspected their true nature. Like

Maggie had told her, though, most were too scared or not scared enough to turn their backs on everything they knew.

"Hold on," Erin said. "This woman gave you a magic badge that makes everyone think you're a cop?"

"That's the legend, right? The Witches' Carnival can go anywhere, move through any barrier."

"So where is it? I want to see it work."

Paul stared at his sneakers. "I burned it."

"Yeah right. If you really had something like that, why would anybody burn it?"

"Because I didn't trust myself with it. Maggie helped me rescue Grandad and Trent. Using her badge to pull stupid shit would have been, I don't know, defiling it. I didn't want to do that, but that's all I could think about. So I burned it before I could."

Erin laughed at him, but Gilly and Sam understood. You spent your life clutching for things with names but no substance. Courage. Freedom. Happiness. Then they appeared in the flesh and blood and glittering brown eyes. A glimpse of the Witches' Carnival inspired awe to the brink of madness.

"So you'll help with the passports?" Vic asked.

"Yeah." Paul nodded, looking at Gilly and Sam. "Yeah. I want to help."

They started laying out plans. The design center closed at nine, but Paul had key access and permission to work there after hours, the main reason Vic needed him. First they had to get Erin's passport, glean everything they could from it, and find somewhere for Gilly and Sam to stay in the meantime.

Vic's first suggestion was that they sleep in Erin's dorm room. Erin shot that down with her first breath. "Hell, no. No offense, guys, but I don't want any connection with this. When the Feds come looking, I sure as hell don't want anybody mentioning that you two were sleeping on my floor."

They decided to get another hotel room. They'd need to go to town tomorrow, anyway, to get passport photos and do some shopping. Everyone exchanged cell phone numbers so they could keep in touch.

"All right. This is going to be easy. This is going to be fun," Vic said. With a long night looming for him and Paul, the group split up.

TWELVE

The Gilman House stood between the Rhode Island School of Design and Brown University. Two-thirds historic and one-third run-down, the hotel catered to visitors of both campuses.

Gilly and Sam ordered pizza, a ham and pineapple on thin crust. They ate while flipping across unfamiliar channels on TV. Through the connecting door they heard a couple talking in a foreign language neither of them could place.

Gilly opened *Doctor Faustus* again.

"Why are you reading that, anyway? It's not like you're going to find a secret message or something."

"It's just interesting, seeing what Chris thinks about and what he's like and stuff."

"You met the guy, G. You need a book to tell you what he's like? You partied with him."

"I know. It's just interesting."

"Speaking of them, you still have that number Jerrod gave us? Maybe we should call now that we know we're getting the passports."

Gilly pulled out the business card she was using for a bookmark. Jerrod had written Peter's number on the back. Staring at it, Gilly made an indecisive murmur. "Let's wait until we get to England. Getting there on our own is our proof that we deserve to join the Carnival."

"So you're going to risk flying with a fake passport before you even know if there's any reason to or not?"

"I just don't want them to think we're just a couple of kids." Gilly's voice was small, almost apologetic.

"Jesus fuck."

"What?"

"Nothing. I'm going to take a shower. Don't answer my phone if it rings, okay?"

"Okay."

Sam went into the bathroom. Grabbing the remote, Gilly muted the TV and went back to reading. She still fought the tangled lines of blank verse but was starting to gain the upper hand. Slowly, a story had begun to emerge from behind the dense thickets of text.

Doctor Faustus had been a professor of religion, not a

medical doctor. He became curious about magic, then obsessed with it. Good angels tried talking him out of it. Bad angels encouraged him. Finally Faustus summoned a demon named Mephastophilis, offering his soul in exchange for the ability to "make the moon drop from her sphere or the ocean to overwhelm the world."

Gilly knew Faustus was the bad guy. He turned his back on Heaven and bartered his soul for power. Like Sam had said, though, Gilly had met the author, who'd spied for France, faked his own death, and joined the Witches' Carnival. Gilly suspected Chris had found something to like in Faustus, brilliant and reckless, gambling the highest stakes possible out of boredom. The more she read and the more she thought about what they were trying to pull off, the more Gilly liked him too.

Sam stepped out of the shower. Having had only a few fitful hours of sleep in the past two days, she'd gone past exhausted into a punch–drunk bitchiness. She was afraid to close her eyes, though. The cruel memories and illusions would come back if she did.

She didn't want to think about her mom or Danny anymore. She wanted to become a zombie and get some sleep. Sam swallowed two Xanax. Even before the flesh–colored pills kicked in, she felt better knowing they were in her system.

The bathroom was quiet and warm with steam. Naked, her hair wet, Sam sat on the toilet. She rested her head in her hands, letting her thoughts drift to the fire-gutted husk of a house she and Josh had explored once when they'd been kids.

Sam remembered the melted toys scattered around, the charred mattresses with jutting metal springs like ribs, and the ragged wound where part of the roof had collapsed. She remembered how serene the destruction had been, rubble covered in silent gray ash. That's how it felt as the drug settled over her body.

Gilly was still reading when Sam stepped out of the bathroom on liquid legs. She walked with the loose, catlike gait she got when she was high or drunk.

Sam curled on the bed. Gilly sat cross-legged with the book in her lap, and as she read, Sam started playing with her toes and tickling her feet.

"You're so adorable," she whispered, slipping her hand under Gilly's shirt.

They started kissing. Sam groped Gilly's breasts, but then Gilly pulled her hand away.

"I'm kind of worn out. Let's just go to bed."

Sam sneered. "Since when?"

"I don't know. We drove all that way, then the plane ride, then–"

"Bullshit. I've spent two years keeping you from dry-humping my leg, and now you don't want to screw me because you're sleepy?"

"I'm tired."

"You're pathetic."

"What?"

"You sleep with some bitch one time–then she ditches you–and you're fucking in love with her."

Gilly stared at Sam. "Why are you so mad?"

"I'm not mad. Just say you're in love with her."

"I'm not in love with Maggie."

Sam laughed. It was a hard, mean sound. "Excuse me, hi. Do you remember me? I'm the bitch you've been in love with for two years. You don't think I know all the signs by now? Trying to figure out every little thing about her"–she kicked Gilly's textbook off the bed–"but you're terrified to just call her and talk to her."

Gilly felt the tips of her ears flush hot. "One, I've never been in love with you. Two, I told you why–"

"Bullshit! The real reason you don't want to call is because you're afraid Maggie will answer. You're such a crackbaby. You're more afraid of her laughing at you than you are of going to jail."

"Fuck you. The only reason you want to have sex is because you're fucking stoned on Xanax."

"I had one."

"Whatever. Like you told Kathy you had two mescaline cookies?"

"They're a prescription, Gilly. I take them because the doctor told me to. I don't get fucking stoned on them."

"Now look who's full of shit."

"Fuck you!"

Voices dropped to mutters, single words, and long pauses. Attempts at humor turned angry halfway through. Every back-and-forth made things worse.

Gilly went to take a shower. Sam started throwing things at the bathroom door, first her shoes then the television remote. There was a loud crash, and when Gilly came out of the bathroom, she saw the lamp, the pizza box, and the Diet Cokes all swept off the nightstand to the floor.

Gilly ended up having sex with Sam, partly to keep her quiet and partly because she was in love with her, at least a little. The motions were mechanical and boring, though. Gilly could come only by fantasizing about Maggie, stripping out of her black bloc uniform.

Afterward, they fell asleep. Sam got the dreamless half-death she'd wanted.

Vic drank coffee and Red Bull to keep himself awake. He and Paul moved to Paul's dorm room after the design building closed at two. They'd gotten clean lifts of the holograms from Erin's passport and scoured every centimeter of it with a magnifying glass, hunting down all of the microprinting.

The word "passport" was hidden twenty-eight times across the inside front cover. The line where you signed your name was actually the word "name" printed again and again. Other symbols were only visible under UV light. They figured out how to implant the RFID tags and had gotten exact color matches for all of the inks used. They knew how to reproduce the gold embossing on the front and the metallic flakes embedded in the cotton paper.

They were making good progress, but the watermarks had them stumped. Holding Erin's passport to the light, an eagle appeared within each interior page along with a metallic strip running across the top. A scanner couldn't reproduce those. Making new pages in the school's paper-making studio would take a lot more time than they had.

Morning came. Getting desperate, Vic called Erin as she got ready for class.

A girl Erin knew had visited Japan last summer. Erin had once mentioned how she left her passport lying on display on her bookshelf, hoping people would see it and be impressed. Vic asked if Erin could sneak in and swipe her friend's passport.

"Here's the thing. With only one passport, we don't know what's the same on all of them and what's different. It's not a big deal. We just need to look at it. We'll put it back tomorrow."

There were more promises and apologies. When Vic told Erin he loved her and hung up the phone, Paul watched him.

"Uh, shouldn't you have mentioned that we're going to destroy both passports?"

Vic sighed. "Trust me. With Erin, it's better to beg forgiveness than ask permission. I'll tell her we planned to put it back, then couldn't at the last minute. She'll be pissed for a while. I'll have to be real, real good for a while. Then everything'll blow over. Don't worry."

Malik walked into the squad room stoop-shouldered and sullen. He looked like a starved wolf. "Come on," he said, approaching Andy's desk. "We caught some luck."

Andy followed him out into the hall. "What luck?"

"Checked the warrant schedule today. It's Judge Dye."

"You want a search warrant for Gilly's place of residence? I'm pretty sure she's not there."

"I want a search warrant for the Grace girl. Remember? We asked her mom if she knew where they might have gone, and her mom starts bitching about how Grace had a debit card and could be anywhere?"

"Yeah?"

"Think, Moonpie. You kid's at least bright enough to not be carrying fifty grand around in cash. Maybe they've used the card for something. Maybe they deposited the money in the account. If they have, we can find out where they are from Grace's financial records."

"You sure you want to do this?" Andy asked.

"No, I don't. Give me another option."

Andy couldn't say anything else.

Judge Dye was young and ambitious. He wanted to be a congressman someday, and in Alabama that meant going to church every Sunday and never letting anybody think you were soft on crime.

At the courthouse, Andy made up a story about how Samantha Grace was tied in with one of Birmingham's better known crystal meth dealers, a three-hundred-pound Mexican creatively nicknamed Big Mexican.

"We know from surveillance of Caesar Puente that Samantha Grace has been running with him for a couple months," Andy said, glancing at the tape recorder on Judge Dye's desk. "And we know that Puente has used girlfriends in the past to hide drug profits."

"I can't issue a warrant on this girl based on what other girlfriends have done for him," Dye countered.

"No, sir. But we can use past crimes to establish the pattern of a current crime." Malik unfolded two sheets of yellow paper and laid them on the desk. "Also, we have an affidavit from Grace's mother. It states that Grace, who works at Domino's Pizza, has made several outlandish purchases during the same time she's been running with Big Mexican. Jewelry, a leather coat, some other things."

Judge Dye grilled them a little more, but once Malik handed him the forged affidavit from the girl's own mother, they were in. Dye signed the warrant.

Climbing back in their car, Andy said, "You know we're leaving a paper trail with all this shit, right?"

"How? We file everything with the records office like normal, and it gets lost. Nobody else is looking for Grace. Nobody else even knows she's missing."

"What if Dye had asked to interview Grace's mother?"

"Dye's never questioned an affiant that I know of. Relax, Moonpie. You're acting like a criminal or something."

They drove to the Compass Bank on Twentieth Street and presented the warrant. Waiting to get Grace's account history faxed over from the regional office, Andy glanced at his watch. It was 9:20. Gilly had ditched school about this time Thursday. His three days were up.

A minute later, the teller handed him a still-warm fax. Andy scanned the last twenty-four hours of activity on Grace's debit card. "There's my money," he said.

Thirty-four thousand, five hundred and fifty-eight dollars had been deposited at an ATM in Saint Augustine, Florida. Then below that were two plane tickets paid for in Daytona Beach and a hotel in Providence, Rhode Island.

"Well?" Malik asked.

"Gilly, you fucking idiot. What are you up to?" Andy felt so tired. He would have given five years off the end of his life just to be able to give up, go home, and go to sleep.

THIRTEEN

"**Y**ou know Colby hasn't called since the day we left home? I haven't talked to Mom since Kathy's house, and I had to call her that time."

"You're always checking that thing. Did you just run away to see who'd beg you to come back?"

"No. I already know they don't give a shit about me." Sam closed her phone and slipped it into her pocket. "What's up your ass?"

"You were a total bitch last night."

It was cloudy, gray noon. A late-autumn snow dusted sidewalks and the shoulders of coats, but didn't stick. Gilly and Sam walked down Thayer Street, new-age shops and open-all-day bars wedged in the chinks between Urban Outfitters and Blockbuster. Neither of them had mentioned the argument until now.

"So were you. Fuck, I didn't mean to piss you off. I was just joking around."

"You smashed a lamp. You were fucking throwing shit."

"And there was a Nazi goat eating my scrap metal!"

Gilly scowled and didn't say anything.

"Oh, come on, G. I'm sorry, okay?"

Gilly thought for a second. "What about when you said I wanted it to be me in the theater with Tracye and not Ben?"

"I didn't mean it. You know I didn't mean it. Come on, G."

Neither Tracye nor Ben had come up during the argument. Sam had been so wasted, she barely remembered last night at all.

"I'm sorry, okay?" Sam said.

Gilly knew she was, except she didn't remember what for, except it would happen again the next time she gobbled Xanax. "Fine. Let's just find this salon."

They'd called Vic late that morning. Fifteen hours in, he was running on caffeine and paranoia. He sent them out to get passport photos at a pharmacy on Thayer and told Gilly to dye her hair a new color.

"It has to look like time's passed since the pictures were taken. So dye your hair blue or something and don't take the clothes you're wearing in the photo. If airport security finds the same clothes in your luggage, it might bring up a red flag."

"That's pretty smart," Gilly said.

"Devil's in the details, baby."

They found the salon on the corner of Bowen. Acoustic rock played on a portable stereo inside. The air held the sharp tang of mousse and shampoo. Gilly picked a brilliant, comic book yellow. Sam stayed outside. She perched on a concrete planter, her hands pulled into the sleeves of her German army jacket.

The stylist tried to chitchat while bleaching the red out of Gilly's hair, but Gilly was too deep in her own thoughts to give more than one- or two-word answers.

Sam had gotten fucked up before, but running away had given her the freedom to spend almost every moment wasted. The image of Sam naked and sobbing in Kathy's bathtub still scared Gilly. The fight last night still made her mad. It didn't look like Sam had any intention of slowing down, and Gilly worried she was raising demons she couldn't control.

She's raising demons? Look at me. Gilly stared at herself in the salon mirror, getting her hair dyed so she could slip out of the country. *What if we don't make it to London? What if I go to jail?* The questions sat like chunks of rusted metal in Gilly's gut.

Even if we get to London, what if Maggie just laughs in my face? Is all of this because I'm in love with her?

No, Gilly answered herself. *But that's part of it.*

Even after the peroxide, Gilly's hair came out orange with

canary-colored highlights. Gilly smiled, said she liked it even better, and tipped the woman twenty dollars for fitting her into her schedule.

When she stepped outside, Sam was smoking a cigarette. "Vic called again. They want us to grab lunch."

Gilly nodded, and they headed to the Meeting Street Café a couple blocks away.

"I really like your hair." Sam ran her hand through Gilly's still-damp hair. Without thinking, Gilly twisted away; she didn't want Sam touching her. Sam got the message, put her hands in her pockets, and didn't say anything else.

I'm in love with Sam, too, Gilly thought. *Half the time I don't want to be, but I am. Why does she have to destroy herself over her psycho-bitch mom?*

Snowdrifts gathered in gutters and windowsills. Gilly's inner voice reeled off questions, demanding answers she didn't have.

What if Dad finds us? What if he never finds us? Should I send Mom and Dad an e-mail or something telling them I'm okay, at least?

Then a deeper voice spoke. *Hush, Gilly.*

She did her best to drown it out. *What if the Carnival's already left London? What if Sam gets wasted again and fucks this up somehow? I don't know what's going to happen.*

The voice spoke softly but with infinite patience. *Hush, Gilly.*

These were the last halcyon hours before their suicide

charge. Reasons didn't matter anymore. Outcomes didn't matter anymore. All that mattered, all that was left, was this moment. Gilly had to shut up and pay attention to now.

Whorls of snow fell from the low, gray sky. The air smelled like dead leaves. College kids and shoppers bustled past under thick coats and caps. Gilly walked along with her best friend, who had a hundred flaws and one virtue.

"Hey, Sam. You wanna know a secret?"

"What?"

"When we were at Kathy's house and I decided to go after the Carnival, I knew you'd come with me."

Sam laughed. "I almost didn't. I'd pretty much decided to go home."

"No." Gilly shook her head. "I knew you'd come with me. Even before I told you." She chewed her lip. "If you weren't, I wouldn't have had the guts to go alone."

"Yeah, well. We're friends, right?"

"Yeah." Gilly bumped Sam with her shoulder. "Bitch."

Sam bumped back. "Bitch."

Crabapple trees grew from the planters lining the street. Gilly watched the wind pluck the smoldering red and gold foliage from their branches. Autumn leaves turned skittering circles through the air and across the asphalt. Dodging cars and passersby, the wind carried them off to unimagined places. They danced all the way.

FOURTEEN

Vic and Paul looked like they'd been embalmed, buried, and dug back up.

"You got them?" Gilly asked, ushering the boys inside the hotel room.

"Hello. How are you? Did you have any trouble making the passports?" Vic sneered.

"You got them?"

Paul unslung his book bag and pulled out two freshly minted passports, wrinkled and still damp from being soaked in water. "All for the low, low price of twenty-five thousand."

Sam grabbed a thick envelope they'd gotten from the bank and tossed it to Vic. Opening it, his glassy eyes grew wide. He pulled a cigar still wrapped in cellophane from his coat pocket. As Vic and Paul took pictures of themselves lighting the cigar with hundred-dollar bills, Gilly inspected her passport.

"Hey, I've been to Glasgow," she said, glancing at one of the entry stamps.

"Yeah, about that." Vic tried to blow a smoke ring. "We couldn't reproduce the watermarks on the interior pages. But only the inside cover has your biometric data, your name and picture and stuff. So we gutted Erin's and this other girl's real passports and sewed the inside pages into dummy covers. Just remember, you've already been to Scotland, France, and Italy. Also, we moved your birthday back a year. You're officially eighteen now, which means you can drink in England."

"Cool."

"Sam, you've gone to Japan."

"Did I have a good time?"

Vic shrugged. "You went with your dad and his new wife. Things were kind of standoffish at first, but after a while, you really bonded."

"That's nice."

"Is Erin pissed?" Gilly asked.

"She doesn't know yet."

Sam grinned at him. "You're a fucking bastard, man."

"Yeah, well . . ." He shrugged again, thumbing the crisp bills. "Hey, now that the deal's done, be honest. I should have held out for thirty thousand, right?"

"You should have held out for forty," Sam snorted.

"Damn."

"Too late. No take-backs." Sam tucked the passport into the front pocket of her backpack. "We do have a bonus for you, though. You know that gift basket we gave you?"

"Yeah?"

"The bath salt is mescaline."

The boys glanced from Sam to Gilly, then back. "Mescaline like . . . mescaline?" Paul asked.

They nodded.

Vic turned to Paul. "Well, want to throw a bon voyage party?"

More planning. Vic called Erin. Paul called his girlfriend, a Brown University junior named Amy. Then Sam and the boys headed to a corner grocery store for supplies.

Gilly stayed behind to buy two plane tickets online. She should have tried talking Sam out of taking mescaline again. The obligation felt exhausted and brittle, though—what she should do but not worth the bother. Sam wouldn't listen, and besides, Gilly wanted to see what mescaline was like. She'd just keep an eye on Sam. Everything would be fine.

In Congdon House's kitchen with the door blocked, Sam and the boys mixed dough and scrounged through the rat's nest of cabinets for something to use as a cookie sheet. Sam mentioned that pot might ease the nausea from the mescaline. Vic and Paul skimmed through the contact lists on their cell phones trying to score. An hour later the six of them–Gilly, Sam, Vic, Erin, Paul, and Amy–sat around the hotel room. Tucked safe inside the weird old hotel, away from the snow and damp wind, they passed a joint.

"I love your hair," Erin said to Gilly. She'd warmed to Gilly and Sam considerably, still unaware that Vic had destroyed her passport.

"Really? It didn't come out like I wanted."

"No, it looks good. Red's too angry. Red's all rage and madness. Orange has the same vibrancy as red, but it's happier. Orange is more sociable."

"I thought about getting my hair dyed some funky color," Amy said. She was a long-faced girl wearing a Ramones T-shirt. "What's blue?"

"Blues and greens are tranquil, very placid. Know what? Go purple. Purple's tranquil too, but there's red just under the surface. Purple looks all sweet and innocent, but if you push it, purple pushes back."

Amy played at her shoulder-length hair. "I'll probably just buy some cool boots instead."

As the conversation turned to boots, Sam picked up two of the cookies and studied them. "They're a little burnt on the bottom, but I think they should be okay," she said.

The six of them gobbled one cookie apiece. A strange metallic undertaste settled on Gilly's tongue.

They lay on the bed and soft carpet. Legs tangled, heads

nestled against shoulders for comfort, it felt like falling while on solid ground. They joked their way through the sweats and stomach-cramps. They weren't scared because they were all falling together.

"Who rolled this?" Vic asked, examining the joint in his hand.

"Me," Gilly said.

"It's coming apart." He sat up, licked his fingers, and performed impromptu surgery on the smoldering cigarette. "Seriously. Get it together, all right?"

After an hour, the tumbling sensation slowed and the mescaline set them down as gently as spun glass. They decided to roam the neighborhood. The impulse hit them all at the same time, the way a flock of birds snaps left or right without a leader. Nobody said anything; they all just pulled on coats and shoes and filed down the hall.

Gilly fell a step behind her friends and watched College Hill move around her. City lights blocked out the stars, turning the sky to black slate. Snowflakes winked into creation a few feet over their heads. They drifted down, touched the wet street, and vanished. The world was darkness and hard light, streetlamps, headlights, and cheery yellow windows. Cars slid past. People marched up and down the street and in and out of doors with the practiced choreography of a musical.

Gilly had spent almost every Sunday of her life at the

Living Waters Baptist Church. Some Wednesday nights her parents could still guilt her into going to youth Bible study with Caitlin. Crammed shoulder-to-shoulder in the pews, they sang, witnessed, and listened to sermons, the hopeful ones and the fiery, apoplectic ones. None of it could prick Gilly's skin. As the preachers wailed, begged, and threatened, Gilly thought about breakfast or the lip-glossed girls in the choir.

She got it now. While Gilly had sat bored and fidgeting, this was what everyone around her had experienced. The night was holy. Snowflakes jeweling hair and eyelashes were holy. Trees lifted their limbs in praise. Vic laughed, and the sound filled Gilly with joy.

"Scarce can I name salvation, faith, or Heaven but fearful echoes thunder in mine ears. 'Faustus, thou art damned.' Then swords and knives, poison, guns, halters, and envenomed steel are laid before me to dispatch myself. And long ere this I should have slain myself had not sweet pleasure conquered deep despair."

"Huh?" Sam turned to stare. Gilly kept reciting. She didn't have to think about the words. Because of the mescaline, because of the silvery snow, she found every line waiting on the tip of her tongue.

"Have not I made blind Homer sing to me of Alexander's love and Oenone's death? And had not he, that built the walls of Thebes with ravishing sound of his melodious harp, made music with my Mephastophilis? I am resolved. Faustus shall never repent."

"What's that from?" Paul asked.

"*Doctor Faustus.*" Amy smacked him in the arm.

"Well, how should I know?"

"You're in college, aren't you? She knows. She's in high school."

"It's not real college. It's more like four years of coloring in the lines."

Vic snickered. "You think that too, huh?"

"Like we're being trained instead of taught? Yeah, sometimes."

Vic, Erin, and Paul talked about school. Before long, their conversation ascended to a strange, three-lobed stream of consciousness.

"The problem is that in class, progress is measured by this linear scale of definable goals. That's bullshit."

"Human consciousness isn't a straight line, it's a circle. It's the same questions over and over. Its art has to be a circle too."

"Not a circle. It's the same questions over and over, but the context changes. The Sistine Chapel and aboriginal Dreamtime paintings answer the same question."

"So it's not a circle, it's a spiral."

"Yes."

While they talked postmodern theory and metaphysics,

Gilly, Sam, and Amy discussed smaller things–*Doctor Faustus*, plans for tomorrow, and cool stores around Providence. They wandered for hours, winding their way down College Hill. The neon glow of Thayer Street far behind, dignified old homes hunched close together against the cold.

"The spiral can't be subjugated. Bricolage and eclecticism evolved as counterattacks against materialist attempts to reign in art."

"So Rodin and a Subaru ad are the same thing?"

"They could be. A urinal was."

"Only after Duchamp forced people to see it that way. Maybe people could see art in a Subaru ad if they wanted to, but they don't."

"Bricolage, eclecticism aren't counterattacks. They're art turned feral."

"Art turning its back on society."

They wound up at an all-night Chinese restaurant, sipping hot tea and munching fried wontons. Sam stepped outside to smoke a cigarette. Her friends were insane, and she loved them because they were insane. She glanced at her watch. She and Gilly had to catch planes in the morning, but Sam couldn't make herself declare an end to the laughter and talk.

"Hey." Paul walked toward her slowly, like approaching a strange dog. "You okay?"

"Yeah, I'm cool. Sometimes the chatter gets too much and I need to chill out a little bit."

She offered him a cigarette. Paul lit it and blew a jet of pale smoke into the black night. "I really hope you find the Witches' Carnival," he said, staring into the distance.

"Thanks." Sam studied his face, the blue eyes and long hair tucked behind his ears. He had a nice chin.

"When we were making those passports, I thought about making one for myself. But I'm too big a pussy to go and leave everything behind."

Sam shook her head. "It's not like that. We just don't have much to stick around for, y'know?"

"Yeah, but still . . ."

"Look. My mom's a bitch. My boyfriend's an asshole. Gilly's parents think she's going to Hell. I'd love a reason not to go. If I had somebody like Amy or any sort of future except working at Domino's the rest of my life, I wouldn't leave either. Trust me. I'm scared shitless about what's going to happen."

"Still. Screw the rules. Screw the law. It's punk as fuck." Paul took a half-step toward her. His hand brushed Sam's waist. "I think you're my hero."

Sam grinned. "Yeah?"

"Yeah."

He kissed her. Sam kissed him back. Paul smelled like green tea and ink. Sam slipped her tongue into his mouth. Vapor rose from the corners of their lips. Pulling him close,

Sam thought the best sensation on Earth might be another person's hot skin on a cold night.

The restaurant's glass door swung open. "What the hell, Paul?" Amy punched him hard in the back. "God, I can't believe you. I'm sitting right there." She pointed through the grease-streaked window. "God."

"I'm sorry, Amy. We just got caught—"

Vic, Erin, and Gilly streamed out the door. Erin grabbed Amy in a hug, cooing, trying to calm her down.

"You always do this when you're high." Amy swung at Paul again. "You're a fucking rat." Her voice quivered with oncoming tears.

Be-Woop! Woop! A siren stabbed the night, making all six of them jump. Everything spun in blue and red light as the patrol car pulled to the curb.

"Shit." Sam watched the police officer climb out of his car.

"Evening." Tall and muscular, with a black mustache and thinning hair, he stepped onto the sidewalk, flexing his gloved fingers at his sides. "What's going on?"

Everybody shook their heads, certain that nothing was going on.

"Well, something is. You're kissing her, and then she's punching you."

They shook their heads again, tripping over themselves to assure him that all was exactly as it should be. The cop cut them off.

"Listen to me. Whatever it is, you need to keep it at home. I don't need you two making out or you two fighting in the middle of the street. Understand?"

It couldn't be plainer. They understood perfectly and felt foolish for assuming anything else. They were thankful to him for pointing out their ridiculous error.

Even though they stood in the golden light of the restaurant, the policeman shined his flashlight in Paul's face. "How much have you had to drink tonight?"

"N–none."

"Nothing to drink? How about drugs?"

"No, sir."

"Your pupils are huge. You're telling me you haven't taken anything tonight?"

"No, sir. I mean, yes sir. I mean, I haven't taken anything."

"All right, come over here." The policeman lined them up against the restaurant's cinder–block wall. While he had Paul follow a pen with his eyes, Sam mentally checked everything on her. The passports were at the hotel, the drugs were hidden safely in her bloodstream. She was in the clear as long as she didn't act stupid. Even if the cop took them to jail, she and Gilly could post bail and still be at the airport by morning.

"Got some ID on you?" the cop asked Paul.

The question sent a jolt up Sam's spine. Paul and the others were legal adults. But once the cop checked her and

Gilly's licenses, he'd know they were underage runaways. Even if he let the others go, he'd have to take them in.

Sam snapped around to look at Gilly. Gilly had already figured it out and stared back with panicked eyes.

The officer finished with Paul and moved to Amy, asking to see her ID too. Gilly cast around for a way out of this, but the mescaline kept sending her thoughts spiraling in strange directions.

Her dad was a cop. She knew cops. She knew what they wanted to hear. She recognized the officer's stance, hands hanging by his sides like a gunslinger. She recognized the soft-toned commands and the duty gear hanging from his belt, the nylon key holder, the Leatherman tool. She wondered if it was a real Leatherman or a knockoff. It looked like a knockoff.

None of that matters. Think, think.

The officer handed Amy her student ID back and started grilling Vic. Gilly was next.

They'd gotten so close. In a few hours they would have joined the Witches' Carnival. They would have become shooting stars, burning across the night. But shooting stars were really just meteors, chunks of rock and debris plummeting toward Earth.

You dumb bitch, stop it! Think!

"How about you? What's your name?"

Gilly stared up at him. They'd come so close, and now it was ending so stupidly, she couldn't believe it.

"Let me see your ID."

Gilly fumbled for her license. She decided to run. She wouldn't get ten paces before the officer caught her. But ten more paces of freedom and fire would be worth more than the rest of her whole stone-cold life put together.

"Gillian Stahl . . . you're from Alabama?"

"Yeah." As he studied her license, Gilly shifted her weight to her right foot, edging out from between the cop and the restaurant's wall.

"How old are you, Miss Stahl?"

Gilly bolted. Rattlesnake-quick, the cop was after her. A guttural order to stop and a hand grabbing her elbow, almost swinging her into the wall.

"Get down! Get on the ground!"

Gilly struggled to pull free knowing she couldn't. They were about to topple together onto the pavement when a shard of night sliced past her head.

"Get on the—shit!" The officer raised his arms to protect himself, letting go of Gilly. The crow shrieked, beating iridescent black wings and clawing the cop's face.

Gilly lurched clear and watched. The officer swung his heavy flashlight but missed. The berserk creature kept up its attack, drawing blood from thin scratches. It was only a distraction, though. In a second or two, the cop would be on top of her again. Gilly knew the crow hadn't saved her; it could only buy her a slender chance to save herself.

Acting before fear or conscience kicked in, Gilly crashed into the policeman. As he staggered back, she snapped the key holder off his belt.

The cop finally seized the bird by its wing and threw it onto the sidewalk. It hit the concrete with a rustling *whap* and lay there, stunned or dead. The cop's gaze whipped side to side. By the time he spotted Gilly, she was sliding into the driver's seat of his cruiser.

"Oh, fuck. Hey!"

With the door open, Gilly cranked the engine. One hand clutching his still-holstered gun, the cop reached around and tried jerking her out. "Get the fuck out! Get out now!"

Gilly swung backward into traffic. Tires squealed behind her and horns blared. She dragged the cop a couple yards before he let go. Jumping onto the sidewalk, he screamed into his shoulder mike. Gilly shifted into drive and hit the gas. Two wheels popped the curb. The cop scrambled farther back.

Driving a wedge between the cop and her friends, Gilly threw the passenger-side door open. "Let's go, Sam!"

"Later, guys." Sam dashed toward the cruiser. She had one foot inside when Gilly turned hard back onto the street. More tires, more screaming horns, and they left the shouting, purple-faced cop and their friends behind.

On the squad car's radio, they heard the policeman reporting Unit 506 stolen, giving their descriptions along with a string of numbers. Two other cruisers answered back with more numbers. Then dispatch told everybody to switch to fire frequency and the radio went silent.

Blood pounded in Gilly's ears. Her chest felt like it was about to cave in. "Oh shit, oh shit, oh shit, okay, where the fuck are we going?"

"The hotel. Get our shit and get out of here."

"We can't," Gilly yelled. "They fucking LoJac these things."

"Then what?"

"I don't know. I didn't plan this far."

"The school. Leave it somewhere at the school and we'll get to the hotel on foot. They'll be looking all over the campus for us."

"Okay. That'll work."

"And get the fuck off the main street. Turn down a side street. And drive slower. No, drive faster. We're gonna get fucking caught."

With the police already looking for them, there was no point in trying to stay inconspicuous. Gilly roared down residential streets and blew through red lights. Somehow, they made it back to the campus and ditched the cruiser near the beach.

Only a few people strolled along the sidewalks. Gilly and Sam cut across lawns crystalline with snow, staying away from the roads and keeping an eye out for campus security.

The yellow cupola of the Gilman House hotel came into view. Riding the elevator up to the third floor, they broke into a dead run toward their room, grabbed backpacks and *The Norton Anthology of Elizabethan Literature*, then slipped out.

Twenty minutes later, two squad cars pulled up to the hotel's front entrance. Gilly and Sam watched from the Kettle Diner down the street.

"Man, I knew Vic and them would tell the cops where we were staying," Sam said, sipping coffee. "Can't trust anybody these days."

"Don't worry. They don't have any reason to ask about fake passports. And Vic and Paul don't have any reason to tell them."

Sam nodded, watching four police officers disappear through the hotel's glass doors.

The only other people in the diner were the cook, one waitress, and a threesome of laughing college students, their fingers and clothes stained with paint. The cook leaned against the counter reading yesterday's newspaper. A portable stereo played rock with the volume turned down low.

Gilly and Sam went to the rest room to clean up. It had just been mopped, and the smell of disinfectant stung their noses. Gilly brushed her hair in the mirror and caught Sam staring at her.

"What?"

"That was, like, the most hard core thing I've ever seen anyone do. Except you were the one who did it."

"Hey, I was born hard core." Or at least, Gilly thought, she was getting there. Like she'd feared, Sam had gotten high, made an ass out of herself, and they'd almost been caught. It was okay, though. Gilly had saved them. "So how much shit do you think we're in?" she asked.

"Let's see. Stealing a police car, resisting arrest, assaulting a police offic–"

"Come on. That was a bird. They can't blame us for what a bird does."

They stepped out of the rest room looking hard–worn but otherwise respectable.

"That was Meek's crow, right?"

"I assume."

Their hearts raced from the mad escape. The idea that they'd gotten away with it made Gilly and Sam swell with giggling swagger. They could barely sit down. Smoking one cigarette after another, they tried piecing the evening together.

They mulled over why Meek had sent his crow to save them and who Meek was in the first place. They didn't come up with much except that Meek was helping them reach the Witches' Carnival. That was enough to make them feel practically bulletproof.

The conversation drifted to other things. Gilly and Sam passed the pitch-black hours of morning discussing which bands were cool and which ones sucked, detailing the reasons they hated Tracye, Ashley, and various other people, and chuckling over misadventures they'd had at school and the multiplex.

"They have Halloween over in England, right?" Sam asked out of the blue.

Gilly shrugged. "It doesn't involve Indians or independence, so I guess so. Why?"

"Look at the date, G."

Gilly checked her watch. It was October 29. "Oh, cool."

"Oh, cool," Sam mocked. "I miss Halloween. Trick-or-treating and stuff. You wander around at night, wear a disguise, demand candy from people, play tricks on them. It's, like, the only holiday that celebrates anti-socialness."

"Yeah. Christmas is for pansies."

Long periods passed when they sat together but silent, sipping coffee and staring in different directions. The cruisers still sat in front of the Gilman House. Yawning, Gilly leaned her head against Sam's shoulder. Sam fussed with Gilly's hair.

"It's always sticking up in the back. You need mousse or something, Gilly."

"Yuck. The dye makes it crispy enough already."

"You think Vic and them'll be okay?" Sam asked.

"They'll be fine."

"You know that cop's pissed as hell. He's gonna fucking find something to charge them with. He's gonna make up laws."

Gilly shrugged. "We just paid them twenty-five grand. They can make bail."

"See? Hard core bitch. That's what I'm talking about."

Gilly shrugged again. She remembered sitting on the beach in Saint Augustine, their lives behind them, the Carnival ahead. They could have whatever they wanted, but only if they were smart enough and fast enough to grab it.

Gilly looked at the cook's radio above the stove, then jumped up. "Give me your cell phone."

"Why?" Sam fished it out of her purse.

"Just wait."

Gilly asked the waitress for a phone book and made a call.

"What are you doing?" Sam asked when Gilly sat back down.

"Just wait."

The song on the radio ended, and the vampire-shift DJ came on.

"We have a dedication here from someone who'd like to remain anonymous, sent out to the brave men and women of the Providence police force. She wants them to know she's sorry about that squad car, and for the record, it wasn't her crow, just a friend's. Sounds like someone's having a more interesting night than me. Also, she'd like to remind everyone that if you aren't pretty, start trouble."

The DJ vanished, and the greatest song in the history of the universe ever began to play.

Runnin' out of time! We're running hot. Running out of time. We're running hot.

Gilly and Sam howled and joined in. "Fever's up to hundred and one! Brain's near oblivion. Let's go have some fun. Raise hell and a back beat!"

FIFTEEN

Indigo morning came. The diner filled with construction crews, beefy men grabbing steak-and-egg breakfasts before heading to the job site. Gilly and Sam decided it was time to go.

Gilly had booked two flights. One had a connection in Newark, the other in Chicago. With two hundred miles between them when they used the fake passports, airport security would have less cause for suspicion. They'd take two different cabs from two different cab companies to the airport. From that point on, each of them was on her own until they got to the Hotel Constantinople in London.

"Listen," Gilly said. "You have to swear. Even if you see the cops in London busting my ass ten feet in front of you, just keep walking."

"Hell, I'll help them smack you around a little before they throw you into the squad car."

"Sam, be serious. Swear."

Dropping the jokes, Sam said, "Okay. I swear. As long as you'll do the same thing."

"Okay."

A green and white taxi pulled into the diner's parking lot. "That's my ride," Sam said, slinging her book bag onto her shoulder.

"Good luck."

"Screw luck. If we had any luck, we wouldn't be running away in the first place. Just remember everything I told you. We'll be fine."

The taxi driver honked her horn. Sam hugged Gilly. "Here. You smoke when you're nervous." Opening her Coffin Nails box, Sam dropped the last three cigarettes onto the table, then pocketed the box. "I love you, G."

"I love you too."

Sam hustled out the door and into the cab. Gilly sat down and watched her best friend slip away through the dusk.

Gilly lit one of the cigarettes. She worried she was getting a habit, but with everything else going on at the moment, that seemed a minor concern.

For more than an hour last night, Sam had drilled Gilly on what to say and how to say it.

"Why are you going to London?"

"I don't know. My grandmother has cancer. I have to go up and see her."

"That's too big a sob story. They'll know you're trying to get sympathy. Tell them your boyfriend lives in London. You met online, and you're going to meet him."

"Can't it be my girlfriend?"

Sam shook her head. "Makes you stick out more. You have to be as unnoticeable as possible."

They decided that Gilly's boyfriend was named Ben. He was twenty-one, worked at a restaurant called Milo's, and played in a band called Merricat. Drums. He'd dropped out of college after a year, and Gilly was trying to convince him to go back.

"But don't just spew all of that in one sentence," Sam said. "Answer their questions, but don't offer any more than you have to. But don't act like you're trying to avoid their questions either."

"So what college did Ben go to?"

"Doesn't matter. If they're digging that deep, you're already busted."

"Don't say that. I'm going to be so fucking scared already, they'll know something's up."

"Scared is fine. This is your first time flying by yourself, you're alone in a huge airport, and now something's wrong with your passport? Of course you're scared. But here's the thing. When you look at the security guard, don't look at him like he may put you in jail. Look at him like he's the only person who can save you. Look at him like he's your rescuer, not your enemy. Tell yourself that over and over until you believe it."

Gilly was smarter than Sam. She'd never say it out loud, but it was true. She knew more and remembered facts better. She could scribble down an English essay during lunch and still get a B. And maybe, when push came to shove, she could jump into a bathtub to help her friend or steal a police car. But Sam saw through people in a way Gilly never would. She anticipated every move. She knew the exact words to say to flatter them, insult them, or move them around like puppets.

The skill depended on some hard-earned wisdom and a certain fox-like cunning. It wasn't something she could teach Gilly, but Gilly prayed she'd gleaned enough to squeak through today with her belt and shoelaces.

A second taxi pulled up a minute later. Gilly grabbed her bag, dropped a twenty on the table, and headed out the door.

At the College Hill precinct house, the police held Paul, Vic, Erin, and Amy in spartan interview rooms. The coconspirators spilled the absolute, unvarnished truth to every question the cops asked. They kept their mouths shut about the rest.

Gilly and Sam were friends from Alabama who'd shown up on Vic's doorstep last night. All four of them confessed to smoking marijuana and, after a little more pressure, dropping mescaline. They didn't know where Gilly and Sam had gotten the drugs or where they were headed. The police didn't know anything about passports, and nobody volunteered to fill them in.

After seven hours of grilling, the investigators couldn't pin anything on them except misdemeanor possession. By eight in the morning, Erin had gone past scared and was just sick of the whole thing. She told the officer to either charge her or she was walking out. The police sent them to lockup knowing they'd wind up with some fines and community service.

Major Campbell smoked a cigarette in the alley beside the motor pool. He had dark rings under his eyes and wore clothes he'd pulled out of the hamper. When uniforms walked past, they didn't wave or chat. They stared at the ground and made sure to look busy. Everybody had heard about last night's grand clusterfuck, and the entire department walked on eggshells around him.

Campbell was commanding officer over the uniformed division. Like a buck sergeant in the army, he was the man in charge where it mattered. While the chief and deputy chief bickered over policy and posed for photo-ops with the mayor, they left it to Campbell to actually get bad guys off the street.

Lieutenant Danby had dragged Campbell out of bed at three that morning, right after the first reporter from the *Providence Journal* called. Since then, reporters from NBC 10 News, ABC 6 News, the *Providence Journal* again, and the Brown University student newspaper had come looking for statements. Campbell had to give them something soon, but he couldn't figure out how to say, "Last night two high school kids distracted an officer with a bird, stole his cruiser, vanished into thin air, and then called a radio station to brag about it," and somehow manage to keep his job.

Cigarette bobbing in the corner of his mouth, Campbell flipped through the statements they'd gotten from the college students who'd been with the perpetrators.

"They're from Alabama?" he asked, glancing up at Lieutenant Danby, who'd just handed him the report.

"Yeah."

"So a pair of shoeless, cousin-fucking *Jerry Springer* guests gave every cop I've got the slip."

"They're big NASCAR fans down there. Maybe they just watched too much Daytona 500."

Campbell didn't laugh. "Listen to me. This shit's about five minutes from hitting the fan, and when it does, we need to at least look like we know our elbows from our assholes. Clear?"

"Yes, sir."

"What about the call to the radio station?"

Danby shook his head. "Cell phone. We don't know where they called from."

"The hotel room?"

"Nothing useful. They left a laptop behind. I got the techies from MIS looking at it now. They may find a clue to where they've gone, but I'm not holding my breath."

"Do you have any good news?"

"I'm pretty sure we can keep the crow out of the news-papers."

Campbell sighed. His eyes skimmed the rows of squad cars filling the motor pool. Unit 506 sat in the back, its front bumper half torn off and the undercarriage wrecked. Across its scraped front door was the department shield and motto: SEMPER VIGILANS. Always vigilant.

A young patrol officer came up the alley. "Major Campbell, the chief's looking for you."

"You put him on hold? Why didn't you transfer him to my cell phone?"

The cop shook his head. "No, sir. He's here looking for you. He's in the squad room."

Campbell stared at him for a moment. "Goddamn it." Turning toward Danby, he said, "I have to go upstairs to get my ass chewed. When I get back, please have something useful on Daisy Duke and her girlfriend here."

"We're trying, but there's not much to go on."

"We've got their names. Call Alabama and see if they have

anything." Campbell was already walking away. "If these two raise this much hell on vacation, Lord only knows what they've gotten into back home."

Beneath bright orange hair, the girl had a dull, dingy appearance, with chewed-down fingernails and a school book bag bulging with clothes. Her gaze buzzed around the terminal like a housefly, landing briefly on people and courtesy carts, anything that made a noise or moved. Jonathan could tell she'd never flown by herself before.

Her passport was wrinkled from water damage. Jonathan passed it in front of the RFID scanner. Instead of the girl's photograph appearing on the monitor, a text box popped up reading: ERROR 208. Jonathan scanned it twice more before asking, "Why's your passport wrinkled like this?"

"I had it in a box in the basement and the basement flooded. But, I mean, you can still read it, right?"

Masking his annoyance, Jonathan nodded. "Yeah, but there's a microchip inside that I have to check. It's not working, see?" He swiped her passport by the scanner again. ERROR 208.

The girl got scared. "O–Oh, no. What do I–" She glanced around the terminal, instinctively searching for a parent to come take her hand. Finally, her imploring eyes settled back on Jonathan. "What do I do?"

Jonathan had the authority to detain her. He'd lead her to

the Pen, a concrete-walled holding area in the bowels of the airport, and have her wait until the State Department verified her identity. He'd done it a couple times to people who acted like assholes, making sure they sat there long enough to miss their flight. This girl wasn't yelling and threatening to have him fired, though; she was just stupid.

"It won't be a problem today." Opening her passport, he started entering her information into the computer manually. "But if the tag won't read, we can keep you here until we get in touch with the State Department. It's a big hassle and usually takes a couple hours, and you don't want to go through it. So as soon as you get home, get this replaced, okay?"

"Okay."

"All right, Miss Stahl, you're all set."

"Thank you so much." Taking her passport back, the girl beamed at him.

Jonathan smiled a tight, company-policy smile. "Not a problem. Have a nice flight." He reached for the passport of a man juggling cell phone, laptop, and Michael Crichton's latest paperback. Jonathan scanned it and forgot about the girl with orange hair.

Walking through the security checkpoint, Gilly allowed herself a glance over her shoulder and a quick sneer. She hadn't even gotten to talk about Ben, her college-dropout boyfriend. Turning back around, she started chewing her lip again and staring around the busy concourse. She played a mousy little nobody. It wasn't hard since that's all she was.

Not pretty or particularly charming, Gilly was easy to ignore. Sometimes her words came out stumbling or slow, so people assumed her mind worked the same way. They'd been happy to underestimate her every day of her life. In Saint Augustine, Gilly had almost given up, unable to find a high-tech solution to get them through airport security. She'd forgotten that she was invisible already.

Stepping onto the BritishAir jet, she found her seat and opened *Doctor Faustus*. A few minutes later, the plane taxied down the runway.

Major Campbell sat in his office, a windowless space cluttered with police manuals, when Lieutenant Danby found him.

"Well?" Campbell asked.

"Not much, and a lot more than we thought. I called Jefferson County down in Alabama. Neither of the girls has a record, but a search warrant was executed against Samantha Grace just yesterday." Danby handed Major Campbell a fax copy of the warrant. "They were looking for drug profits. Something about racketeering. The warrant hasn't been returned yet, so there's no inventory, so we don't know if they found anything. Still, it's strange."

Skimming the warrant, Campbell's gaze snagged on a name. He grabbed the statement from one of the college kids and read the first page.

"What's going on here?"

"What now?"

Campbell turned the sheets of paper around to show Danby. "The executing officer for the search warrant on this girl has the same last name as this other girl."

"Stahl." Danby's eyes flickered from warrant to confession and back. He shook his head. "That can't be a coincidence, can it?"

Campbell raised his hands. "I give up. I don't know what the hell's happening. I'm going back to bed." He slumped in his chair and fell silent. Lieutenant Danby stood waiting for orders.

"Call Alabama back. Get me in touch with whoever's in charge over there. Maybe they can explain this crap."

"Yes, sir."

Danby left to call the law clerk at the Jefferson County Courthouse again. She put him in touch with Lieutenant Swopes, head of Birmingham's robbery unit.

Swopes talked to Danby, then Major Campbell. The second time through the story, he scratched notes across a yellow legal pad.

"What did you say the other girl's name was?" he asked.

"Gillian Stahl."

Swopes thanked Campbell and promised to keep him informed. Hanging up, he felt sick. His mind groped for an answer he knew wasn't there. More calls. First to the law clerk to have her fax him a copy of the warrant, then to Judge Dye to hear his part of the story. Finally, Lieutenant Swopes called dispatch on the backline and told them to find Andy and Malik.

> Cut is the branch that might have grown full straight,
> And burned is Apollo's laurel bough
> That sometime grew within this learned man.
> Faustus is gone. Regard his Hellish fall,
> Whose fiendful fortune may exhort the wise
> Only to wonder at unlawful things,
> Whose deepness doth entice such forward wits
> To practice more than heavenly power permits.

Surrounded by the rustling quiet of the plane cabin, Gilly finished *Doctor Faustus*. She reread the final lines and felt gypped.

The story just stopped. Faustus traded his soul, played around with black magic for a while, and got dragged down to Hell. Gilly had assumed there'd be some eleventh-hour miracle; Faustus would trick Mephostophilis into giving him his soul back or something. Instead, it ended with a finger-wagging morality lesson.

Closing the book, Gilly rubbed her eyes. The cabin's dry air made them itch and gave her a dull headache.

Maybe the point was everything that didn't happen. Maybe the tragedy wasn't that Faustus traded his soul but that he wasted his power pulling pranks and showing off. She'd have to ask Chris about it when she saw him.

The fat woman sitting beside Gilly had fallen asleep. Leaning over her, catching a whiff of her musky scent, Gilly lifted the window shade. The plane sailed over cloudscapes tinged rose quartz pink. They flew west, away from the sun. As evening closed its wings around her, Gilly's world started to crumble six miles below.

Andy stood with Malik in Lieutenant Swopes's office. The warrant lay on Swopes's desk beside a stack of blue equipment acquisition forms.

Feeling the sharp edge of panic, Andy became hyper aware of everything around him: the dark wood paneling on the walls; a cheap ballpoint pen that had fallen to the dirty carpet.

"Some serious questions have come up about this warrant you got from Judge Dye yesterday," Swopes said without looking at Andy or Malik.

Malik started to say something, but the lieutenant held up his hand. "I've called the FOP. They're sending two lawyers over now."

Malik stood with his arms across his chest. Looking down, he shook his head back and forth like an ox. "We don't need lawyers. We can keep this in the family. Andy's daughter ran away. She's tangled up with some bad stuff; that's why he didn't want the department involved. He asked me to help find her before she got into serious trouble, and I agreed. It was stupid." Malik spread his hands and let them drop to his sides. "Whatever you need to do now, no hard feelings."

Lieutenant Swopes sighed and wiped sweat off his bald forehead. "Andy, why didn't you come to me?" He was angry but not suspicious. He believed Malik.

"Because . . ." Andy stared at his commanding officer. He could get away with it. They'd suspend him, probably fire him, but he wouldn't go to jail. All he had to do was not mention the money. All he had to do was make sure they never found Gilly. He'd be in the clear.

And maybe she'd come home on her own after all.

"Me and Malik have been skimming money off perps. Better than a hundred thou–"

"Shut up!" Malik screamed, spit flying from his mouth. "Goddamnit, Moonpie, Shut up!"

Andy shouted over him. "Gilly took the money when she–"

"Goddamn–" Malik punched him full force in the jaw. Crystal stars circled Andy's vision. Blood filled his mouth, and he heard Lieutenant Swopes yelling for help. He clung to the bookcase, about to collapse to the floor. Far away, Malik was screaming, "Just be quiet! Be quiet!" His voice cracked with a sob. "I can handle this."

The office filled with blurred figures and the voices of friends. Andy felt them grasp him under his arms and sit him down. A gray fog had settled over the room. It would feel so good to slip into it. Andy wanted to lose consciousness and not wake up, but he refused.

"Gilly has the money. That's why I didn't say anything."

Lieutenant Swopes's light brown fingers pressed a handkerchief against Andy's split lip. "You need to wait for a lawyer, Andy."

"Fuck a lawyer." Andy pushed the handkerchief away. "I'll tell you everything, okay? But listen. Gilly's gone. She might be hurt or dead, and I don't know where she is, and you've got to find her, okay? Swear you'll find her, and I'll tell you everything. She's my daughter. It's supposed to be my job, but I fucked everything up. Please, just find Gilly and get her home."

SIXTEEN

For Gilly, London was built from words and pictures in books. It felt strange plunging into a living city. Through the taxi's window she watched men in soccer jerseys and women with dreadlocks walk along in laughing clusters. The wind snapped at awnings above bars and Indian, Italian, and Japanese markets. The McDonald's arches glowed bright and familiar against the neon static. Homeless people sold a magazine called *The Big Issue*. Graffiti attacked movie posters. Skeletons and jack-o'-lanterns decorated windows. Finally, the Hotel Constantinople's wedding cake finials rose above convenience stores and tchotchke shops.

"Is this it?" Gilly asked, staring up.

The taxi driver grunted, "Yup," and steered down the circular drive leading to the hotel's glass doors.

Hushed light filled the lobby. A fountain in the center burbled. In T-shirt, unwashed pants, and the blue Converses she'd bought in Atlanta, Gilly moved through the elegance with an assassin's cool. She got a key from the desk clerk, found the elevators around a corner, and rode to the sixth floor.

Sam sat propped up in bed eating a room-service hamburger. When Gilly walked in, she turned and grinned with her mouth full. "Are we punk as fuck or what?"

"You know what's the most nerve-racking thing about traveling on a fake passport?"

"How easy it is?"

"They really need to fix that." Gilly shrugged off her backpack. "The whole trip I'm staring around at everybody else, thinking, *All right, who's doing the same thing I'm doing, except they've got a bomb?*"

"I ordered you a hamburger by the way." Sam pointed to a wooden tray sitting on the table. "And there's Diet Cokes in the fridge."

"You're so good to me." Lifting the plate cover, Gilly grabbed the burger and took a bite. It was lukewarm, but she was starving.

"Hey, you got us to London, right? That's how this friendship works. You come up with the brilliant plan, I order dinner."

"Whatever. You're the one who got us through security."

Sam laughed, licking mustard off her thumb. "Yeah, right. My fiendish plot to 'just walk through like normal.' I'm an evil genius."

Eating, they compared their flights, both uneventful. Sam complained about the weird shows on TV. She'd already showered and changed clothes. When Gilly jumped off the bed to do the same, Sam spoke up.

"Now that we've made it to London, you wanna call the witches?"

Gilly hesitated. When Sam had gotten wasted in Providence, she'd accused Gilly of being more afraid of humil-iation than going to jail. Gilly wouldn't have flown into a rage if it hadn't been the truth.

"What if they say no?" she asked. "What if we've come all this way and they just laugh at us."

Sam shrugged. "Then we go back home and the Providence police take us to jail. Unless your dad gets his hands on you first."

"You're not helping."

"I don't know what's gonna happen, G. I do know we've completely fucked our lives up over this. Maybe Maggie'll laugh at you. Maybe she'll say you weren't that great a screw, anyway. But it doesn't really matter, because your last chance to be a pussy was about two fake passports and a stolen cop car ago."

There were lines of reasoning so elegant in their simplicity, they were impossible to argue against. Finding Jerrod's business card, Gilly picked up the phone and dialed. She listened to the ringing on the distant end with a knot in her stomach and a prayer in her throat.

The CD spinning in Peter's Discman was burned with eleven different covers of "Cross Road Blues." Robert Johnson, the Mississippi bluesman who supposedly wrote the song about meeting the devil at a crossroads and trading his soul for musical talent, worked a beat-up guitar on one track. Eric Clapton followed him note for note and just missed it. Some college jazz band poured every thump and wail they had into another.

High on his own product, Peter stood in the archway of the suite's kitchen. Surrounded by boxes and trays of cookies, four boys with acne scars and pierced lips played quarters with the Witches' Carnival. Peter turned up his Discman's volume until their voices slipped beneath the music. He watched the motion of their bodies as they bounced a ten pence and downed shots of Guinness. The boys were part of the brigade of punks and modern-day street Arabs they'd raised to take Battersea.

"I went to the cross road . . . Fell down on my knees . . ."

Peter was a child of the great culture wars, too young for Woodstock but not by much. He knew the glorious victories by rote. Civil rights. Sexual freedom. The Beatles. But he couldn't help looking back at the scorched earth they'd left behind.

It had to be done. The other guy started it. They killed King and Kennedy. They bombed a church in Birmingham. The young fought back, hurling rocks and Molotovs. But the cops and politicians were just cogs in the system. The system itself was evil; it had to be torn down. And what was any system except belief in that system?

Total war. For thirty years they bombed everything worth believing in. They seized classrooms and TV studios, and trust became a thoughtcrime. Justice was a myth. Nothing was certain. You were alone. They ushered in an age without heroes, and the system collapsed. They won.

While the saviors sang victory songs and told their war stories, the dead-eyed children huddled in the ruins. They cried for warmth, sustenance, and beauty. The revolutionaries gave them *Being and Nothingness*.

No wonder they all turned into credit card fascists giving their lives for hype. Abercrombie & Fitch worn as crisply as Nazi uniforms. Band logos displayed like loyalty medals. In a world stripped to its Freudian core—greed, fear, and animal rutting—it was the only way they could be part of anything greater than themselves.

"Standing at the cross road, baby, risin' sun goin' down. I believe to my soul now, I'm sinkin' down."

Peter thought of himself as a coyote. A hustler and a survivor. He'd bummed around with squatters and porn stars, framing houses or dealing drugs to pay the rent. He'd spent five years in Bombay, had an ex-wife and a kid in Montana, and in fifty-nine years had never had a dental plan or 401(k).

The coyote life suited Peter, but it demanded a high price. He couldn't remember the last morning he hadn't woken up in a coughing fit, his lungs full of fluid. His diabetes would kill him soon. His lower legs stayed swollen now, the scaly skin a dusky bluish-red.

His life had entered its dusk. Peter accepted the imminence of his death without bitterness but feared the circumstances. He didn't want his corpse to bloat on the bathroom floor of a studio walk-up for three days until somebody noticed the smell. He didn't want the end to come in a piss-stinking charity ward with a fat nursing assistant bent over him.

Peter wanted to die comfortably. He wanted to rent a cabin in Zurich overlooking the emerald lake. He wanted to spend lots of money on a vacationing college girl even though his dick barely ever got hard anymore. Peter wanted to greet the abyss with a glass of Burgundy in his hand, not lying in his own shit. All in all, he didn't think that was too much to ask.

He needed one last hustle. Like an aging boxer, Peter had lost some speed over the years, but he'd earned some brains.

Studying the brave new world he'd helped create, Peter realized that all he had to do was sell the children the cure for the disease he'd infected them with.

Mescaline was the ultimate antidote for Existentialism. Along with gentle hallucinations and intense empathy, it made users certain that God was moments away from speaking. It made them feel safe, cradled by a loving, ordered universe. Peter would make a fortune.

Other entheogens existed. LSD and Ecstasy had sold in their day, but they'd long since glutted the market. They'd become vulgar, nothing but chemicals and a fun Saturday night. Image is everything in any marketing operation, and mescaline still held mystique.

Peter spent a lot of time deciding where to set up shop. He had a few contacts in London that would make distribution easier, and British police spent less energy hunting down recreational drugs than the DEA did. As long as Peter kept a low profile, he'd be safe. Even more important, an ocean separated the average London club-rat from the nearest peyote cactus. Peter had the perfect commodity and the market all to himself.

After hunting down a chemist who'd teach him how to synthesize mescaline hydrochloride, Peter bought a double-wide trailer and some land in South Dakota, stringing razor wire around the whole operation. It took a year and a half to produce six kilos of bile-colored crystals. His savings gave out in the first three months, but he borrowed money from friends and lived on beans and rice to keep going.

The whole time, Peter never thought bigger than his chalet on Lake Zurich. Then the Witches' Carnival descended from myth and whispered in his ear. The time had come for the synthesis between the wasteland's absolute truth and the system's sense of unity and purpose. Peter was dying. He only had one bullet left, but if he aimed well, he could start the next revolution.

They'd sold one key of mescaline to raise capital but kept the rest to throw a party. A really, really big party. A party big enough and loud enough to shake Bacchus, Puck, Anansi, and Abbie Hoffman out of their graves. Tomorrow, the trickster gods would return to rescue humanity from itself.

"Phone! Hey, Peter!" Hijack pointed to Peter's cell phone sitting on the mosaic countertop. "Answer your phone."

Even though they still had a dozen details to work out, Peter was avoiding calls. When the dealers he'd lined up learned Peter had stiffed them and was planning on selling in their territory, they weren't happy. A gentleman named One-Nut Joe had promised to bash Peter's skull in with a hammer.

"They'll leave a message," he said.

"Come on, Chief. It might be important. One-Nut can't find you."

"Fuck it. They'll leave a message." Peter slipped the earphones back over his ears.

Closing his eyes, he stood alone in the dark with Robert Johnson, listening to that voice that had seen so much and just wanted peace.

In the middle of the fourth ring, Maggie grabbed the phone. "Hello?"

"H—"

Maggie heard canned laughter from a TV. "Hello? Peter's phone."

At the other end of the city, Gilly pressed the receiver to her ear. When Maggie answered, she'd forgotten how to speak. All she wanted to do was sit and listen to her voice.

"All right. I'm hanging up now."

"No, wait. Maggie, wait. It's Gilly. I'm in London."

"Gilly?" She paused. "How'd you get to London?"

Her words tripping over themselves, Gilly skimmed across the last few days—the flowers on TV and the drugs in her pocket, getting Kathy and Jerrod to tell them what they knew and paying Vic to make the passports. Maggie never laughed or scolded; she just listened. Finally, Gilly mumbled, "Anyway, we're here. And I'd really like to maybe see you again. So . . . maybe . . ."

"So Sam's still with you?"

Gilly heard the worry in Maggie's voice but didn't understand it. "Uh, yeah. She's right here. You want to talk—"

"It's all right. It's just . . . I'd really like to see you again too."

Gilly felt lighter than air. The exhaustion and fear it'd cost to get here, the anxieties she'd carried with her, all of them burned away in an instant.

"Really?"

Maggie laughed. "Of course, really. Listen, there's going to be a party at the Battersea Power Station tomorrow night."

"Battersea Power Station," Gilly repeated. "Tomorrow."

"Come around midnight. Just go to Nine Elms Lane. Don't worry about getting in; it won't be a problem. I'll see you then, all right?"

"Okay."

"Now go have fun, sweetie. I'll see you tomorrow."

"Okay. Bye."

Maggie hung up. Gilly held the phone to her ear for a couple seconds listening to the dead line.

"So?" Sam chewed her thumbnail.

"So she wants to see me again."

Sam let out a war-whoop. "We're gonna be witches! We're gonna be motherfucking witches!" She jumped up and down on the bed, sending her plate bouncing to the floor. "I told you, G. I fucking told you we'd make it! I told you!"

Gilly started jumping with her. "We're gonna be witches! We're gonna be witches!" They hugged and laughed, collapsing into a panting heap, still chuckling. Gilly wanted to cry.

237

After Sam got her breath back, she asked, "So where do we go?"

"Somewhere called Battersea Power Station. Tomorrow night."

"Why tomorrow?"

"It's a party or something. That's just what Maggie told me."

"Well, remember what Vic said about us being old enough to drink here? Let's go out and celebrate."

"Let me take a shower first."

"Cool."

Rolling off the bed, Gilly headed toward the bathroom.

"Oh, Jesus fuck Mary," Sam said. "I thought they'd tell us to fuck off for sure."

Gilly smirked. "I knew we were in. Never doubted it for a second."

sEVENTEEN

Sam was brushing her hair when Gilly came storming out of the bathroom wrapped in a towel. "My fucking dye job started running in the shower." She held up canary-stained fingers for Sam to see.

"Your hair still looks okay."

"What about my back? I tried to wash all the yellow off, but I couldn't see."

"No, you're cool. Hurry up and get dressed. I want to get outta here."

"I tipped that hairdresser twenty bucks too." Gilly vanished back into the bathroom. Fifteen minutes later, they headed out. There was a bar off of the hotel lobby, but after hours trapped in planes and airports, they wanted to walk around and see the city.

Joining the bustle of people in the sparkling night, they sang and danced down the London streets. Sam jumped on Gilly's back and rode piggyback, howling as Gilly barreled through the crowd. Gilly's lungs burned after half a block. She dropped Sam back to her feet, and they walked along with their arms around each other.

"I–I don't think Maggie likes you all that much," Gilly blurted, the sentence coming out as one long word.

"What? She barely fucking knows me."

"I know. I don't think she hates you or anything, but when I told her I was in London, her first question was, 'Is Sam with you?'–kinda almost upset like that."

"Bitch."

"She still invited us to come. It's like you said, she just doesn't really know you."

Sam shrugged. "Fuck her. She probably just doesn't like to share."

"Huh?"

"Well, she likes you, right?"

Gilly grinned. "Yeah."

"And she's probably figured out that me and you . . . we've got benefits, right? And she doesn't like to share."

"Oh." Gilly turned to look at some coats in a display window. She chewed her bottom lip, afraid of the question hanging in the air.

"You're not going to leave me for Maggie, are you, G?"

Gilly snapped around to look into Sam's hurt face. "No. I mean–"

"Gilly, I love you." Sam squeezed her hands. "Every moment I'm with you is like rolling in a field of daisies. A field of daisies with bunnies hopping through it. Pink bunnies."

Gilly snatched her hands away. "Fuck you."

"Fuck you. Think I'm going to get into a catfight with Maggie over you." Sam's phone started ringing. "Oh, go to hell, bitch," she growled, staring at the number.

"Who is it?"

"Mom. She hasn't called in five days. Why the fuck does she want to make up now?" Switching her phone to vibrate, Sam slipped it back into her purse. "Come on, let's hit an ATM and find something to drink. And it's got to be a good bar, not like a bitter, angry drunk bar."

"A happy bar."

"There you go."

Walking two blocks, they passed several doorways before finding a bar that looked promising. The Wednesday night crowd was sparse. Men in oxford cloth shirts sat at corner tables. Everybody ignored the musician perched on a stool near the window.

With Sam half a step behind her, Gilly crossed the wear-polished floor and asked for a Tennet's, reading the name off one of the taps. As the girl behind the bar handed them glasses of amber beer, Sam scowled and fished her cell phone out. "What the hell?"

"Your mom again?"

"No. Colby. About time he got worried about me."

Two guys walked up smiling. Sam started joking around with them and forgot her boyfriend. The four of them grabbed a table by the wall. Between the music and their accents, Gilly barely understood a word the men said, but they seemed cool and bought a second round.

While the black-haired one laughed with Sam, the sandy-haired one, his name might have been Todd, leaned toward Gilly. "So you're here on holiday?" he asked, lifting his voice above a melodramatic cover of "Leaving on a Jet Plane."

Her brain skidding toward panic, Gilly tried to think up a lie. Then she realized she didn't have to. "Actually, we're looking for the Witches' Carnival," she answered.

"I'm sorry?"

"The Witches' Carnival."

Both Todd and the other guy stared at her. Uncertain grins spread across their faces. Gilly stared back with level eyes and sipped her beer.

"Seriously? And you think they're in London?"

"We know they're in London."

"We've got their phone number," Sam added.

The guys exchanged a sideways glance. "The Witches' Carnival?" Todd asked again.

"All right. Last Thursday, right? We're hanging out at the gas station where her brother works."

"Josh."

"Her brother Josh. Anyway, Josh is in the back, and this homeless guy . . ."

Buzzing from her first pint and halfway through her second, Gilly didn't leave anything out, not Meek's bargain, the mescaline, her night with Maggie, or the fake passports. She half-expected the guys to bolt for the door. Instead, they listened to every word. Their bright expressions verged on childish delight. They didn't believe her, but they wanted to. After she'd finished, the sandy-haired one asked Gilly to marry him. Gilly snickered and didn't answer.

A while later they all walked out with their half-full glasses and headed for another pub. This one was louder and more crowded, a twisting series of basement rooms with blue tubes of light tracing the ceiling.

The guys kept buying drinks, beer then Aftershock, a liqueur that had the same taste and color as mouthwash. Gilly drank until a liquid numbness spread across all five senses.

She never forgot what Todd and the other one hoped for at the end of the night. Still, they were fun to talk to and it beat watching TV back at the hotel.

Another bar and more neon-hued drinks. The men told them about the magazine where they worked and minutia about the publishing industry. They compared this and that about England and America. Everybody insisted their country sucked worse. They were all happy–drunk and talking too loud.

It was almost one o'clock when Sam whispered in Gilly's ear, "Ready to go?"

Gilly shrugged and nodded. Sam stood up, swaying a little. She whispered something to Todd that made him grin. Before he could answer, Sam grabbed Gilly's wrist. They turned a corner toward the rest rooms and slipped out a back door.

"Fever's up to hundred and one! Brain's near oblivion. So let's go have some fun!" They sang bright and clear, stumbling down the block. Neither of them had any clue where they were.

"Let's just get a taxi. Fuck it. It's too cold to walk, anyway."

The cab smelled like mud and other people's boots. Sinking into the seat, Sam pulled out her phone. "Jesus fuck. Mom's called again. Colby's called again, and Dawn's called."

"Stop checking that thing." Gilly swiped the phone out of Sam's hand. Sam cussed at her, making Gilly giggle. She tried shoving Gilly off the seat, and they both tumbled squealing to the taxi's hard rubber floor.

They wrestled for the phone. Gilly grabbed it, and Sam grabbed her wrist. "Let go, bitch."

"Ow! You let go."

"Something's going on." Sam pried her phone out of Gilly's grip.

"It's nothing that matters."

"Then why are they all calling all at once?"

"Because they still think they're real. But they're not." Gilly nestled her cheek against the curve of Sam's neck. "Home doesn't exist anymore. It's just you and me and the Carnival and the big, big world. And nothing back there can hurt us ever again."

Sam stared at her phone. She closed it and tossed it up onto the seat. They lay still, folded together on the floor. Outside the cab's window, the city floated past like a dream.

"Know why I ditched Todd and Steve back there?" Sam asked.

"Why's that?"

"I was thinking, you know? Tomorrow we're going to be in the Witches' Carnival."

"Yeah?"

"And you and Maggie are gonna start dating and get married and adopt Cambodian babies. And that means me and you have to be just like regular friends." Sam's head lolled back and forth. "No more benefits."

Gilly watched Sam in the bands and glimmers of passing light. "But we'll always be friends, though, right?"

"Yeah." Sam's hand crept to the small of Gilly's back. The touch felt as familiar to Gilly as her own fingers might be.

Through the alcoholic haze she remembered Maggie and thought maybe she shouldn't do this. Then Sam flashed her Cheshire Cat smile. It was a smile nobody else on Earth had, not even Maggie.

Gilly kissed her, tasting liquor and cigarettes.

"We're at your hotel, ladies," the driver said as he pulled to the curb.

Heading up to their room, they clung to each other to keep from falling down. They whispered and giggled. Hands wandered some more. They'd almost made it into the elevator when Sam's phone started ringing.

"Fuck! These people need to quit." Glancing at the number, her face softened. "It's Josh. What's going on, Gilly?"

"I don't know. I don't care."

Sam turned her phone off again but didn't put it away. The sixth–floor hall seemed to be spinning very slowly. "If I don't call him back, he's going to think I'm dead. I've got to tell him why, before I just vanish into thin air."

"He won't believe you."

"I know." Entering the room, Sam slumped onto the bed. "Josh is like the only person who ever gave a shit about me, G. I can't let him spend the rest of his life thinking I was murdered or something."

Sam would stick by her brother after cutting all others loose. "You should probably call him, then," Gilly said. "Excuse me, but I've got to piss like a racehorse."

Gilly went to the bathroom. Through the door, she heard Sam making her call.

"Hey, big brother."

. . .

"I'm all right. Don't worry about me, all right?"

. . .

"No. I'm pretty fucking far from Atlanta. And, um, I don't think I'm–"

. . .

"Yeah, she's with me."

Shaking off some of her drunkenness, Gilly turned toward the closed door. Josh was asking about her.

"Fuck."

. . .

"What happened?"

. . .

"But how the fuck did they–"

. . .

"Oh, Jesus fuck."

Gilly finished and stepped out of the bathroom. Sam stared at her, eyes brimming with pity. The look terrified Gilly.

"She's here. I need to tell her."

. . .

"I don't know. I'll–Look, I'll talk to you later, okay?"

. . .

"Don't worry about me, all right? I love you, all right?" Sam hung up.

"Your dad got arrested," Sam said. "They found out about the money. It's all over the news."

Gilly was struck dumb for a long moment. Then she shook her head. "Wait a minute. How could they've found out about the money? We've got it. It's not even there anymore."

"He was looking for it. He put out a warrant for me or something, and somehow they figured everything out. The cops showed up to talk to my mom about it."

"But the money's not there. How can they arrest him if the money's not even fucking there?"

"I don't know, but they did. Your dad's in jail."

"But . . ."

"Sorry, G," Sam whispered.

Gilly saw her dad scared and alone in a cell. He was a cop. The other prisoners would beat the shit out of him, maybe kill him. She'd never meant to hurt anybody.

"I've got to do something."

"Gilly, you can't do anything. They've already arrested him."

"No. I–" Her mind soaked with liquor, Gilly lurched for the door. Her voice cracked. "I've got to do something."

"Gilly. Shit." Sam jumped off the bed and took her wrist. "Stop for a second."

Gilly jerked away. She had the door open before Sam grabbed her in a bear hug, pinning one arm to her side. "Stop!"

"Let go!" Gilly reached back and yanked Sam's hair. "Let go!"

Heaving Gilly off her feet, Sam kicked the door shut and slammed Gilly belly–down on the bed, collapsing on top of her to keep her still. Gilly tried thrashing free. Sam held her tight, pressing her face against Gilly's cheek, cooing to her as Gilly snarled.

"Let the fuck go of me!"

"Shhh . . . shhh . . . calm down, baby."

Before long, Gilly quit fighting. She lay limp on the bed with fat, hot tears trickling down her face. "Sam, I fucked up. I didn't mean to . . ."

"I know, G." Sam loosened her grip. Her scalp stung where Gilly had pulled her hair. She rubbed Gilly's back. "It'll be all right."

Gilly didn't answer. Her dad was in jail. They'd strip-searched him and put him in an orange jumpsuit. He was sitting there right now, trapped behind concrete and steel. The scene made her sick, but Gilly forced herself to imagine it.

She wasn't a rebel, she was just a stupid fucking spoiled bitch who had to have whatever she wanted. She'd sent her whole family into free fall without giving it a second thought.

"It's not like you framed him," Sam said. "He stole the money."

"Yeah, well, we've sure as fuck been enjoying it, haven't we?"

"So? It doesn't matter. Like you said, it doesn't even exist anymore."

Gilly wiped her eyes. "It was a lot easier to say that before my dad got arrested."

"Here." Sam grabbed her purse off the floor. Finding SpongeBob, she shook out a Xanax and offered it to Gilly. "Just take it and you'll stop thinking about your dad. And tomorrow, we join the Witches' Carnival and leave everything behind."

Join the Witches' Carnival and all your responsibilities, all your loyalties, blew away like dead leaves. They'd learned it so long ago, alongside Puss 'n Boots and Cinderella, that they couldn't remember a time when it wasn't sitting at the base of their hearts.

"He don't exist anymore, right?" Gilly asked.

"Right."

Gilly swallowed the pill dry. They talked about something, but the moment the words left her mouth, Gilly couldn't remember what they'd been. Sam was laughing. She lay on her side, head propped on her fist.

Gilly smiled at her. "What are you laughing about?"

"You're really fucked up."

"No. I'm just . . ." She spread her hands across the thick blanket. "Everything's fluffy."

Time slithered by. Sam was laughing. Kneeling at the foot of the bed, she pulled off Gilly's shoes.

Gilly smiled at her. "What are you laughing about?"

"Nothing, baby. You're just funny is all. Sit up."

Helping her sit up, Sam tugged Gilly's T-shirt over her head, leaving her in her pants and bra. Crawling into bed beside her, Sam was laughing.

Gilly smiled at her. "What are you laughing about?"

For some reason, that made Sam laugh harder. "Shhh . . . go to sleep, okay?"

"Okay."

Sam turned off the lamp. Deep shadow washed across the room. Gilly closed her eyes, curling under the cool sheets. Traffic noise from the streets below drifted away.

EIGHTEEN

"What do you mean?"

. . .

"No. Did you put the number in wrong?"

. . .

"Did you push the green button? I work there. You have to push the green button when you put in a debit card."

Gilly drifted up through mirror hall dreams, emerging in the glaring sunlight. She listened to Sam argue with somebody on the phone.

"Well, not there. At another Domino's. Just push the green button, okay?"

Gilly's head throbbed. The pillow and sheets were clammy with sweat. "Who are you talking to?" she asked, annoyed.

"Domino's won't take my order. How're you doing?" Sam rubbed Gilly's arm, then turned to speak into the phone again.

"Listen. I promise you; there's plenty of money in my account."

Flipping the pillow to its dry side, Gilly tugged the covers over her head. Money her dad had stolen. Money he'd gone to jail for. He'd filed a fake search warrant. He'd been trying to find her and got busted for it.

"Fine. Just forget it. It's cool." Sam dropped the phone back in its cradle. "Fucking idiot."

Gilly heard the *snick* of Sam's lighter.

He'd been trying to find the money, not her. It wasn't her fault he was crooked. It wasn't her fault he'd gone to jail.

Muscles in Gilly's arms and back ached, totally given out. Sprawled under the covers, she felt like someone had filled her chest with gravel. Within her dried-up body, her brain refused to quit.

Even if it wasn't her fault, it was. But what did he think? He could just leave fifty grand lying around the house and she'd never–*They're coming.*

"Oh, shit." Gilly sat bolt upright. The thought sliced through the Gordian knot of tangled emotion. Everything else became meaningless. She kicked off the blanket and rolled out of bed. "Fuck, fuck, shit."

"What's the matter?"

"Why did Domino's reject your card?"

"Because they're crackbabies. Don't worry, we've got–"

"We need to get the hell out of here. The cops are onto us."

"What?"

Gilly shoved clothes into her backpack. "Josh said the cops came and talked to your mom, so they know you're involved, right?"

"Yeah? So?"

"So they've figured out the money is in your account. And they need it as evidence against dad."

Sam watched her for a second. "Fuck. They froze my account."

Gilly nodded. "Next, they'll track us down by seeing where we spent the money."

"Like this hotel."

"Come on. Let's go, go, go."

A minute later, Gilly and Sam were sneaking out of another hotel. They avoided the lobby just in case. Going through the fitness center, they slipped out a side door and around the pool emptied for fall. Clouds obscured the sun. In the cement-gray afternoon, London had become sinister, a rust-ing chasm sunk between tall buildings. A city full of wolves.

At an ATM two blocks away, Sam tried withdrawing some cash. The machine bleeped and flashed a message onto its screen:

WE'RE SORRY, BUT THIS ACCOUNT HAS BEEN SUSPENDED. FOR ASSISTANCE, PLEASE CALL 0800 00 55.

Gilly stared at the terse message. They'd almost lost everything, snatched up by the police while sleeping it off at the hotel. The thought made her hands shake.

"Almost" didn't count for shit, though. Gilly forced herself to calm down. "Okay. We're okay," she said, glancing at her watch. It was a quarter until one. "We're meeting the Carnival at the Battersea place at midnight. That means we've just got to not get arrested for eleven hours. How much money do you have?"

Sam rifled through her purse. She found twenty-one pounds and one hundred and fifteen dollars. Gilly had eight pounds and over two hundred dollars.

"Let's get the American money exchanged just in case."

"Sounds like a plan."

They were both sick from liquor, Xanax, and not enough sleep. They passed a deli full of baking bread and spicy meat. The smell made Gilly's stomach lurch.

Sam slipped her sunglasses on despite the overcast sky.

She glanced over her shoulder at the Hotel Constantinople. "Hung over, broke, and a thousand miles from everything, and we're still too quick for them, G."

They turned up a side street, and Gilly remembered her dad. When she'd had time, she'd felt guilty. She'd yanked her heart one way then another, torturing herself with all the things she couldn't do. Then the hammer hit the pin, and she'd dropped all pretense. Slip the trap. Dodge the police. Join the Witches' Carnival. That's all that mattered.

Gilly loved her dad. She wished he wasn't in jail, and she wished he wasn't a crook. But she'd come too far to make believe she'd ever turn back.

The Bayswater area hosted a high concentration of out-of-towners. An exchange bureau or souvenir shop stood on almost every corner. The bureau they walked into was run by a Middle Eastern man brooding behind bulletproof glass. "I don't give change," he said after passing them a hundred and eighty pounds through a steel drawer.

"Thanks for telling us." Gilly took the money, flipped him off, and they left.

Gilly and Sam spent their final day in the ordinary world doing ordinary things. They bought a map of London and pinpointed Nine Elms Lane, just across the Thames. A block down the street, Sam got her pizza, a ham and pineapple on thin crust. Too queasy to eat, Gilly sipped a Diet Coke.

"You think they know about the passports?" Sam asked.

"If they don't, they'll figure it out soon."

"Think Vic and them are in trouble?"

Gilly drew her name in the grease on the tabletop. "Probably."

When they left the pizza place, a drizzling mist crawled across the city. Gilly put on her faded black hoodie but didn't pull the hood up. Her skull throbbed, and the cool rain felt nice against her face.

At a drugstore they grabbed aspirin and bottled water to fight their hangovers, plus toothbrushes, toothpaste, and deodorant for their rendezvous with the Carnival. They wandered nowhere. The occasional tired joke broke long stretches of quiet.

The sun sank away. The streets burned from the diffused glow of headlights, store windows, and jack-o'-lanterns. A pack of costumed children, herded by a woman in a pointy witch's hat, flowed around Gilly and Sam on their way to a party.

"Let me get a cigarette," Gilly said.

Sam handed her one, and her eyes grew wide. "Your dye job's ruined."

"What?" Gilly ran her fingers through her hair. They came back streaked watery yellow. She'd forgotten the cheap dye had started running in the shower last night. She'd been walking through the rain for hours. "No. Goddamnit."

"Maybe if you dry it right now, it'll be okay."

Gilly wiped her hand on her sweatshirt. "I wanted Maggie to see it."

"Well, let's find a bathroom or somewhere. Maybe it'll be okay. C'mon."

Alan Craft, an inspector with the Metropolitan Police's special branch, walked through the hotel room. He poked at strewn clothes with the toe of his shoe. A textbook, *The Norton Anthology of Elizabethan Literature*, sat on the writing desk. He touched the TV and the mattress; both felt cold.

"Left their toothbrushes," Neil said, stepping out of the bathroom. "Some makeup stuff too."

"Good. They're coming back, then."

"Unless someone tipped them off and they left in a hurry."

Alan rolled his eyes. "They're two runaways. Who's going to tip them off?" A round red fruit wasn't necessarily an apple to Neil. It might be a pear in disguise.

"Have you read the report? These runaways are either criminal masterminds or the luckiest, stupidest kids on planet Earth. I'd prefer not to take chances on this either way."

Neil had him there. Samantha Grace and Gillian Stahl had apparently taken up humiliating police departments as a hobby. Two officers were in jail because of them. Another would spend the rest of his career explaining how a teenage girl swiped his cruiser. Then, as if that wasn't a full day, they'd hopped on two different planes, both headed to Heathrow.

The Home Office and the American State Department were pissing themselves. Neither of the girls had a passport. Nobody could say how they'd gotten into the country or why they'd come.

The hotel room didn't offer any clues. Alan gave it one last sweeping glance, then nodded. "All right, let's send an advisory to the boroughs to keep their eyes peeled. You want to stake out the lobby in case they do show back up?"

"Sounds good. I can use the overtime."

They left the room and headed toward the elevator. Alan snickered. "Did you read how they got away from that cop in America?"

"The crow? Yeah, what the blue hell was that about?"

"Goddamn it." Gilly combed her hair in the gas station bathroom's grimy mirror. Pale drops of yellow splattered the sink. "I can't believe this. I wanted Maggie to see it."

"Don't worry. You look fine."

"No, I don't. It looks all washed out."

"Um, G? Isn't that about your natural hair color?"

Gilly stared. "Oh, God." The violent red peroxided out, the cartoon yellow faded, her hair had become strawberry blond. "The salons probably haven't closed yet, have they?"

"Christ, Gilly, we've got bigger problems right now than your fucking hair."

"I know, but—"

"Like that Nazi goat eating all our scrap metal!"

Gilly smirked. Her reflection seemed like a younger self, someone Gilly had spent years trying not to be. "Fucking Nazi goat," she said.

"I like it." Sam smoothed the rain-tangled ends of Gilly's hair. "I always liked it. And Maggie's gonna like it too."

"Promise?"

"I promise. Just quit panicking, okay?"

"Yeah, okay."

"So what do you want to do now? I'm getting bored just walking around."

Gilly shrugged. "There was that theater a few blocks back. Wanna go see a movie?"

"Sure."

They left the gas station and headed the way they'd come. A wrought-iron fence bordered a sprawling park, black trees and empty trails at night.

"Look at this shit." Sam handed Gilly the Winston Lights she'd had to buy to get the key to the bathroom. The box was half the size of a normal pack and only contained ten ciga-rettes. "This cost me just as much as a regular, American pack."

Gilly turned the tiny box over in her hand. "It's probably for kids. You know, like they make little cups and saucers for them to play kitchen with?"

The theater blazed up ahead like a sunset sculpted from

neon. Roof-to-sidewalk posters flanked the ticket booths, advertising a two-hour-long sequence of fight scenes and exposition. It was the kind of movie that cost millions of dollars and still looked like cardboard. It was exactly what they wanted to see.

Staring at the screen in the flickering dark, Gilly felt a strange disconnect. As far as she could tell, she was in London, about to join the Witches' Carnival. But somehow she'd wound up doing exactly what she would have been doing back home if none of it had ever happened.

An explosion filled the screen. Gilly didn't notice what had blown up. She missed her friends and the run-down multiplex where they hung out. She missed the popcorn-butter smell and the Crazy Taxi video game in the lobby. She missed wandering from movie to movie with Colby, Dawn, and Alex. She missed running and yelling around the empty parking lot.

Her friends. Their patois of inside jokes and stolen phrases. The posters pinned to the walls of her room and the clothes cluttering the floor. Mr. Byrne's photography class. Wasting time at Josh's Texaco. As a brand-new life blossomed, an old one folded closed.

Gilly remembered the bleakness, too. She remembered every one of their snickered insults and her own trembling cowardice. She remembered clinging to clothes and posters, praying they could transform her. She remembered keeping her television on all night so the darkness wouldn't feel as lonely.

Looking back from London, though, Gilly wondered what she'd been so afraid of. Ashley's giggling clique, Tracye's casual betrayal—all of it seemed so small now.

More explosions filled the screen. The good guy got in a few more one-liners, saved the day, and the credits rolled. Filing out of the theater, Sam checked her watch. "You about ready?" she asked.

They hailed a cab. Heading toward Nine Elms Lane, Gilly watched Sam from the corner of her eye. She remembered the day Sam had swooped out of nowhere and into her life—crashing into Ashley for no reason except she was crazy and liked starting trouble.

"Watch where you're going!

I did. I slammed into you on purpose."

Gilly clamped down on a mean chuckle thinking about it. She should have known from that moment; nothing could hurt them. The Four Horsemen of the Apocalypse might have rode into town. Gilly and Sam would have knocked Death off his pale steed and swiped War's sword for a souvenir.

NINETEEN

The taxi carried them across Vauxhall Bridge into an industrial region stretching the southern bank of the Thames. As streetlights and passing headlights grew sparse, the darkness tightened around them.

Nine Elms Lane was warehouses and anonymous office buildings. The air smelled like the muddy, slow-moving river. Above the austere landscape, four smokestacks vaulted into a starless sky.

"When you said we were meeting them at the power station, I kinda figured it was the name of another club or something," Sam said.

Gilly gazed at the Cyclopean building and nodded. "Me too."

A chain-link fence, railroad tracks, and fields of cracked

asphalt separated them from the power station. Gilly and Sam started toward an open gate near the end of the block.

The Battersea Power Station had been built seven decades before, a cathedral consecrated to the electric dynamo. As its smokestacks breathed black haze over London, parquet floors and Italian marble filled the control rooms inside. Frescoes turned turbine halls and workshops into naves, side-chapels, and sanctuaries.

The London Power Authority decommissioned the station in 1983. They sold the building, and plans began to turn it into an amusement park, then a museum like the Tate Modern, and then a shopping plaza, but nothing ever worked out.

Contracts were signed. Blueprints were drawn up showing tree-shaded paths and glass elevators. From time to time swarms of workmen attacked the building like leafcutter ants. They wrenched up sections of railroad track, knocked down walls, tore away part of the roof, and lifted out the eighty-five-ton turbines.

Then engineers would discover that half the support beams needed replacing or the foundation was cracked. Renovations would grind to a halt. Investors got edgy. The owners announced they were confident and planned to move forward. A year later they'd sell the station at a loss. While the deed passed from hand to hand, the brickwork titan sat derelict, sinking slowly into the clay bank of the Thames.

On Halloween, an invading army of dreamers marched on Battersea.

A party at the power station, late tonight. No one knew where the whisper began–a friend of a friend and back and back. One and a half million text messages moved around London every day, even more phone calls, e-mails, and words passed on the street. Most people who heard the whisper smirked it off. They weren't tromping all the way out to Wandsworth on some impossible rumor. By the time they'd lain down in their comfortable beds they'd forgotten all about it.

But the whisper did reach a desperate scattering. Peering through the chain-link fence, Gilly saw people trickling through other entrances. They were the ones who wanted to believe in impossible rumors, the ones whose curiosity could always get the better of them. They followed the whisper like the children of Hamelin.

The gate in the fence was wide enough to admit earth-moving equipment. Just inside, a mud-splattered porta-cabin served as a guard post. Someone had spray-painted a message across its windows, writing backward so the guard inside could read it. It took Gilly a second to mentally reverse the words.

It's nothing. Go back to sleep.

"We have some weird fucking friends," Sam said.

"Psst. All right?"

Gilly and Sam turned to watch a girl in pumps sprint clumsily across the street. Glitter dusted her arms and cleavage, and her top shimmered red in the wain light. She wore a pair of devil horns on top of her head.

"Do either of you know what's going on up there?" she asked, stepping onto the sidewalk.

"Not exactly. But don't worry, it'll kick ass."

"We sort of know the people behind it."

Three figures emerged from the shadow of a government building's doorway and jogged across four lanes of empty asphalt, a couple holding hands and a boy smoking a cigarette. They all wore masks. Gilly wished she'd thought of buying one.

The boy in a pig mask asked the same question devil girl had and got the same answer.

"But this is still breaking and entering, right?"

"Oh, yeah." Gilly nodded.

"And the people ahead of us are doing the same thing?"

"Yep."

"What about the guards? They're not going to notice all these people?"

"Of course not." Sam pointed to the spray-painted portacabin. "There's a sign, see?"

"But . . ."

"Don't worry about it. It's going to be fun. C'mon."

"I'm not going in there. This is nuts." Tiny jewels covered

the girl's mask like dewdrops. When she shook her head, they winked beneath the streetlight.

Pig mask wrapped his arm around her waist. "Come on. We've got to at least see what it is."

"The police are probably going to show up any minute now. I'm not going to be here when they do."

"Let's just see what it is, and then we'll go."

"Noel," she whined.

"How can you turn back now?" Gilly snapped, startling herself by jumping into the argument. But she recognized her own pleading tone from a few days ago, whining to Sam that they'd get in trouble for skipping school.

The girl blinked at her. "Easy. I take a cab back to my flat and let the rest of you spend the night in jail."

If Gilly told her the Witches' Carnival was behind it, she'd never believe her. "What if this is meant to be the greatest night of your life? Right here, right now, and you're letting it slip away. It's going to take a little risk to find out, but it'll be worth it. Trust me, it'll be worth it."

The girl looked up at her boyfriend. "Don't listen to her, Noel. She's some crazy American. Let's go."

It made Gilly sad to see the girl stand at Eden's gates, too timid to take one more step. It terrified her how close she'd come herself to turning away. But there was nothing she could do except hope Noel was as bad an influence as Sam had been.

Gilly turned and started walking. Sam followed. They passed the security post, and glanced at the guard inside watching TV. He rested his chin in his hand and never looked up.

The sprawling parking lot hadn't been repaved in either girl's lifetime. They had to pick their way around grave-wide cracks. A hard wind blew off the river making their teeth chatter. It carried faint music from the station ahead.

Gilly counted rows of windows. The station was seven stories tall. Two massive wounds in its belly, each large enough to fit her house through, spilled yellow-pink light.

"So what happens if we lose them this time?" Sam asked.

Gilly thought about it. Her dad in prison, the police after them, there was no way home.

"Think only on Hell, Faustus," she answered. "Thou art damned."

Sam nodded. "And raise hell and a back beat."

They clambered over a hill of broken bricks into Turbine Hall B. Someday a comet would smash into Earth, snuffing out all life. Gilly imagined the party on the eve of the apocalypse would look a lot like the party at Battersea.

Music boomed against weather-damaged frescoes; it pelted down like a hard rain. Three thousand dervishes danced beneath drifting motes of light. The air was hot from the roiling throng. People bounced, shouted, and made out in recesses along the walls.

Holding hands so they wouldn't get separated, Gilly and Sam edged through the hall. Joy burned across faces and sweat-slick bodies all around them. These were the always-hungry ones. These were the ones driven mad searching for something they couldn't name, something they only knew by the ragged hole where it should have been. But tonight it was closer than ever before. The crumbling power station was the threshold. Just one more dance, one more screw, one more hit of drugs would carry them to the other side.

Half the people wore costumes, a crowd of ghouls and pixies. The other half wore the usual club disguise of hyperbolic style and designer logos. Gilly noticed a boy with a spiked blue mohawk and a pirate costume. In the middle of the merry frenzy, he was all business. People clustered around him. He had to-the-point exchanges with one after another, never more than a few words. Money was handed over for a cookie or two wrapped in cling wrap. Gilly spotted another pirate by the wall. She guessed Peter and the witches had plenty more posted around the station.

The turbine hall mocked Gilly's sense of scale and made her dizzy. When she focused on the distant walls, her brain refused to believe she was inside. She kept glancing up, checking to see if a ceiling actually enclosed the soaring space.

"Gilly!" Sam had to shout for Gilly to hear her. "Up there!"
She looked up. A singer stood like Mussolini on a

balcony high over the crowd, belting out lyrics with a pack–a–day rasp. Two guitarists flanked him on the left. To the right, their DJ swayed behind his turntables.

"What am I looking at?" Gilly screamed back.

"The big machine! Look up!"

Gilly almost had to lean back to see where Sam was pointing. A massive crane hung close to the ceiling. Built from steel beams painted warning–stripe yellow and streaked with rust, it spanned the width of the hall. A pair of drive chains would have moved it parallel to the floor so its retractable hook could lift and maneuver heavy equipment.

Three figures watched the celebration from a catwalk on top of the crane. They stood half–lost in shadows above batteries of lights, but anyone who saw them would know they were the priests of this church.

Gilly peered at one of the silhouettes. She saw the curve of a body that she'd danced against, the dark hair that had been tangled and damp, the bow of the mouth that had kissed her mouth.

Maggie stood with her hands on the catwalk's railing, eyes skimming the crowd. She was searching for someone. It took Gilly a second to realize that someone was her.

Squeezing past slithy toves and mimsy borogoves, Gilly kept her eyes fixed on the bridge crane, terrified the Carnival might vanish if she glanced away.

"How do we get up there?" Sam asked.

Archways lining the turbine hall opened into a labyrinth of offices and machine shops. Somewhere in the decrepit station, a staircase led to the balcony where the band played and then to Maggie. Gilly spotted a more direct route, though. Grab irons, U-shaped bars fastened to one of the support pillars, formed a ladder up to the crane. Tugging on Sam's arm, Gilly shoved her way toward the pillar and started up. Grumbling, Sam followed her.

Years worth of dust covered the rungs. It made Gilly cough and drifted into her eyes. Thirty-five feet. Forty. Forty-five. Gilly's arms and calves began to burn. Dangling fifty feet above the party, Gilly cussed and wanted to throw up. She forced her muscles to move, hand over hand, until she'd reached the top.

The grab irons led to a channel holding one of the crane's drive chains. No railing protected them from slipping over the side. Clutching the chain for balance, its links so thick, they couldn't close their hands around them, Gilly and Sam edged toward the crane. They climbed on board. With careful steps and racing heartbeats they picked across its steel skeleton to the control cabin, then up a ladder and through a hatch to the catwalk.

Maggie heard someone approaching and turned. Gilly emerged from the hatch on quivering legs. She looked up at Maggie. It was like looking up at the stars.

"Hi." After days of madness and scrambling, after burning every bridge, it was the only thing Gilly could think to say.

Maggie smiled, painted lips parting just a little. "Hi, there."

Jack and Peter stood on the catwalk too. "All right, Atlanta," Jack said. "Heard you two were in town." As Sam climbed up, he opened a battered military rucksack and produced some cookies. "How was the trip? Mescaline?"

"Pretty fucking wild. Thanks." They both took one. The cookies were orange this time, covered with candy sprinkles, white ghosts, and black witches.

"So what are you dressed as?" Sam asked.

Jack wore a royal blue vest over a shirt with ruffled sleeves and collar. A sword hung at his side. The tall feather of his Three Musketeers hat brushed girders overhead. "Christopher Marlowe," he said, spreading his arms to show off the costume.

Unwrapping her cookie, Sam started telling Jack, Maggie, and Peter how they'd gotten to London.

Gilly stayed quiet and snuck peeks at Maggie. She wore a silk brocade dress with a mandarin collar. Embroidered dragons twined down her body. A purple flower sat tucked behind her ear.

". . . So then, everybody back home starts calling my cell phone. Like all at once, right?"

Listening to Sam tell their story, Gilly peeled back the cling wrap and raised the cookie to her mouth. A gentle hand touched her wrist. Watching from the corner of her eye, Maggie gave a single, solemn shake of her head. Gilly gave her a confused look, but lowered the cookie without taking a bite.

Jack turned to Gilly. "Your dad got arrested? You all right?"

She shrugged. "I guess so."

"I think I'll go and check on the others," Maggie announced. She climbed down the ladder and off the crane. Gilly watched her vanish through a narrow doorway leading into the machine shops beyond the turbine hall.

Sam nudged her. "Go, bitch."

Handing Sam her cookie, Gilly went. Sam stepped onto the catwalk's lower rail. Both cookies in one hand, lighting a cigarette with the other, she bounced in time with the music. "This place is great!"

Ducking through the doorway, Gilly found herself on an unlit stairwell. The music turned distant and thudding, like she was hearing it from underwater. Over generations, the smell of machine oil had seeped into the power station's concrete walls. Feeling her way down in the dark, Gilly reached the next landing when a voice startled her.

"You're a very interesting girl," Maggie said.

"Thanks." Gilly grinned. It was the best compliment anyone had ever bothered giving her.

Maggie kissed her. Gilly dreamed of red wine and warm

quilts, good pot, the exact right song playing on the radio, lush forests after it'd rained.

Pressing her face into Gilly's hair, Maggie breathed deep. "I'm glad you came."

As soon as Maggie said it, the air turned brittle. Gilly pulled out of Maggie's arms. She answered in a hard, small voice like a pebble.

"Then why'd you leave in the first place?"

In the darkness, Gilly heard the silk of Maggie's dress rustling. "Because . . . it's a hateful world," Maggie said.

"That's bullshit. That doesn't mean anything."

"I didn't do it to be cruel."

"Then why?"

"I'll tell you. But you have to dance with me first."

"Just tell me."

"I will. I swear. But you have to dance with me first."

Gilly scowled. "Promise?"

"I promise." Maggie wore a small vinyl backpack. Gilly heard the zipper open, then a flashlight clicked on. "Let's go."

Down the stairs, they found themselves in a musty corridor. It belonged in a ransacked palace more than a factory. Vainglorious moldings traced the ceiling and framed stairwells. Doors were dark wood and ocean-green glass. They passed some kids taking bong hits and rolling around in old office chairs. Glow sticks surrounded them with eerie chemical-light halos.

"You tricked me, by the way." Maggie ran her fingers through Gilly's hair. "I knew you were coming, except I was looking for a redhead."

"Yeah, it's . . . less angry."

Maggie laughed. "All right."

They stepped through an archway into the motion and shrieking rush of the dance floor. Maggie led Gilly toward the center of the ecstatic sea.

They bumped into Chris, acting as a runner between Peter and the pirate-punks working for him. Tonja talked to a man with glasses in a corner of the hall. She hugged Gilly, told her she liked her hair, and then waved them off.

A new band took over the balcony. They filled the echoing space with rhythms so breakneck fast, Gilly could barely catch her breath. Sweat plastered her hair to her forehead.

Everybody was radiant. Everybody was glorious. Gilly danced with Maggie, close enough to feel the damp heat radiate off her skin. She danced with glitter-covered girls and boys with bat wings.

Peter smoked a joint with two of his hirelings. There was some minor problem with the sound system, and he'd come down to the band balcony to check it out. While they worked to sync three mismatched amps through the same line driver, Peter couldn't take his eyes off the celebration below. The crumbling power station had become Zion.

It was partly the drugs, partly the music, and partly the illegal thrill of it all, but the night transcended its hedonistic parts. Peter saw it on the faces of the children. They knew they were alive, and they knew that mattered. It was an age without heroes, but they could become their own. They would never be the same. They'd carry the truth far past this night and spread it through the streets.

After forty years of wandering, the Witches' Carnival had delivered them to the promised land. Peter stood and watched the death of meaninglessness. All that, and he was making money hand over fist.

"It's my best friend!" Sam appeared from the crowd, Jack and Qi beside her. "We made it, G!" Sam squeezed Gilly's shoulders. Two LED-studded bracelets flashed red-yellow-green whenever she moved. Her pupils were as wide as the night sky. "We're here. We made it!"

Gilly laughed and hugged her. "If you ain't pretty—"

"Start trouble!" Sam gave Maggie a rough hug. After they all chattered some, Sam, Qi, and Jack disappeared back into the mob.

Time telescoped in on itself. Gilly gasped when she glanced at her watch; four hours had passed. She and Maggie decided to take a break.

The corridors surrounding Turbine Hall B were a crush of

people, laughter, and pot smoke. Plastic bottles and pieces of cling wrap cluttered the floor. Gilly and Maggie sat with their backs against the tiled wall, drinking water.

Gilly's hands shook. She'd pulled off her hoodie and lost it somewhere. Her muscles quivered on the verge of collapse. Her pulse throbbed against her temples. It was a good feeling. She had to check and recheck her memory to make sure she hadn't taken any drugs that night. She wanted to do this forever. Her mind and body grasped the original, ecclesiastic meaning of wonder-full.

Maggie grabbed Gilly and scattered kisses across her flushed-hot face. They pawed each other and toppled to the floor in slow motion. Maggie lay sprawled on her back. Gilly rested half on top of her, feeling her chest rise and fall.

"Tell me why you left us."

Gilly already knew. Maggie had slipped away because she hadn't thought much of her or Sam. Nice enough, maybe, but no different from millions of kids wasting nights and lives in nowhere towns across the world. Not anyone who could keep up with the Witches' Carnival.

Gilly wanted Maggie to say it out loud so she could tell Maggie she wasn't mad. She didn't blame her. Before the last few days, Gilly hadn't thought much of herself either.

Instead, Maggie's gaze drifted into Gilly's. She studied her. Their hearts beat together.

"Do you remember in Florida, you told me how Sam became your friend? When she stood up for you to those other girls?"

"Yeah?"

"Did you ever thank her?"

"No. Not yet."

Maggie nodded. Wiggling out from under Gilly, she got to her feet. The purple flower had fallen out of her hair. She tucked it back behind her ear. "Come along."

Gilly sensed another stall. When she hesitated, Maggie said, "I'm going to tell you. Come along."

Taking the flashlight out of her backpack again, Maggie led Gilly up some stairs at the end of the corridor. They climbed past one landing after another. Feedback-as-a-weapon rock receded below, leaving only their footsteps to crack the silence.

Boring through stone-solid darkness, the flashlight beam halted against a steel door with rust boiling through its paint. Maggie touched the handle. Gilly heard the metallic *cli-click* of tumblers and pins unlocking themselves. She remembered that the Witches' Carnival could pass through any barrier. She couldn't wait to try that.

They stepped out onto the roof. Like when she and Sam had first entered the turbine hall, the power station's massive scale left Gilly's head reeling. Four smokestacks loomed above them, monoliths glowing bone-white under the moon. Red lights blinked at their very peaks to ward off airplanes.

Head down against a vicious wind, Gilly followed Maggie to the edge of the roof. The sparkling geode of the city lay gathered beneath them. London had become small enough for Gilly to cup in her hand.

"Like it?" Maggie asked.

"Yeah." Gilly nodded, not sure what Maggie wanted to hear. "It's really cool."

"It's yours if you like."

Gilly smirked. "I'll take it."

"Not just London, either. Have you ever been to New York?"

"I've never been anywhere."

"Wait until you see New York when the snow is falling. And spring in Okinawa. And the white nights over Saint Petersburg, the Cape Town jazz clubs. Budapest. Tokyo. Rome. And wherever you go, Gilly, doors fling open, rules bend for you. Everyone loves you."

Gilly stared down at glimmering London and imagined flowing through its night like music. She would never misstep or trip over her words again. The huddled gray people would glimpse her from the corners of their eyes. Heads would turn; conversations would drift to quiet. They didn't have to know she was a witch to see she was beautiful.

Not just pretty, beautiful.

"Sounds great," she said.

Maggie nodded. "Even more than you think. And it's easy, too. No magic rings. You don't have to sign your name in blood anywhere. All you have to do is leave everything behind, and the Witches' Carnival whisks you away. It's as easy as jumping off a bridge."

Gilly could have said something about the easy part, but didn't. "Well, we're here. Let's jump."

"You have to leave everything behind first, sweetie."

"We have. Everything's ten thousand miles away. It's all an ocean away. I got my dad arrested. We can't go back. Ever. What else do we–"

The last word caught in Gilly's throat. She looked at Maggie, but Maggie wouldn't look at her. She knew Gilly knew, and she was sorry.

"Maggie."

"It can never be 'we,'" Maggie whispered. "Join the Witches' Carnival and leave everything–and everyone– behind."

When Gilly couldn't answer, Maggie half-turned and mustered a bitter smile. "I told you it was a hateful world."

"I can't." Heat prickled Gilly's skin. She felt sick. "I can't leave Sam."

"You have to."

"But the police are onto us. The money's gone. They know about the passports. She'll go to jail."

"I know, sweetie."

"This is bullshit. You might as well say only left-handed people can go, or girls named Mary."

"Except no one daydreams about being left-handed. Run away, join the Witches' Carnival, and leave everything behind. That's the fantasy everyone has sometime, some-where in their life. Those daydreams make the Carnival real, and they shape it, too. So if you want to become part of it, you have to go through with it. You have to leave your whole world behind."

Maggie squeezed Gilly's hand. Gilly felt Maggie's warmth in the cold night and smelled the wildflower scent of her skin.

"I know it's awful," Maggie went on. "But it's the one law the Carnival has to obey. You go alone or you don't go."

"No. I can't leave her." Even as she said the words, callous thoughts flickered through Gilly's mind. Right now Sam was downstairs, burning herself out on music and mescaline and whatever else would do the trick. She'd be wasted soon, groping some boy who'd caught her eye or yelling things she wouldn't remember tomorrow.

All Gilly had to do was slip away, out of the power sta-tion, out of London, out of her grubby little life, and never look back. She wouldn't have to watch the betrayal dawn across Sam's face or hear her swear, snarl and cry.

As easy as jumping off a bridge.

• • •

Inside, Peter glimpsed the stairs that seemed to stretch the wrong way. Metal pressed against his hip and the knobs of his spine. He tried to sit up. He tasted metal. Metal tore into the side of his chest. He could feel it inside him, beneath his ribs.

They pushed him back to the floor. Their faces were red-purple and screaming. The thumping music sounded far away. Peter didn't think anything or wish for anything. He couldn't figure out what was happening. Indifferent metal sliced into his body again.

TWENTY

"If I'd known, I wouldn't have come," Gilly whispered.

"I didn't tell you because I never thought you'd try to come. You'd go back home and probably hate me, but you'd never know it was Sam who stood between you and the Carnival. I figured that was kinder than telling you the truth. And the truth is, this will haunt you the rest of your life whatever you decide." The taut line of Maggie's mouth wasn't pity, only understanding. It was hurt for Gilly and for herself.

Gilly wiped her eyes. "Who'd you leave behind?"

"My family. My mother and sisters and brothers."

"That's not so bad. I mean, none of them went to jail because of you, at least."

"No. But I was born a long time before welfare or

government assistance. Back then, if you didn't earn enough to buy food, you didn't eat. That was that. When my father finally left for good, I was about your age. Mother worked at a hog-butchering plant, but it wasn't enough money, so she got me a job cleaning offices at the plant."

The wind twisted Maggie's dark hair around her face. She pushed it back with her fingers. "Things from your old life start slipping away after a while. I can't remember Mother's voice or the apartment I grew up in, but I remember the plant. It was dark and sweltering hot. It was like Hell. The machines ate workers piece by piece, fingers, hands. Ever heard of the Haymarket bombing?"

When Gilly shook her head, Maggie waved it off. "Forgotten history. Some union organizers held a rally, and I went to see what they had to say. Just as it was ending, though, the police moved in and started busting skulls. Then someone threw a bomb into the police line, killed eight of them. The whole thing turned into bedlam. I was scrambling, trying to get out of there, when I saw Chris for the first time."

Maggie laughed at the far-away memory. "He had this diamond-pattern vest with silver threading and that grin. He wanted me to go dancing. He asks me right in the middle of the shouting and smoke. I didn't plan it, but one thing led to another. I never went home again. I don't know what happened to my family." Plucking the trumpet-shaped flower from her hair, Maggie twirled it between her fingers, then started tearing it to scraps. "I don't know if they ended up on the street or if one of my sisters left school to take my place at the plant. Sometimes I hate myself for what I did, Gilly, but when Chris showed up . . . that was my one chance to escape, and I took it, and I don't hate myself half as much as I should."

She let the wind snatch the shredded flower out of her hand. "I like you a lot, Gilly. You're cute and bright and braver than you think. But I won't stay for you. I've got too many ghosts on my own trail to stay behind for anyone."

Gilly stared at her sneakers. She couldn't think of anything worth saying.

Be-blip. "Maggie? Where are you?"

A two-way radio hung from the strap of Maggie's backpack. She unclipped it and pressed a button. *Be-blip.* "On the roof. What's going on?"

Be-blip. "Peter just got killed." It was Tonja, sounding annoyed. The music played on behind her.

Be-blip. "What happened?"

Be-blip. "Some guys jumped him, probably some of the dealers he was supposed to sell the mescaline to. Jack got sliced up pretty bad too, and nobody's sure where the killers are. We need to get out of here."

Maggie sighed. *Be-blip.* "Sounds like good sailing weather."

Be-blip. "Meet us in the control room."

Maggie turned toward Gilly. "It's time. You have to decide."

A panicked shadow crossed Gilly's eyes, then she dropped her gaze. The cavalier attitude she wore, polished to gleaming by the past few days, turned out to be just a trick of the light. Like so many other times in her life, Gilly stood docile, waiting for someone else to choose for her.

Maggie took her hand. "It's going to be amazing. You'll see. Just don't look back."

Down stairs and through corridors, it felt like falling sideways. Gilly tumbled after Maggie as Maggie got directions to the control room over her radio. They crossed the teeming turbine hall. There was a dead man somewhere, a killer somewhere, but the children danced on.

When they found the control room, everyone except Qi had gathered. In the twitching beams of the witches' flashlights, Gilly saw tarnished copper pipes and banks of dials covered in bird crap. Jack sat on the parquet floor. An unsettling amount of blood smeared his chest and the geometric tiles underneath him. Two ragged holes in his forearm and one in the side of his hand terrified Gilly. They didn't look like knife wounds. It looked like something had chewed on him.

Laughing and cussing at once, Jack poured gin over his arm to wash away the gore. Chris knelt beside him, wrapping the slashes in strips torn from Jack's ruffle-collared shirt.

"Are we sure Peter's dead?" Maggie asked.

"Yeah. They damn near chopped his head off."

"So where are they?"

"Ran away. Probably gone by now, but I'd rather not risk it."

"What about Qi?"

"Do they know we were working with Peter?"

"I'm guessing." Jack held up his bloody hand.

"Qi's coming. I called her on the radio."

"That shirt isn't really doing anything."

"How long ago did you call her?"

"Well, I don't have any bandages at the moment, so it'll have to do."

"I don't know. After I called you."

Questions and answers bounced around the room. Qi showed up a minute later, groaned at the sight of Jack and added to the clamor.

Gilly kept quiet, hovering behind Maggie. Finally, Chris glanced up and asked, "Coming with us, Atlanta?"

Gilly managed a single nod. Maggie smiled. Wrapping an arm around Gilly's waist, she pulled her close. "Patch Jack up so we can get out of here."

"What happened? They just popped out of nowhere?"

"One of the damn pirates showed them up. When they jumped Peter, the little shit vanished."

"So was the pirate working with the dealers?"

"No, but hopefully they tipped him on the way out."

They bandaged Jack's wounds the best they could. He climbed to his feet and leaned on Tonja. Gilly noticed two scars like knot holes on his shoulder, old bullet wounds.

"Gonna live, Hijack?" Qi asked.

"Fucking Koreans couldn't kill me. Fucking Feds couldn't kill me. Fucking Brazilians couldn't kill me. Think those little fucks can kill me?"

"That's my soldier." Qi saluted him.

Jack took a swig of gin and saluted back. "Hell, I ain't even having a bad day yet."

"All the same, can we get out of here now?" Maggie asked.

They left the control room. Forming a loose circle around Jack, the Witches' Carnival slipped through the faerie mob of gossamer wings, kitty ears, and shiny vinyl.

Gilly walked beside Maggie. Bodies rippled around them like a storm-wracked sea. Nothing felt real. Forward motion had become dreamlike. There was no jostling or stumbling. People instinctively moved aside to let them pass. Then, on the edge of Gilly's vision, Sam's sharp-cornered smile emerged from among the anonymous faces.

Sam pushed toward Gilly. She screamed something, her voice lost beneath the music.

Maggie squeezed Gilly's hand so hard, it hurt. Whipping her head around, Gilly met cool, glittering brown eyes. "You can't look back," Maggie hissed. "You can't worry about her."

If they stayed together, they stayed behind. Gilly loved Sam, but she couldn't make herself stand by her. Fingernails digging into Maggie's hand, Gilly followed her out of the power station.

"Fuck." Sam stared at the point in the churning crowd where the Carnival had vanished. "Fuck!"

Gilly had glanced in Sam's direction but hadn't seen her. A second later, she and the witches disappeared again among the angels, pimps, and girls in bloody prom dresses.

"Was he bleeding?" Ronald asked.

Ronald was one of the pirates working for Peter. He and the others had been recruited from the hangers-on at a club promotion business either run or half-owned by either an old friend or business partner of Peter's; Sam hadn't gotten all the details.

Ronald had told Sam about the murder. He also knew the killers in some roundabout way. After telling Sam that they were serious men, not to be fucked with, he'd trailed her on her panicked search for Gilly and the witches.

Sam tried to remember what she'd just seen. Jack had been half-naked and stumbling. Congealing blood streaked his torso and covered his pants.

"Did they stab anybody but Peter?" she asked.

Still wearing his three-cornered hat and a patch over his left eye, Ronald shrugged. "Don't know. I didn't see it."

Relief that Gilly was okay gave way to fear again. "C'mon." Grabbing Ronald's sleeve, Sam started ramming through the crowd.

Outside in the frost-hoared night, dance music was swallowed by the roar of an industrial generator sitting on the bed of a truck. The Carnival's footsteps swished through tall weeds toward a rented Escalade at the edge of the station's coal yard.

"So was it One-Nut Joe?"

"One-Nut said he'd smash Peter's head in with a hammer. These guys had knives."

"All right, where to?" Tonja asked, climbing behind the wheel.

"Zurich." Leaning over the backseat, Qi rifled through an overnight bag. She pulled out some computer printouts and a glossy brochure.

"Oh right, Peter's chalet."

"Be a shame to waste. He's already got the reservations."

"It looks nice." Maggie took the brochure from Qi and opened it. The resort was called Glänsande Lac. Beside Maggie, Gilly stared at slope-roofed wooden cabins beside an azure lake. The scene was glazed with snow and twilight. A medieval city rose through the distant haze.

"Switzerland then." Tonja cranked the ignition. Icy blue Xenon headlights sliced across the industrial ruins. The

Escalade jolted along the broken ground away from the power station. Maggie laid the brochure in Gilly's lap. "This'll be our room," she whispered, touching a photograph of a bedroom with a roaring fireplace and canopied bed.

At the station, the party raged on. Word passed among the pirates. The hippie was dead, the other bosses had split, and a murderer was on the loose. Some of them pocketed the money they'd made and got out. Plenty more stayed, stripping off their pirate costumes and, mescaline tending to negate one's capitalist drive, handing out the last of the drugs for nothing but good karma in return.

There was a brief meeting on what to do about Peter. Someone found a plastic tarp. Two boys wrapped Peter up and carried him out to the weedy lot between the power station and the pier.

DJs and bands changed whenever one needed a break or wanted to try a new song. They jammed together and goofed around on the balcony. A few kids got fucked up, but strangers stepped in to care for them, feeding them bites of fruit until they felt better. Even without anybody in charge, the power station's community refused to disintegrate. Everyone danced, took free drugs, screwed, and had a good time.

• • •

It was five in the morning. Beneath the pale, predawn sky, a steady trickle of headlights flowed across Vauxhall Bridge.

"Tonja, where are you headed?" Maggie asked.

"Heathrow."

"No flights are going to leave for a couple hours. Let's go to Victoria Station. The trains should already be running."

"Then we'll be cramped up in a train all day," Jack said.

"I'd prefer to get out of town as soon as we can."

Everybody turned to give Maggie confused stares. Then they glanced at Gilly and nodded. Gilly stayed quiet, pretending she didn't realize Maggie wanted to hustle her out of London before she could think too much. Her greedy side relished Maggie being greedy for her.

"Goddamn it." Sam raised her arm to throw her cell phone at something. Catching herself, she dropped it into her lap. "They don't have Peter's phone."

"Relax. If one of your friends is hurt, they'll take them to the casualty department."

"The what?" Sam snapped.

"The hospital. The emergency room. If somebody's hurt, Gordon is the closest hospital. We'll meet up with them there. Everything's going to be all right."

Sam felt Ronald rub her back and knew he wanted to get laid. She ignored him. The two bracelets on Sam's wrist blinked different colors every time she moved. Their flashing became the sudden focus of her frustration.

"Stupid, fucking–" Yanking the bracelets off, she threw them onto the cab's floor. That wasn't enough. She stomped on one and heard the plastic crack. It didn't make her feel any better.

Sam's glimpse of the witches leaving the power station replayed in her head. Gilly had been clinging to Maggie. Had she gotten stabbed too? Her hoodie had been gone. Why had she taken off her hoodie?

Worse than any battle Sam might fight and lose, the sense of helplessness bowed her. Slowly so Ronald wouldn't see, she clasped her hands together. *Please, please, just let everything be okay.*

"I think that's them up there."

Sam lifted her eyes. They were almost off the bridge. Six car-lengths ahead, an Escalade stuck out among the smaller vehicles.

"You sure?"

Ronald nodded. "I helped set things up this afternoon. That's what they showed up in. See? No worries."

They fell into a tense silence. Picking up the two bracelets, Sam slipped them into her pocket. The taxi passed a ceremonial guard of bronze statues and exited the bridge. Another minute had passed when Ronald grunted a soft, "Huh."

"What?"

He motioned to a side street. "Gordon Hospital. It's down Vincent Square."

He tapped on the Plexiglas partition separating them from the cab driver. "Hey, just follow that gray SUV up there, all right?"

The driver nodded, and Ronald leaned back.

"Who knows. Maybe they just left to get something to eat. No worries."

Sam watched the Escalade. She'd seen Jack bleeding. She'd seen Gilly clutching Maggie. "Yeah. Maybe."

Victoria Station formed a nexus for metro, train, and bus lines in and out of south London. The station was an architectural dreamscape–columned arcades, glass, and white stone–pressed into service for thousands of businessmen and tourists passing through each day.

Gilly's ears rang from the party, a soft, steady whine that muffled voices and footsteps. A Eurostar train left in five minutes headed for Paris. The Witches' Carnival stalked through the station like a pride of lions, heading for platform nine. Jack was still bare-chested and streaked with dried blood, but no one stepped up to challenge them. Nobody even seemed to notice anything strange about it. The Witches' Carnival traveled wherever, and apparently however, they pleased.

Gilly followed the other witches. She filled her mind with the moment around her, struggling to keep guilt and thoughts of Sam at bay. Passengers dozed, stretched out on metal benches with backpacks under their heads. A swallow fluttered through the steel girders high overhead. Most of the restaurants and shops stood dark. A too-perky woman sat at a kiosk selling coffee and bagels.

Chris grabbed some napkins from the kiosk and handed them to the other witches.

"What's your last name," Maggie asked Gilly.

"Stahl."

"First rule of the Witches' Carnival, sweetie. Always carry a pen." With a ballpoint pen from her backpack, Maggie wrote across two of the napkins and handed them to Gilly. One read *United States Passport. Gillian Stahl.* The other declared itself a *Ticket to Zurich, Sweden. First Class.*

"Will these really work?" Gilly asked.

"Good for any train, plane, subway, or horse-drawn carriage in the world."

Remembering Paul's homemade police badge and the message across the security guard's portacabin, a fragile smile touched Gilly's lips. "Cool."

The platforms smelled like ozone and diesel fuel. Passing through metal barriers, they approached the train. Mechanical hisses trembled through the air around it. Boarding had already been announced. Two college-aged boys walked ahead of them, sleepy-eyed and unshaven. They showed their tickets to the conductor, a little sleepy-eyed and unshaven himself, and climbed a set of portable stairs into the train.

Gilly didn't know what she was supposed to do, so she hung back to watch the others. Chris showed the conductor his ticket. With a bored smile, the man glanced at it and waved him into the car. There was no sleight of hand involved.

Qi went next. The conductor gave her a few more moments of his time. "Zurich, eh? You've got a long road ahead of you." He offered his hand to help her up the wobbly steps and never noticed her ticket was written on a paper napkin.

"Gilly!"

Pounding footsteps echoed across the platform. Thought lagging a moment behind instinct, Gilly turned toward Sam's voice. "Don't," Maggie snapped. "Don't worry about her. You can't worry about her."

"Gilly! Fuck! Gilly!"

Gilly forced her stare straight ahead on the train's door. Dark metal showed through scraped blue paint. The conductor shouted over her head. "Stay behind the barrier, miss. If you don't have a ticket, stay behind the barrier!"

Someone else barked orders. Sam shrieked, "Let the fuck go of–Gilly!"

Jack then Tonja climbed aboard. Maggie pushed Gilly ahead of her, hissing, "Just go. It'll be amazing. Just go and don't think."

Gilly showed the conductor her ticket and started up the steps.

"Gilly, stop! Please!"

She told herself she couldn't save Sam, only go to jail with her. It wasn't the same as all the times people had betrayed her, ignored her when she was hurting. It was different. Gilly tried to make herself believe it was totally different.

Gilly looked over her shoulder; she didn't want to, but she couldn't help it. Sam was pulling against the uniformed man holding her. She yelled Gilly's name and met her glance with wide, terrified eyes. Gilly only regretted it for a second, but even a second was too long. The illusion shattered.

Grabbing Gilly's arm, the conductor growled, "What's this? Get out of here."

Gilly spun back around. "N-no."

He shoved the scrap of paper back in her hand. "Get off the platform."

She'd just looked back for a moment. Weakly, Gilly held up the ticket. "But it's–"

The conductor yanked her out of the train. "I don't have time for this rubbish."

"What the fuck, Gilly? What the fuck?"

Gilly couldn't face Sam. She had to get away. The conductor held her arm and pulled a radio from his belt. "Victor One, send security to platform nine."

As he called for security and Gilly wrestled against his grip, Maggie slipped around them both and up into the train.

"It's a ticket!" Gilly shrieked. "Just take it. Wait, I'll buy a ticket, okay? I'll pay anything you want, okay?"

Two transit cops rushed toward them. Gilly let out animal wails when they grabbed her arms and jerked her back. The conductor tossed the portable steps into the train and slid the door closed.

"Maggie!" Gilly snatched a final glimpse of the Witches' Carnival. Maggie never turned around. The door banged shut, and the Carnival vanished like the daydream they were.

"No," Gilly whimpered. "I just want to get on the train. Please, I just want to get on the fuck–" Her throat clenched with a sob. It was over.

The police escorted her, Sam, and a boy Gilly had never met outside, warning that if they came back, they'd be arrested.

On the sidewalk, Gilly shivered in her T-shirt. She clutched the make-believe ticket and passport in her hand. The Eurostar's wail pierced the dawn as it pulled away from the station. Gilly hated the witches, and she hated herself for ever dreaming she could be one of them.

"What the fuck, G?" Sam sniffed. Gilly stared at the pavement, bearing the weight of her stare without a word.

"That was it, wasn't it? They're gone?"

Gilly nodded.

"You tried to ditch me."

"No." Shame burned Gilly's face. "It wasn't like that."

"Fuck you. 'Wasn't like that.'" Sam shoved her hard.

"Sam—"

"Fuck you! You think I'm just stupid white trash, and all of a sudden you're part of the Witches' Carnival, and I'm a fucking embarrassment."

It wasn't true, but it was true enough.

"What's in your hand?" Sam asked.

"What?"

She reached for the ticket and passport in Gilly's fist. Gilly jerked her arm back. "Nothing. Just some . . ." Even ashamed, hating herself for what she'd tried to do, Gilly couldn't keep from thinking, *What if the ticket still works?*

"You know where they're going, don't you?"

"No." Gilly stuffed the napkins into her pocket.

"Fucking liar." Tears spilled down her cheeks. "You're the one person I—go to Hell."

Sam turned her back on Gilly and started down the street. Gilly didn't move.

Sam was the only girl Gilly knew who casually called other girls "bitches." She cussed like a poet, using a handful of swears to express a hundred nuanced emotions. This time was different, though. This time Sam meant it, and all past blasphemies couldn't blunt the force of Gilly's best friend casting her into a cold, alien city. Anything Gilly said after that would be meaningless.

The boy Gilly didn't know, one of the pirates from the party, trotted after Sam.

"I'm bailing, man," she told him. "And I'm not going to fuck you. You might as well go back to the party."

The pirate made soft protests. Ignoring him, Sam hailed a taxi and climbed inside.

"Take me to the Hotel Constantinople on Bayswater."

The driver sneered. "Come on, kid. I'm not driving halfway across—"

"Just do it, and I'll tip you twenty pounds. I'll tip you another twenty if you can keep your fucking mouth shut until we get there."

The driver pulled away from the curb without another word. Gilly watched Sam through the rear window. Wiping her eyes, Sam never looked back.

TWENTY-ONE

The city yawned and stretched itself awake. Cars still had their headlights on. A man wearing a ratty coat set up his newspaper stand beside the station's south entrance. A woman inside the grocery store across the street pulled Halloween decorations from the windows.

"Gonna be all right?" The boy who'd come with Sam stood at a cautious distance from Gilly. He held his black pirate hat in his hand and still wore the patch over his eye. "Don't worry about it. She just got scared by all that stuff at the power station. Let her get some sleep, calm down, then give her a call. You'll be mates again."

Gilly managed a nod and began walking away.

"Hey, I'm going back to the party. Why don't you come with me?"

Ignoring him, Gilly kept walking. She crossed a major road, then another, then turned left for no reason. She wandered alone through the strange city.

It was the same London she and Sam had gorged themselves on, pub-crawling and killing time at the movies. Everything was different now. Gilly saw gashes in the city's skin revealing the barbarism underneath.

Graffiti marked walls like prehistoric rock paintings. Alleys rustled with stray dogs and stray men scavenging for food. A pair of lilac panties lay on the sidewalk covered in shoe prints, the tossed-away trophy of some sexual conquest. A sewer-stink hung in the air, perfumed with exhaust and baking bread. Gilly passed a thousand bored eyes.

Civilization's gears never stopped, never slowed. Everybody had somewhere to be. Watching people go through their motions while her life collapsed made Gilly seethe. She wanted the world to stop for a minute so she could figure things out.

Paul's badge had worked after Maggie had left. Gilly guessed that the ticket would too. Even if it didn't, getting arrested at the airport today or on the street tomorrow didn't make enough difference to matter. She just had to forget about Sam. She had to be willing to leave everything and everyone behind.

Gilly couldn't figure out what had happened. She tried

stringing together the days and events that had led up to this, but none of the pieces fit. It had been a stupid game. Ditch school, blow some money in Atlanta, come home, get screamed at, and then it was over. Now the police had arrested her dad. They knew about the passports and were tightening the noose around Sam's neck. Gilly had fucked everything up, and all she could do was run away.

She walked until each step sent a dull jolt through the bones in her feet. She was hungry, and the November morning's chill made her teeth chatter. She passed a souvenir shop with toy double-decker buses in the window and a rotating rack of postcards on the sidewalk. Gilly stopped and snapped around, staring at a postcard with a picture of the Tower of London on it.

Ducking inside the cramped store, she found the cash register in the very back. Approaching the man behind it, she asked, "There are ravens at the Tower of London, right?"

The man grinned. "I certainly hope so."

Long ago, an alchemist had warned King Charles the Second that if the ravens ever left the Tower of London, first the tower would fall and then all of Britain. A royal decree had protected the birds for centuries, and today they were a tourist attraction in their own right. Gilly didn't remember where she'd first heard the story. Probably from one of those paperbacks filled with Wiccan symbols and empty promises she'd poured over years ago. But she remembered Meek and prayed she could find her and Sam's guardian angel at a place legendary for its blackbirds and soothsayers.

"I need a map or something. I need to know how to get there." As Gilly spoke, a rivulet of hope began welling up inside her.

Crossing the lobby, the dark-haired girl passed within an arm's length from Alan. He glanced up at her, noted the dried tears streaking her face, then went back to reading yesterday's *Sun*. The girl turned the corner toward the elevators. Two minutes later, Neil stepped over from the other side of the lobby.

"That was one of them, wasn't it?"

"Yep." Alan slipped a pair of grainy pictures from the folds of his paper. Neither of the girls had a mugshot, but the American police had faxed two photos that probably came from a school annual. "That was Grace," he said, reading his handwritten notes at the bottom of one photo.

"Looks like she had a bad night."

"Poor dear."

"Wait? See if Stahl shows?"

"Yeah, that one's been up all night." Alan nodded, indicating the girl who'd just passed through the lobby. "She'll stay put for a while."

"I'll call command, then, tell them what's going on," Neil said.

"All right. And see if you can find some coffee somewhere. And see if you can find a copy of today's paper. I've read this one twice already."

Upstairs, Sam let herself into the hotel room. Housekeeping had made up the bed. Other then that, the room was untouched since she and Gilly had rushed out the day before. She was a little surprised a phalanx of cops wasn't waiting to grab her.

Clothes lay strewn across the floor. The stupid textbook Gilly had lugged from Florida sat on the desk.

"Fucking bitch." Sam threw the book against the wall, making a satisfying *thud*. The corner smashed a triangular dent in the plaster.

Slumping onto the bed, she stared at her hands, the chipped nails and fingers half–closed like dead spiders. She knew she shouldn't be here, but it didn't really matter. More than scared, more than angry, Sam felt hollow.

Gilly had turned on her, used her until she became inconvenient and then dumped her without a second thought. Sam shouldn't have been surprised. She knew she was a fuckup, that she got wasted all the time and got her friends into trouble. She just thought Gilly was the one person who might forgive her for all that.

Sam started crying again. She dug SpongeBob from her purse and shook out a Xanax. She stared at the tablet for a while, then tipped the whole box, a dozen pills, into her palm.

For a dead-silent minute, Sam thought about taking them all and downing them with some liquor. She wouldn't go to jail. Everyone could get on with their lives.

On the street, car horns bleated.

Dust motes drifted through the morning sunlight.

"Fucking bitch." Sam sent the pills scattering across the carpet. She didn't want to die. She sat motionless for a while longer, listening to herself sniff and blubber. Her stomach growled. Finally, Sam leaned over and grabbed the room service menu. She was going to jail. It'd be stupid to go hungry.

The train car rocked side to side, rattling through the tunnels below London. Gilly rubbed her eyes to keep the gentle motion from lulling her to sleep. She tried counting how many hours she'd been on her feet, but she was too tired to think. She remembered Sam waking her up arguing with the pizza boy. It felt like weeks ago.

A soft chime sounded over hidden speakers followed by a woman's recorded voice. *Now approaching Tower Hill. Tower Hill. Next station, Monument. Monument.*

The train slowed to a stop, and the doors hissed open. Gilly got out, clutching the travel guide she'd bought at the souvenir shop. Outside again, everything seemed too bright, too loud, and too frantic. Gilly followed London Tourism Board arrows past small restaurants and shops and finally to the top of a wide, green slope. At the bottom sprawled ancient stone walls scrubbed almost to gleaming. Gilly bought a ticket and found the short line of autumn tourists.

A boy with a shaved head, gold earrings, and a security uniform swabbed every backpack and purse, checking for explosives. Gilly shivered in the cold sunlight. Except for her, all the people in the stub of a line were with families or friends. Everybody around her talked, posed for pictures, or pointed out parts of the Tower to one another. It made Gilly feel more miserable than she already was.

Passing the security check, Gilly walked through a wooden gate and up the cobblestone rampway. She'd always heard "Tower of London" and imagined a single tower. It was more like a town square surrounded by high walls. Several towers, a church, a gift shop, and other buildings stood separated by clipped lawns and winding paths.

People snapped pictures of the royal guards and the executioner's block. Gilly watched them form a second line to see the Crown Jewels. She walked toward the ravens' grassy enclosure. Blue-black birds hopped around the base of White Tower, stabbing at the ground with their pickax beaks.

A Beefeater in his immaculate uniform was giving a tour.

Gilly listened to him tell the legend of King Charles the Second and the ravens, explaining that if the birds ever left, England would collapse.

"Now this is, of course, silly, medieval, superstitious non-sense," he barked out to the crowd gathered around him. "And we in the modern era would never believe such prattle." He paused for a moment. Gilly waited for the punch line. "But just to be sure, we clip their wings so they can never fly away."

Everybody laughed, and the beefeater made sure to mention that the birds were all well fed and very happy before moving on with the tour.

Gilly stayed by the fence watching the ravens. They fluttered in, out, and on top of their wire roosts. None of them took any notice of her.

"I'm looking for a friend of mine," she whispered under her breath, only half-joking. "I thought one of you might know where he was."

"They're just birds," Meek said.

Gilly turned. He stood at her shoulder, tall, thin, and slightly bent. His good right eye looked at her, alert and kind. The scummy blue orb of his left eye stared out at the world as dead as a pebble.

Meek held one side of his jacket closed. A bulge in the olive drab fabric rustled. His crow had come back to life again and sat cradled inside.

"I figured this was the best place to try to find you," Gilly said.

Meek shrugged. "Only because I knew this would be the place you'd look for me. So, how are you enjoying England?"

Gilly glanced away. "You know what FUBAR means?"

"Yes. Do you know what SNAFU means?"

Situation Normal, All Fucked Up. A sour smile crossed Gilly's face, remembering the stories and dirty jokes her dad told about life in the Marine Corps. "No. This is way beyond the normal level of fucked up–ness."

"And how's that?" With stiff steps, Meek walked over to a park bench along the flagstone path. His crow gave an irritated squawk when he reached inside his jacket. "Hush," he said, pulling out a half–empty pack of Marlboros.

Gilly sat beside him. Certain Meek knew everything already, she was glad for anybody willing to listen.

"After the Providence thing, we came here and found the Carnival again."

"What do you think of Qi? Interesting young lady, huh?"

"Yeah, she's pretty cool."

"Rule of thumb, Gilly. A girl who climbs from concubine to ruler of China by the time she's twenty makes a good dinner companion."

"She ruled China?"

"Behind the curtain. She didn't tell you? You didn't ask?"

"Actually, I didn't talk to her all that much."

Meek heard the words hidden behind her words. "Ah. How's Maggie then?"

Gilly grinned. She could talk about Maggie for hours, but not now. "Anyway, the cops know about the passports. They're looking for us, but only one of us can join the Carnival."

Meek nodded. "Join the Witches' Carnival and leave everything behind."

"Yeah, you could've . . ." Gilly stopped herself. Reaching into her pocket, she pulled out the ticket and passport written in Maggie's careful script. "Before she left, Maggie gave me these."

She handed them to Meek. Cigarette smoldering between his lips, he glanced at the napkins, then handed them back.

"There're people who'd kill for those, Gilly."

"So they'll still work?"

"They'll work. Go to the airport and get on a plane. Your trouble will be over by this evening."

"Right, but Sam's won't, see? I'm not asking you to break the Carnival's golden rule and let us both go, I just need you to make it so Sam doesn't go to jail over this."

"Sam's not my problem."

Hope turned to ice. Gilly watched Meek smoke his cigarette. His eyes were slits facing the sun, watching tourists wander back and forth.

"But . . . you could."

"Probably. If I had to."

"Then why not? Why'd you save us in Providence if–"

"I was only there to save you, Gilly, not her. My bargain was with you. I offered to help Sam find her way home in exchange for a pack of cigarettes, but she laughed. Then I offered to make you beautiful. You took me up on it, and I've done everything I can to keep my end of our bargain. But I don't owe Sam a thing."

"What? That's fucking crazy." But it was true. Gilly remembered the night in the gas station. She was the one who'd bought the cigarettes. She was the one Meek told about the Witches' Carnival, and she was the one he rescued from the cop in Providence. "Fine, I'll buy you another pack of cigarettes to help Sam. I'll buy as many damn cigarettes as you want."

"No, thanks. I'm good." Meek flicked ash onto the cobblestones.

Gilly stared at his gruesome, blinded eye. She couldn't see a guardian angel anymore. She saw something repulsive, offering glittering baubles at great prices. Gilly saw Mephostophilis. Dropping her head between her shoulders, Gilly started crying and didn't care who saw her.

"Come on, now." Meek sighed. "You have a ticket to join the Witches' Carnival. How bad can it all be?"

When Gilly didn't answer, he made a phlegmatic *humph* deep in his throat and watched another Beefeater stop nearby, giving the tour.

Climbing to his feet, Meek walked to the raven's enclosure. Gilly watched him. He leaned over the guardrail and whispered something. When Meek came back, he didn't sit down.

"Let's go," he said.

"What?"

"Just come on."

Gilly got up and followed him, edging past the knot of tourists surrounding the Beefeater.

". . . That of course is just silly, medieval nonsense. And we in the modern world would never–"

A manic flutter-beat of wings cut him off mid-joke. As the Tower ravens took flight, murmuring tourists fell silent. Everyone craned their necks to watch the birds wheel high above the courtyard and vanish over Traitors' Gate. Staring around in a rising panic, the Beefeater's mouth opened and shut without any words coming out.

Meek fought to keep from bursting out laughing. He shuffled through a turnstile with Gilly close behind. The exit led to a pedestrian street running between the Tower's outer wall and the murky brown Thames.

"Come on, now. That was funny. Didn't that cheer you up just a little?" Meek spoke in raspy chuckles that made his thin chest shake.

"Please. It wasn't even Sam's idea to come. It was mine." Gilly sniveled. Meek could save Sam whenever he wanted.

Instead, he was using his power to pull idiot pranks. Gilly was ready to beg and kiss Meek's feet, knowing the whole time it wouldn't matter. "Just let her go home. Please."

Meek had let his crow out from under his jacket. It perched on his shoulder, stretched its wings, and watched Gilly with eyes like flint. Meek raised his hand and wiggled his fingers to show Gilly he wasn't holding anything. With a flourish, he pulled two coins from behind Gilly's ear and dropped them into her palm.

It took Gilly a second to figure out the denominations and add them together. Thirty pence. "What am I supposed to do with this?"

"Call Sam." A mild smile crossed Meek's face. "Tell her good-bye."

She glared at him. Gilly wanted Meek to know how much she despised him, but her all-consuming hate was a spark to him, an ember already dying. Stuffing her hands into her pockets, she refused to disgrace herself with another word. Gilly started back toward the tube station.

TWENTY-TWO

Safe within the anonymity and droning clatter of the Underground again, Gilly stared out the window at the passing darkness, sometimes glimpsing lengths of pipe or dim red lamps as the car sped by. Everybody around her minded their own quiet business. They read books or newspapers and ignored her.

Touching the ticket and passport in her pocket, Gilly remembered the name of the chalet from the pamphlet Maggie had shown her. Glänsande Lac. She wished there was another way, but she'd tried everything. She'd hate herself for it, but she had it inside her to leave Sam behind.

She was about to join the Witches' Carnival. She would travel the earth with wings stitched from millions of daydreams. She would become something limitless, something purged of fear, something beautiful.

Sam knew what we were risking. Why's it my fault if I make it and she doesn't? I can't save her.

Gilly had every logical reason to head to Zurich and never look back. But she knew that, if the tables were turned, Sam wouldn't give a damn about logic.

Sam could be just as dangerous to her friends as to her enemies, but she was the most recklessly loyal person Gilly had ever known. If the tables were turned, Sam would rip the ticket up without a second thought, and if they couldn't join the Witches' Carnival together, then they'd go hand in hand to jail.

But Sam only had herself to blame. From the day she had saved Gilly, whimpering and squirming under Ashley Brown's shoe, she'd known Gilly was a coward.

Ashamed of herself and afraid for Sam, Gilly started crying again. Two men holding on to the pole close by glanced at her, then turned back to their conversation.

Last night, Gilly would have placed her life in Sam's hands and trusted her to guard it more jealously than she herself would. Then Maggie told her the final price for joining the Witches' Carnival. She'd never see Sam again, and it wasn't even noon.

Gilly just never imagined it'd end so suddenly. She always thought there would be time for one more rambling conversation or another lunatic adventure. She always thought there would be time to thank her.

Call Sam. Tell her good-bye.

Gilly reached into her pocket and touched the coins Meek had given her. He'd been serious. A wave of nausea crested over Gilly as she realized several things with preternatural certainty. Sam was at the hotel. She'd pick up the phone if Gilly called. The call would cost exactly thirty pence.

The recorded voice fizzed over worn speakers. *"Now approaching South Kensington. South Kensington. Next stop, Gloucester. Gloucester."*

Emotions warred against one another. Facing Sam, facing what she'd done, terrified Gilly. But she owed Sam every-thing; couldn't she at least say thank you? No. Sam would think Gilly was making fun of her. And Gilly was free now; she didn't have to do anything she didn't want to. Finally, a medieval shade of Gilly's soul won out, the dark, awful thing inside her that wanted Gilly to hurt.

By the time the train pulled to a stop, Gilly's breath came in unsteady gulps and her legs quivered. Somehow she made it up the escalator to street level.

The light was ashen, coming from flickering fluorescents overhead. Gilly walked down a corridor of grimy white brick surrounded by echoes and the loneliness that haunted all the passing-through places.

She followed signs to a pair of hyper-modern pay

phones. The phones took cash, credit cards, and phone cards. They had Internet access and computerized directories. Her hands shook as Gilly looked up the number for the Hotel Constantinople and deposited the money.

After two rings, Sam picked up. "Hello?"

She'd been crying too. She sounded exhausted and hoarse. Gilly fought the urge to slam the phone down without saying a word.

"It's me."

A second of dead air passed between them. It seemed to last forever.

"What the fuck do you want?" Sam finally asked, each word dripping venom.

"I-I'm sorry it ended up like this. I'm-"

"Yeah, right. You got your fucking Witches' Carnival and your fucking bitch Maggie. So get your goddamn dyke ass out of my-" She was about to hang up. Gilly screamed, "Wait! Sam! I just-thanks, okay?"

"What?"

Tears blurred Gilly's vision. "That day we became friends. That-that day Ashley was making fun of me in the hall. And you jumped in and made her stop just out of the blue. Just because you felt sorry for me, I guess. I never thanked you for that. Or any of the other times you stuck up for me. I'm sorry. I'm sorry for everything. I know I'm a goddamn bitch. I know you don't fucking care. But thank you, okay?"

Another eternity passed. Gilly clutched the receiver with white knuckles, waiting for a hail of abuse or some shadow of forgiveness, desperate for anything Sam was willing to give.

"That's not when we became friends."

Gilly stood motionless, still waiting. The words had come clear as cut glass through miles of fiber-optic cable, but she didn't understand. "What?"

"I didn't do it out of the blue. That's not when we became friends. We were in biology class that whole year before that."

"Yeah. We sorta knew each other, but–"

"'I don't want acceptance. I don't want understanding. I just want to be left the fuck alone.'"

"W-what?"

"You said that, Gilly. The day Tracye turned on you and started making fun of you with Ashley and them. Remember?"

Gilly vaguely remembered muttering it to Alex and Sam, not really caring if they were listening or not, trying to make herself laugh so she wouldn't cry.

"What about, 'Two-thirds of this school think I'm going to Hell, the other two-thirds want to watch me make out with a cheerleader.' You remember that?"

"Kind of, but–"

"You don't think I know how much shit they gave you?

You don't think I know how they are? And you showed up every damn day and laughed about it. I thought that was cool as fuck. You didn't try to hide or kiss their asses so maybe they'd be nice to you. Fuck, you sat at that goddamn lunch table and didn't give a crap until I made you sit by me."

Deep in the corridors of South Kensington Station, Gilly felt the planet shift beneath her feet. "No," she said. "It wasn't–"

"Shut up! I didn't stick up for you, almost get suspended for you that day because I felt sorry for you. I liked you. I thought you were funny and smart and had more guts than Ashley or Tracye or any of those bitches could ever imagine having."

"Sam, don't–"

"I said shut the fuck up! This is the truth, Gilly. I never, not once, thought you were some pathetic little stray kitten. You thought that. You. Not me."

"You're making shit up!" Gilly screeched. "You're just making shit up!"

"Yeah? Then why did I ask you to go search for the Witches' Carnival with me?"

"None of it happened like that!"

"Why, Gilly? Why didn't I ask Colby or Dawn? Why didn't I just go by myself?"

"I don't know."

She heard Sam choking out each word. "Because you're the one person I've ever met who's smart enough and stubborn enough to actually find the Witches' Carnival." She forced a laugh. "Turns out I'm right, huh? See you around, G."

The line went dead in Gilly's ear. People walked by, busy with their own lives. She could hear the trains shuddering in and out of the platforms below. "None of it—" She sobbed out to nobody. "None of it happened like that."

"This call has been disconnected. Please hang up to place another call."

The message scrolled across the phone's monitor, accompanied by a cartoon hand placing the receiver back in its cradle.

"It fucking didn't—" Hot tears veiled Gilly's face. She threw the heavy plastic receiver against the touch screen.

"This call has been disconnected. Please hang up to place another call."

Snatching the receiver again, Gilly clubbed the screen over and over. The monitor cracked. LCD colors oozed underneath, then blinked to a flat, sickly green. A shard of glass cut her cheek.

Gilly smashed the screen because Sam had fended off wolves for her, she'd faced sticks, stones, and insults, all because she saw something in Gilly that no one else ever had—something beautiful.

Gilly smashed the screen because she couldn't scheme halfway across the world and keep telling herself she was a coward. Because she was terrified of losing Maggie, of going to prison, but Gilly would face it. For Sam, she would face it.

The receiver struck the ruined screen, and slivers of glass flew up. A searing heat pierced Gilly's eye. The world turned red.

"Ow. Fuck." Dropping the phone, Gilly clapped a hand over her eye. "Fuck."

The pain snapped Gilly into the real world again, into the grungy corridor of the South Kensington Station again. Gilly pulled her hand away from her eye. Blood and tears streaked her fingers. She'd just smashed apart a pay phone. Everybody was staring at her.

She glared back. Londoners and tourists quickened their steps, casting her cautious, backward glances. A man in a charcoal gray suit edged away from her. A gold pen stuck out of his pocket. Gilly took a step forward, watching his eyes widen toward panic.

"Could I borrow your pen, please?" she asked.

The man fumbled for his pen and handed it to her. "Keep it."

Gilly nodded. "Thanks. It's . . . it's been a really long week," she mumbled, not sure what else to say. Turning, she rushed back toward the subway platforms, only stopping in front of a large Tube map for a few seconds to figure out the fastest way to the hotel.

TWENTY-THREE

"That was cool," Sam said.

Gilly gave a nervous laugh.

They lay mostly naked in the narrow bed belonging to Ben's thirteen-year-old stepbrother. The room held the sweaty, unwashed scent of boys. A poster of some basketball player going for a slam dunk was the only thing on the wall.

The clock read 4:22. Gilly had told her dad she'd be home by eleven, but Sam had broken up with Alex, her boyfriend, two weeks ago. She'd been full of beer and laughter, and even though Gilly kept telling herself, *Stop hoping. It's enough that she lets you hang around her,* she couldn't pull herself away. She spent the night fluttering around Samantha Grace like a moth.

It hadn't been a party, exactly; less than a dozen friends

sat around drinking themselves stupid. They kept playing the same Green Day song over and over. Someone had found a porno Ben's dad kept hidden in his closet and popped it into the DVD player. Ben's stepbrother had already thrown up and fallen asleep on the couch when Gilly and Sam stepped out onto the front porch.

Sitting on the glider, they spent hours smoking cigarettes and talking, dropping butts into an empty Budweiser can. They sifted through Sam's breakup with Alex piece by piece. Every detail unfolded like a paper fortune–teller, revealing another layer of things said and not said, events that occurred or should have. They talked simple philosophies and complicated lives. Sometimes, their conversation drifted to a smiling quiet, both of them gazing out at the dark neighborhood.

For no reason, Sam kissed Gilly's cheek. It startled her. She stared into Sam's eyes, too terrified to move. But when Sam started to laugh and turn away, Gilly plunged forward, kissing her lips.

"American Idiot" banged out of the stereo inside. Sam smelled like beer and soap, and she still had a cigarette held between two fingers. When she took Gilly's wrist and led her through the house and up the stairs, the whole world seemed to drop away under their feet.

Now it was 4:22 in the morning. Gilly knew her dad would kill her when she got home, but all she could think about was the downy hair on Sam's arms and how hot her skin had felt.

A fist banged on the door. "This is the police! Open up!" A clutch of snickers followed the growl.

"Fuck off, Ben!" Sam shouted back. Bodies tensed, she and Gilly listened to murmuring voices in the hall and the soft scrape of metal on metal. The boys popped the door lock with a bent paper clip. As Gilly swore and jerked the blanket over herself, Sam was already out of bed. Crossing the room in one bounding step, she crashed her shoulder into the door.

"Ow!"

Sam had pinned Ben's arm, a beer can clutched in his fist, between door and frame.

"Hey. This is my brother's room. I have a responsibility to—ow! Shit!"

Sam dug her fingernails into his beefy forearm, leaving crescent-shaped marks. Before Ben could yank his arm back, she snatched the Budweiser from him.

"Come on," Colby Reeves whined. "We won't get in the way. We just want to watch."

"Dude, she stole my beer," Ben laughed.

As the boys begged to be let in, Gilly grabbed a desk chair and wedged it under the doorknob. In the hall, Dawn shouted, "Just leave them alone. God."

"She stole my beer, Dawn. That ain't right."

"Get another beer and leave them alone."

In the dark bedroom, Gilly and Sam pulled on their clothes. Gilly gave the door a hard kick.

"You guys are, like, no fun at all," Colby answered back.

"Let's get out of here." Sam opened the window and knocked out the screen. A shed stood in the side-yard below. Climbing onto the window sill, clinging to the frame, Sam jumped. Both feet hit the shed's corrugated metal roof then she half-slid, half-toppled over the side. She landed in the soft grass and lay there laughing as Gilly clambered out after her.

The shed was six feet to her left. Gilly swung through the night, legs cocked ahead of her like a long jumper. Drunk and filled with the kind of madness that frees, she never thought about what might happen if she missed.

The roof came up hard. The impact numbed both legs and slapped her flat. Gilly dropped sideways to the ground beside Sam, which made Sam laugh harder.

"Fuck. I hurt my shoulder."

"You okay?" Sam asked.

"Yeah. Luckily it ain't my drinking arm." Sam had managed to hold on to Ben's beer. Grabbing it, Gilly took a sip. "You okay?"

"Yeah. Let's go walk around or something."

Waking birds chirped, and occasionally a dog barked at them from behind a fence. Empty, sleeping streets Gilly had known her whole life became an exotic country, everything strange and wonderful. She and Sam wandered alone through Byzantium.

"Those guys are such assholes," Gilly said.

Sam grinned a wide, sharp-cornered grin. "They're okay. Ben's cool at least."

"Yeah, I guess."

"Kevin Carney lives over there." Sam motioned to a brick home with blue shutters. "I dated him for, like, half an hour in ninth grade. That's his room," she said, pointing to a darkened window.

Gilly looked and nodded. "Listen." She drop-kicked the empty Budweiser can and watched it skitter down the street. "I've never, um. I've never actually had sex before."

"Oh. Seriously?"

"Yeah, I mean . . . I don't know. I know we're . . . I don't know. I just wanted you to know that, okay?"

Sam stopped dead beneath the orange glow of a street-lamp and stared at her. "Fuck."

"W-what?"

"You're not in love with me now, are you?"

"No."

"Good. 'Cause even if I were gay, I would totally fuck your life up."

Gilly snorted. "No, you wouldn't."

"Hell yeah, I would. I do it to everybody. Their lives are

great, then I come along, start trouble, and totally fuck everything up."

"Well, my life needs a little more trouble, so I like you."

"Ah . . ." Sam squeezed Gilly in a tight, drunken hug. "Let's dance."

Before Gilly could say anything, Sam started spinning her, mimicking waltzes she'd seen on TV. Everything fell still around them. The earth held its breath watching two girls giggle, twirl, and step on each other's feet.

Time stopped. The sun would never rise. The tattered, petty daylight world would never come. Gilly was certain she and Sam could dance through that glory-filled night forever.

TWENTY-FOUR

Ah, Faustus,
Now hast thou but one bare hour to live,
And then thou must be damn'd perpetually.
Stand still, you ever-moving spheres of heaven,
That time may cease, and midnight never come;
Fair nature's eye, rise, rise again, and make
Perpetual day; or let this hour be but
A year, a month, a week, a natural day,
That Faustus may repent and save his soul.
O slowly, slowly run, horses of the night!
                                    —*Doctor Faustus,* Act V, Scene 2

Gilly didn't remember her trip deeper into the city except that time and stations sped and crawled by at once. The other passengers around her weren't real. Their words sounded muffled. Only the dull burning in her eye convinced her she was awake.

Gilly's reflection stared at her from the dark window. Blood and tears baptized the side of her face from cheek to chin. Strands of strawberry-blond hair stuck to the gore. When she forced her eyelid open, she couldn't see anything except bright bubbles of color. She'd lost her left eye. That knowledge seemed distant and unimportant.

Gilly pulled two scraps of paper out of her pocket. With careful, shaking fingers, she unfolded the most precious artifacts in the world.

United States Passport. Gillian Stahl.

Using the borrowed pen, Gilly drew a line through her name. Above it she wrote, *Samantha Grace*.

At the Bayswater Station, Gilly got off the train and stepped out into the cold, clean sunlight of the November morning. Music played. Car engines grumbled. Voices in English, Sufi, and French rose and fell around her. Gilly stalked through the babble unmoved.

The Hotel Constantinople came into view. Gilly tried using her sleeve to wipe away the encrusted gore on her face, but it didn't help. As she pushed open the glass doors, conversations cut off mid-word. People stopped and stared. She glared back, hackles raised, silently daring any of them to get in her way. Then Gilly noticed one man with the exact opposite reaction as everybody else.

He sat in a leather chair near the front desk. He glanced up at her for a second and, his face blank beneath a day's worth of stubble, went back to reading his newspaper.

He was a cop. Gilly's steps halted slightly, but she caught it and forced herself to keep walking. She'd already sprung the trap. If she bolted now, he'd catch her. Turning the corner, Gilly saw a pair of Coke machines standing opposite the two elevators. Checking over her shoulder, she ducked behind them.

The facts came to Gilly as calmly as she might note the weather. Plainclothesmen had probably staked out the lobby since yesterday. Had they already grabbed Sam? No. They wanted both of them and didn't know about the fight. Sam had walked past them that morning. They'd been downstairs when Gilly had called her. Patient, professional hunters, they'd sat still and waited for either Gilly to show up or Sam to lead them to her. Now the cops were giving Gilly time to go to the room. Then they'd come through the door—Gilly and Sam together with nowhere to run.

She didn't panic. She wasn't scared. She didn't need Meek. She didn't need Sam or the Witches' Carnival. She'd spent seven full days outsmarting everything polite society could rally against her. Ten more minutes would be easy. She just needed a plan.

The hall branched off to her right, leading to the fitness center and pool. A door at the end of the corridor was marked with a large white-on-blue exclamation point and the legend FIRE DOOR. KEEP CLEAR. Maybe she could pound up six flights of stairs quicker than the elevator, but not by enough. Gilly turned her attention to the elevators.

A man walked up and let his four- or five-year-old son push the call button.

If Gilly smashed the control panel somehow, the cops couldn't use it, but they'd figure it out in a matter of seconds and be on her heels up the stairs.

One of the elevators opened with a soft *bing*. The man and little boy stepped inside. Gilly thought about dashing in, riding up to the second floor, pulling the emergency stop, and breaking it off. That would disable one elevator but not both, and she still had the stairs to worry about.

Gilly watched the light above the brushed aluminum doors blink from L to 1.

The plan came to her all at once, as if she were reading instructions from a book. Smiling, Gilly flattened herself against the Coke machine's warm, humming metal. Her pulse pounded against her temples.

The cop she'd spotted and his partner walked up to the elevators. Badges hung around both their necks. Pushing the button, they stood and waited. The one Gilly hadn't seen, a heavyset man in dull clothes, held a two-way radio.

"Signal five. Going up now."

"Ten-four, sig-five. Going up. Be careful. The Americans said these two've got wings."

The plainclothesman chuckled. "Ten-four. I got my trainers on."

Sweat trickled into Gilly's dead eye, sharpening dull pain into a white-hot burn. One suspicious glance would reveal her behind the vending machine. She didn't move. She didn't breathe. She prayed no one would come from the other direction and ask what she was doing. If anybody did, she'd make a dash for the stairs. Maybe both the cops had bad knees.

The elevator doors opened. The detectives stepped inside, and Gilly slipped out of hiding with smooth, unhesitating motion. When the two cops turned around, they had a clear view of the Coke machines. Gilly stood against the other elevator, out of sight again.

She listened to their conversation full of jargon and as many numbers as words. The doors shut, and their voices faded away. A dozen reasons why this wouldn't work suddenly came to mind, but she couldn't do anything now except try.

The light above the cops' elevator moved from L to 1. Gilly jammed her fingers between the doors and strained. She pulled them wide enough apart to fit her hands inside, then enough to wedge her shoulder against one.

The other elevator opened, and two women stepped out gossiping. They stared at Gilly for a second before one of them managed to speak.

"What are you doing?"

Gilly ignored her. She heard metal snap, and one of the doors telescoped into the wall.

"Stop that!–Go get someone, Linda!"

The bottom of the shaft was two feet lower than the hallway floor. Gilly stepped down inside. She had no clue what would be there but prayed for something breakable. Guiderails ran along the walls, and a huge spring was bolted to the concrete, a last–ditch shock–absorber if the elevator fell. Two roller chains, like extra–large bicycle chains, rose through a gap between the elevators. One stood motionless while the other worked link–by–link through a flywheel bolted to the shaft's steel support structure.

Gilly tugged on the moving chain; the car continued creeping toward the sixth floor. The woman shrieked. "You're going to kill somebody!"

"Shut up! Relax." Gilly patted her pockets, looking for something useful. "They have all kinds of safety stuff," she said with confidence. She didn't actually know, but her hope depended on fail–safes and redundancy systems stopping the car if she did even minor damage.

The woman remained unconvinced. She stood at the edge of the shaft, screaming for help.

Gilly was about to pull off her shoe when she glanced up at the lady. With a happy yelp, she snatched the woman's purse off her arm. The bag was heavy and made from calf-skin. Gilly fed it into the flywheel.

Sprocket teeth chewed into leather. Makeup and a package of tissues bulged out. Gilly squeezed her eyes shut, ready for everything she'd assumed to turn out wrong and the elevator car to thunder down on top of her. Instead, the chain ground to a halt. An alarm clattered to life.

Gilly could see the doors leading to each floor. The elevator had stopped between the fourth and fifth floors.

The woman's friend came back. Charging ahead of her was the desk clerk.

"Whoa! What do you think you're doing?"

"She's got my purse."

Gilly climbed out of the shaft, her clothes streaked with grease. The clerk grabbed her arm. Everybody clamored at once.

"Did she hurt anyone?"

"Jaimi, call the police," the clerk shouted to a girl behind him.

"She jammed my purse in that machine. I tried stopping her."

"The fire department too, Jaimi."

The clerk was a bony man wearing a dark suit. Gilly let him clutch her arm until she'd climbed all the way out of the inky shadows. Then, without a word, she turned to look at him dead on, opening her left eye as wide as she could.

"Holy sh–" The clerk flinched, loosening his grip on her arm. The ruined orb glistened scarlet. Shimmering, almost luminescent jelly clotted the lower rim of the girl's eye socket.

Gilly glanced around. A small crowd gathered. Down in the shaft, each second had stretched for hours. Back in the golden-lit hotel, so little time had passed that the other elevator still stood open from when the two women had come down.

Gilly stepped inside and pushed the button for the sixth floor. Nobody moved to stop her. As the doors closed, Gilly smirked at their gaping faces and flipped them off.

Listening to the alarm bell the whole way up, she hoped neither of the police officers needed regular insulin injections or anything.

The elevator reached the sixth floor. Gilly pulled the emergency stop, and a second alarm wailed. Pounding down the carpeted hall, using her key card to unlock the door, she opened it as far as the security latch let her. Through the gap, she saw Sam pacing and smoking a cigarette. When the door banged open, she whirled around.

"Sam, it's me."

Sam stared at her in openmouthed disbelief. "What the–"

"Open the damn door. The police are–"

Sam was too angry to hear. "Fuck you, bitch. I don't have shit to do with you anymore!"

Gilly stepped back and kicked the door with the flat of her foot. It took two solid kicks to wrench screws out of the jamb and send the security latch flying. As Gilly came through, Sam jumped back.

"What the fuck happened to your eye?"

"We have to go, Sam. The cops are here."

"Where?"

"Here. I trapped them in the elevator."

"Is that how you hurt your eye?"

"No. I smashed up a phone. Don't worry about it; I'm fine. We have to go."

"We can't. The money's gone. Our passports are junk. They're onto us, Gilly. We can't go anywhere."

"One of us can. You can." She handed the ticket and passport to Sam. A sharp stab of fear and all the things lost pierced Gilly's chest. "You have to go, okay? There's, like, no time."

Sam stared at the passport, her name written above Gilly's in a shaky hand. "Wait. Why do you think I'm going to ditch you like you ditched me? I'm not like that."

"I know, Sam. I know you love me, but you don't need me."

"Yes, I do." Sam's voice trembled. "Gilly, I need you all the time."

"Not like I needed you." Gilly shook her head. "Never as much as I needed you."

• • •

They were trapped in the lift with a Chinese delivery boy stinking of pot. Once the car had jolted to a halt, he backed into the corner and tried to remain inconspicuous.

Alan had already advised command of the situation. He could hear laughter in the background as they told him to stand by; if he and Neil weren't out in a few minutes, they'd send uniformed police to execute the arrest warrant.

"You know they're loving this," he grumbled.

Neil shrugged. "At least the power didn't go out." He tried cutting off the alarm by pushing and pulling the emergency stop, then started stabbing random buttons on the control panel.

Alan was getting edgy. With nothing else to do, he grabbed the emergency phone again. It rang once before somebody at the front desk picked up. "Hello? Is everything okay up there?"

"No. We're caught in the lift."

"Yes, sir. We already have people working on it. Just try to stay calm and we'll have you out as soon as we can. And I'm sure you're upset with us right now, sir, and you have every right to be. But management is committed to doing every-thing possible to make this up to you."

Alan sighed. "We aren't guests. My partner and I are spe-cial branch detectives. We're in the middle of arresting some bad people, so is there any way you could hurry this along?"

"You're policemen?"

Alan gave his badge number.

"Well, Officer. Um, it's going to be awhile. Half an hour or so," the clerk said, dropping the company-speak. "Some crazy girl jammed the governor wheel, and the technician needs to come and reset the computer before it'll run again. We've already called them and–"

Alan blurted in. "A girl? How old?"

"I don't know. Seventeen, eighteen? Why?"

Alan didn't answer. He started spitting out cuss words and kicking the wall. Dropping the phone, he grabbed his radio.

"Signal five to command. Signal five. The suspects jammed the lift. They spotted us and are probably ten-eighteen right now."

Howling laughter crackled through the radio. "Ten-four, signal five." The dispatcher paused to choke back a chuckle. "Sending available units in pursuit."

"You ate lunch?" As Gilly dug through her pockets for pound notes, she stared at the remains of a cheeseburger and fries.

"Last meal," Sam said, pulling on her coat. A cigarette dangled from the corner of her mouth.

"Okay, there's, I don't know, like, sixty pounds here." She shoved the money into Sam's hand. "You have the ticket and passport?"

"Yeah." Sam stuffed the napkins deep into her pocket.

"Okay. Let's go."

They rushed out of the room and down the hall. Sam started for the elevators, but Gilly grabbed her sleeve. "Stairs. We need the stairs."

Pushing the fire door open, they hurtled down flight after flight. In contrast to the posh hotel, the stairs were bare concrete. Thick dust lay everywhere.

"Okay, listen. When you get to Zurich, find the Glänsande Lac chalet. Remember that name, okay? Even if they aren't there yet, just keep your head down and hope they show up."

"Got it. Glänsande Lac. Glänsande Lac."

"There's a subway line that goes straight to the airport. That'll probably be the quickest way, but the police might be watching it, so whatever you do, just be careful, okay?"

"Are you sure about–"

"I'm sure."

They reached the bottom of the stairs. Shoving another fire door open, Gilly and Sam stepped out into brilliant sunlight falling across a back street. They ran past the hotel's emptied pool. Sirens wailed close by. Hungry, exhausted, and hurt, part of Gilly felt relieved it was almost over.

"Listen . . ." She had a thousand things she needed to tell Sam: I'm sorry. I love you. Thank you. God bless you. Good luck. Tell Maggie I miss her already. I miss you already. A thousand things to say and no time at all. "Listen. You have to leave everything behind. Everything, including me. If you worry about me, you're going to stumble and lose them just like I did."

Sam's eyes shined with fresh tears. "Gilly . . . I . . ."

"Swear you'll leave me behind, swear you won't worry about me, and I swear to God I'll be okay. No matter what happens, I'll be okay."

Choking on her words, Sam nodded.

"Police! Don't move!"

They snapped around. A squad car had crept up on them, its lights and siren cut off. Two uniformed officers climbed out, a blond woman and a crew-cut man. They started forward with cautious steps. "Get down on the ground and put your hands behind your head," the woman bellowed.

Gilly watched the cops. From the side of her mouth, she whispered, "Ready?"

Sam thumped her cigarette to the pavement. "Yeah."

"Come on, ladies, it's over," the man said. "You hear the sirens. There's no point running, so why bother?"

Gilly laughed. He'd accidentally asked the ultimate question.

"Why the fuck not?" They whirled around, making a dash for the traffic rushing along Bayswater Road. Gilly heard the cops charging after them, the jangle of their duty belts and their breaths coming in hard pants. She glanced at Sam. Dark hair flying behind her and that mad smile, she looked like a feral angel. That had been Gilly's first memory of Sam, and it would become her last.

They'd almost reached the busy road. The police were right behind them. Gilly spun on her heel and barreled into the cops. As the man grabbed Gilly, Gilly grabbed the woman's uniform. Momentum sent all three of them pinwheeling to the ground. Gilly's head cracked against concrete, but she held on as tight as she could.

"Let go! Let go, or I'll break your damn arm!" the male officer yelled in Gilly's face. The woman pressed down on the pressure point between her thumb and forefinger. Gilly screamed. It hurt like hell, but she wouldn't loosen her grip.

A few more seconds of scuffling and the woman managed to tear Gilly's fingers free, ripping two buttons off in the process. They slammed her hard onto her stomach. Gilly felt handcuffs snap around her wrists and heard the woman shout into her shoulder mike, "Three Zed Eight to dispatch. We have one suspect in custody. One suspect in custody. One more ten-eighteen on foot."

She gave a description of Sam and which way she was headed, but Gilly just laughed. Sam would be part of the Witches' Carnival by nightfall. Gilly knew it, and as they led her to the squad car, joy burst up from her throat in glorious, off-key singing.

"Sorta, kinda feels like flying. Or maybe we're just falling. Who cares–we're hauling. Raise hell and a back beat! We're running! We're running! We're running!"

TWENTY-FIVE

Gilly's joie de vivre didn't last long. Neither cop spoke during the ride through London's noontime streets. When the glowering precinct house came into view, Gilly was scared, cowed down in the squad car's hard plastic backseat.

They took her inside and sat her, still handcuffed, at a desk in a hallway. Uniformed cops, people in T-shirts and people in suits walked past. Gilly glanced up at a pair of prisoners in stained orange jumpsuits. One flashed a snaggletoothed smile and blew her a kiss. She lowered her gaze to her lap, telling the custody sergeant her name, date of birth, and address.

"That's in America, right?"

"Yeah."

He asked her about her eye. How had she hurt it? When?

How bad did she think it was? Gilly told the truth, figuring whatever trouble she'd get into for smashing a pay phone was the least of her problems. He typed out a statement saying Gilly had sustained the injury prior to her arrest and had her sign it.

After mug shots and fingerprints, the sergeant led Gilly into a busy room full of desks and filing cabinets. Gilly sat mute for close to an hour while the cops went back and forth on whether they should take her to the hospital or if they had to wait until special branch arrived.

"Bloody hell, I'll take her," one officer finally groaned. He walked over and took Gilly by the arm. "Special probably got stuck in another lift on the way over. Come on, let's get your eye looked at."

More waiting. First in the ER corridor, then in a darkened room set aside for eye injuries. A nurse came in shadowed by a nursing student. As Gilly leaned back in something like a dentist's chair, they shined a bright lamp in her eye and prodded at it with gloved fingers until Gilly yelped.

The doctor came in, poked at her eye some more, and told the officer that she needed an operation.

Everyone talked about her instead of to her. What was wrong with her eye. Security precautions in case she tried to run. The cop didn't know if the American Embassy had been told she was in custody. He didn't know whose job it was to tell them.

Numbness settled over Gilly, and she was eager for it. She didn't want to think because she couldn't think about anything except how much trouble she was in. Years in prison. Gilly could only grasp it as an abstract, not her real future. She didn't want to feel because all she could feel was fear and chasm–deep loneliness.

Sitting as still and quiet as possible, Gilly tried to become a thing, a piece of furniture to be moved from place to place but mostly ignored. The police and hospital staff were happy to oblige.

Gilly had never had surgery before. That alone was terrifying. After drawing some blood and sticking an IV in the back of her hand, they wheeled Gilly into a room full of alien-limbed machines and people in green gowns. Someone held a breathing mask over her face. A courteous voice, the hiss of cold gas, and Gilly slipped through a long, colorless gap in time. When she woke up, deep evening glowed through the venetian blinds. The only light in the room was the flickering blue of a TV turned down low. She lay between warm sheets with a thick blanket pulled to her chin.

For a few drifting seconds, Gilly thought she was in her bed at home. Her eye itched. Gilly raised her hand to rub it and jerked upright when she discovered her wrist hand-cuffed to the bed rail.

She didn't know where she was. Panicked gasps escaped her throat as hoarse rattles. A policewoman sat beside the bed watching TV. Grumbling, "Look who's awake," she walked out the door.

Casting her gaze around the sparse hospital room, Gilly started to remember. She toyed with the handcuff keeping her from escaping. Her free hand touched the gauze bandage taped over her eye.

The light and motion of the TV drew her groggy attention. It was the evening news. The big story was the ravens flying off from the Tower of London earlier that day.

"Good morning, Gillian. How are you doing?" A nurse with an accent Gilly couldn't place walked in, followed by the cop.

"Okay." Her throat felt scraped clean. It hurt to talk.

"Do you remember you had surgery?"

Gilly nodded. The nurse paused for a beat, waiting for her to ask how the operation had gone. Gilly didn't bother.

"We talked to your mum."

"Oh, no." Gilly looked up. "No, no, she hates me."

"She doesn't hate you. No, she's thankful you're all right."

Gilly sniffed back tears and didn't say anything else.

Stooping down, the nurse brushed a lock of hair away from Gilly's face. "Look at me, Gillian. Everyone's just happy you're safe. They've been worried sick about you. Everything's going to be all right."

"No, it's not! I'm going to jail. I put my dad in jail. It's not going to be fucking all right!"

"Watch your language," the cop snapped.

"Don't worry about all that right now," the nurse said. "Just concentrate on feeling better." She straightened the bedclothes around Gilly and stroked her cheek. The small acts of tenderness made Gilly profoundly grateful, but she still couldn't bring herself to answer.

"I'm going to get you a dinner plate. You need to eat some–"

"Wh–what the hell?" the policewoman sputtered. "That's you!"

Gilly and the nurse looked up, following the cop's stare to the TV. Security camera footage played, showing the ravens escaping the Tower. At the bottom of the screen, Gilly watched herself stand up from the bench and walk off-camera with Meek.

The cop went to call her commanding officer. The nurse brought Gilly a microwaved dinner tray. Even though Gilly hadn't eaten in more than a full day, she was too frightened to be hungry. After a few bites of breaded fish sticks, Gilly laid her head on the pillow and let painkillers carry her down into sleep. She dreamed about Sam and the Witches' Carnival.

Late the next morning, a doctor told Gilly she'd lost her eye. In the hours after she'd busted the pay phone, the glass shard had chewed across her retina, finally slicing into a bundle of nerves.

"There was just too much damage. If you'd come here immediately after, maybe."

Gilly nodded, staring out the window. "Yeah. Maybe." But she'd known the eye was gone the instant the glass pierced it.

Gilly was under a twenty-four-hour guard. The doctor wrote out an antibiotic prescription for her and gave it to the cop watching her. A post-op nurse came to replace the blood-clotted foam inside her eye socket.

People who didn't fit into the hospital's rhythm had hovered around the nurses' station all morning. Gilly recognized the casual wariness in the way they walked. When they spoke to one another, instead of meeting eye-to-eye, they stood looking over their shoulder. They acted like her dad.

After the hospital discharged her, the interrogations began. The police handed her over to two men in ugly suits along with a folder full of paperwork.

"Gillian, we're with the Security Service."

"Oh. Security for who?"

"The National Security Service. We're like the FBI."

"Oh."

It turned out that the Tower ravens officially belonged to the queen.

They took Gilly to a sprawling building on the waterfront, a gleaming palace turned dark with state secrets and special dossiers. They grilled her for hours. Why was she in England? Why'd she gone to the Tower? Who was the man she'd been talking to? Why didn't she want to help herself?

"You expect us to believe that, while special branch is on your tail, you just decide to visit the Tower of London? Then, at that same time that you're there, the ravens just happen to fly off?"

Gilly sat in a metal chair bolted to the floor. She hugged her belly in a posture of defense but not defiance. "Lots of people were there."

"But none of them bought fake passports to get there, did they?"

"I didn't get the passport to go to the Tower. I just went to the Tower once I was here."

"That's right. You bought a fake passport, committed a felony, so you could chase some girl you met in Atlanta."

"Yes."

"She must have been some girl. I mean, I know people who've done stupid things for love, but she must've been bloody gorgeous."

Gilly stared at the floor. "I liked her," she whispered.

"Come on, Gilly. Why don't you want to help yourself?"

And they started through it again.

Gilly confessed everything she thought they'd believe. She didn't mention the Witches' Carnival or Meek's omnipresence. Because they'd never seen the curve of Maggie's bare throat or felt the warmth of her hand taking theirs, they didn't buy a word of it.

The inspectors picked at Gilly searching for more. They threatened, cajoled, assured Gilly that they could help her and swore she'd never see daylight again. In the end, after hours of the same questions over and over, Gilly didn't offer them anything new.

With a final epitaph that she could have saved herself if only she'd talked, they shipped her across the river to an immigration detention facility. Guards told Gilly to take off her clothes and handed her a pair of thin pajamas like hospital scrubs. She wasn't allowed to keep anything of her own except her sneakers.

They put her in a stifling hot jail barrack with steel bunks lining the wall. All the other detainees were grown-ups. They stared at the ceiling and their own hands. Mumbling back and forth, their foreign words didn't mask the doldrums in their voices.

One woman asked Gilly where she was from. It took three tries for Gilly to understand the question through the woman's jagged English. When she finally answered, other women turned, staring at her with looks ranging from incredulity to open anger. Americans didn't try to sneak into other places. It worked the other way around.

After that, nobody had much to say to her. Gilly climbed

onto a top bunk and lay down, her arm over her eyes to block out the light.

For days, Gilly was moved back and forth between the overcrowded cell and interview rooms. She told her edited version of the story to so many people from so many different agencies that their faces and threats blurred together.

The Home Office wanted to know what she was doing in England. An internal investigator with London's metro police wanted to know how she'd trapped two cops in an elevator. The only person who made Gilly cry was a nebbishy man from the U.S. consulate who, after three hours of insisting they'd been Sam's friends and she didn't know their names, made Gilly sign an affidavit that Vic and Paul had made the passports for her.

Special branch found Peter's phone number among the clutter in the hotel room, traced it back to a mysterious corpse that had turned up at the Battersea Power Station, and a pair of homicide inspectors paid Gilly a visit.

"How do you know Peter Spiegelman?"

"I don't, really. I just knew some people he was staying with."

"And where are they?"

"I don't know. Gone."

"Gone where?"

"I don't know!"

She let it slip that Peter dealt mescaline, and the interrogations started all over. This time, everyone dangled drug–smuggling charges over Gilly's head like the sword of Damocles.

"This isn't a game, Miss Stahl. We're going to figure out what's going on. Do you understand?"

"I've already told you everything that's going on."

"Listen to me. We're going to catch up with Samantha and your other friends soon. They already cut you loose once. You don't think they'll do it again to cover their own asses? You need to help yourself now before one of them gives us a better offer, because honestly, everybody's sick of your bullshit."

But no matter how tantalizing the pieces were, no one could fit them into a larger picture. The worst any authority in England could charge Gilly with was obstructing a constable in the exercise of his duty, a summary offense and, especially since she was a minor, a complete waste of time. Meanwhile, the Home Office was getting pressure from America to extradite her. Finally they stepped in, and after going to the tiny jailhouse infirmary to take her antibiotics, a guard told Gilly she'd be flown back to America the next morning.

The guards moved her to a cell set aside for detainees about to be transferred. It didn't have bars, just cinder–block walls and a metal door without a window. Two bunk beds, thin mattresses stripped bare, filled most of the space. Gilly was the only prisoner.

Through the door, she could hear gates clang and guards talk back and forth over their radios. Gilly used the toilet; then, with nothing else to do, she paced around until she spotted mouse droppings in the corner. Gilly lay down, tucking her hands between her knees.

It had been six endless days now, and the police were still pressing Gilly to tell them where Sam was. None of them even knew enough to mention Zurich. As far as they could tell, Sam had simply dematerialized. That meant she'd made it. Sam had joined the Witches' Carnival.

The knowledge filled Gilly with a brittle sense of nobility. Sam was okay. She'd escaped. Gilly didn't regret her choice. But she was still scared, wondering what would happen to her now.

Through the torpid hours stretching between interrogations, a daydream danced in front of her. The Witches' Carnival would come bursting through the door. Alarms blared. Guards shouted. Sometimes it was Maggie and sometimes it was a laughing Sam who grabbed Gilly's hand and spirited her away.

It didn't work like that, though. Gilly had made Sam swear to leave her behind, and she had.

Gilly had also promised Sam that whatever happened, she could face it. That promise had been the one thing giving Sam the strength to never look back and join the Carnival, and Gilly was determined to keep it. Sam had thought she was brave. So had Maggie. Gilly clung to that with white knuckles, telling herself again and again that she could survive this. But staring at her cell wall, alone and forgotten, Gilly couldn't help imagining the white nights over Saint Petersburg and spring in Okinawa.

TWENTY-SIX

The Thomas Jefferson Reception Room, with its eighteenth-century furniture and view overlooking the Washington Mall, was more ceremonial than anything, where the secretary of state received presidents, kings, and dictators. She did her real work in a cluttered office down the hall, buried under paperwork and Post-It notes. She'd prefer to be there now, but an aide had come in saying someone had dropped by to talk about the Stahl case.

The secretary exploded, demanding to know how anyone just "dropped by" to talk to her about anything. Finding the Stahl report under a stack of files, she rushed off to welcome her guest, fixing a beaming smile on her face.

A rail-thin man sat in one of the Penn armchairs by the window.

"Good morning, Mister . . ."

"Meek," he said, flashing a toothy grin and standing up as the secretary walked in.

"Of course. Mr. Meek. Good morning." The secretary of state sized the man up with a handshake and a glance. Neither his bent back nor the eye clouded by cataracts diminished the air of dignity Mr. Meek carried. The two-thousand-dollar Gianluca Isaia suit didn't hurt either.

Gripping his hand, the secretary noted thick calluses earned from years of manual labor. It felt markedly different from the handshakes of the lawyers and politicians she met with day in, day out, and somehow made her resign herself to being the lesser of the two people in the room.

"Please have a seat. Would you like some coffee or anything to drink?"

"Thank you, but no. I'll try to take up as little of your time as possible."

"I appreciate the consideration." She sat down in the other armchair. "So what can I do for you today?"

"I'm sure you've been assessed of the case your department is building against Miss Gillian Stahl."

"Yes. I haven't had time for a thorough review, but I've been advised of it several times. Are you acting as her attorney?"

"Not officially. I'm an acquaintance of Gilly's."

The secretary nodded. She knew where this was headed.

"Well sir, if you'd like to say something on her behalf, I'm happy to listen, but the fact is, she's confessed to a serious felony."

"Very serious. I agree with you absolutely."

"I'm glad. And you understand that in this day and age, we can't afford to treat any breeches in national security lightly."

"Certainly. Which is why I'm curious about what your response will be."

"Response to what?"

"To the reporter who asks how two high school kids went joyriding on bogus passports."

"Well, I–"

"Despite the fact that they didn't have those little microchips that were supposed to make passports fraud-proof."

"Now, no one has claimed–"

"And that nobody in your department would have ever realized any of this except for pure dumb luck."

"Mister–"

"Plus the fact that you don't have any clue how many other passports are out there in the hands of individuals with more nefarious intentions than Miss Stahl and Miss Grace."

The secretary gathered herself behind a wide, empty smile. "I can assure you, and anyone who might ask, that we

are looking into the hows and whys of this. And any problems our investigation might–"

"They got them in less than twenty-four hours. Did you
know that?"

"No. But as I said–"

"For God's sake, they're both C students."

Another smile. "And what do you think we should do
with her, Mr. Meek?"

"Let her go."

"Let her go?"

The man spread his hands. "Free as a bird."

"Mr. Meek, she forged passports. She's already confessed
to it. There's no way Miss Stahl can walk away from this
with a slap on the wrist."

"Think about it, though." Mr. Meek leaned forward. "It's an
ongoing investigation, which means that so far, the details
haven't gotten past these four walls. But even if you let Gilly
plead to a lesser charge and avoid a trial, she can talk to the
press all she wants, once she's in jail. And Madame
Secretary, I know this girl; she's a talker. But what if you
gave her probation? Then it'd only be logical to attach a
condition that she can't tell anyone, including reporters, the
details of her crime. To keep anyone from copying her, of
course. But a side benefit would be no embarrassing questions for you or the president."

For a moment, the secretary relished how easy it would

be. Then she pushed the idea out of her mind. "Mr. Meek, I will not trade the safety of our country for political convenience."

"Yes, you will," the old man said. "You'll put it off awhile. Remind yourself of the duties of this venerable office. But then you'll once again accept that, doctorates be damned, your main qualification for this job is the ability to . . . how did your father say it? Eat a shit sandwich and keep grinning?"

The secretary stared at him, wondering how he knew what her dad had said years ago. She began flipping through the Stahl report, trying to hide the shaking in her hands. "Do you think so, Mr. Meek?"

"Oh, yes. All your gilt and glitter can only dazzle one of my eyes, Madame Secretary." He winked at her. "The other one sees you just fine."

A sharp screech made the secretary jump. A crow perched on the windowsill outside. It began beating its wings and pecking at the glass.

"And, as you can see, I have lots to do today, as I'm sure you do." Mr. Meek pushed himself stiffly to his feet. "Also, you'll want to offer similar deals to Vic Handler and Paul Greenfield. Have a nice day."

The secretary of state couldn't answer. She sat in her chair and stared. The old man smiled faintly, nodded, and turned to walk out.

TWENTY-SEVEN

Gilly stepped off the plane at the same Providence airport where she had left for England. The FBI agent escorting her led Gilly away from the bright streams of fellow travelers and through an unmarked door.

In the busy, hidden guts of the airport, among a clutch of strangers in suits and state trooper uniforms, Gilly saw her mom. Tears made her vision swim. She fought the urge to break away from the agent grasping her arm and run to her mom. She wanted to be held and babied and promised that everything would be okay.

Then Gilly noticed how pale and hollow-cheeked her mom looked, and she remembered that she'd gotten her dad arrested. Managing a soft "hey," Gilly stared at the floor, ashamed for making her mom see her in handcuffs, for putting her family through all this, for her hair being a mess, for being a royal fuckup.

"Gilly . . ." Her mom hugged her, squeezing her tight and saying her name over and over. "Gilly, Gilly, oh Gilly."

Gilly started to sob, burying her face in her mom's shoulder. "I'm sorry," she mewled.

After a minute of shuffling silence, one of the strangers introduced himself as Mr. Mosley, a lawyer her mom had hired. The federal prosecutor had offered Gilly three years' probation for the fake passports. Mr. Mosley beamed through the flurry of paper signing, telling her over and over what an amazing deal it was.

As soon as they were done, a Rhode Island state trooper put Gilly back in handcuffs. Her arraignment for stealing the squad car was that afternoon.

Gilly's mom started yelling. "Wait! She's only been home for ten minutes."

"It's cool, Mom. I'll see you in a little bit. I love you, okay?"

They took Gilly to the courthouse and put her in a holding cell for three hours. Nobody pretended that she hadn't done everything she was accused of, but Mr. Mosley came through again. Instead of pleading innocent or guilty, he asked that the trial be moved to family court. The judge scheduled another hearing for late December. When he banged his gavel, Gilly just stared. She knew she was lucky to have survived the whole thing. The realization that they were going to let her go home was bewildering. Once her mom posted bail, though, Gilly was free."

Her mom bought Gilly a T-shirt to replace her prison uniform. Apple green with white lettering, it read PROVIDENCE, RI. AMERICA'S MOST LIVABLE CITY. They set out for home that evening.

And that was it; the mad adventure ended.

Gilly started school on a Wednesday with a flesh-colored patch covering her empty eye socket. Nothing had changed. Alex and Dawn were still attached at the hip. The school halls still smelled of chemical cleaners and mildew. The same teachers droned on about the same subjects. Gilly needed to find Josh and try telling him all about his little sister. She kept putting it off; she had no idea what to say.

At school, a storm of rumors swirled around her. Whatever classroom Gilly stepped into, kids and teachers watched her with the same startled curiosity they might have for a bird who'd fluttered through one of the windows. Her friends, and people who'd never spoken to her before, kept asking what had happened. Gilly said she didn't want to talk about it and then that she wasn't allowed to.

Not able to tell anyone all the things she'd seen and done, Gilly felt them start to slip away. Meek and his crow, passports written on napkins, Christopher Marlowe. None of it fit with Gilly's day-to-day world. More and more, Gilly found herself killing time with Keith, Vic's younger brother, the one Sam had thought was Mormon. Maybe it was because he was gay too. Maybe it was because he was the only person who knew even a piece of what had happened.

"Vic got expelled from college," he told her one day. "Vic and his friend both."

"Oh. Sorry."

"Don't worry about it. He wasn't real happy there, anyway. He's going to try to stay in Providence, see if he can get a job at a studio or something."

"That's cool."

On Thanksgiving, with a lump in her stomach, Gilly went to visit her dad. The visiting room was frantic with chatter and running kids. Gilly's family sat around a folding table in the corner. Her dad smiled a lot and made nervous jokes as they ate turkey slices and green peas from plastic lunch trays. He told Gilly he loved her and that he'd prayed she'd come home safe. He acted like she'd been kidnapped, like none of it was her fault.

Gilly told him she loved him too. She promised to visit again as soon as she could.

A few days later it started to snow, a dusting of white that settled in the dead grass and in the crooks of trees. Gilly went to school, took tests, ran errands for her mom, and the world continued its stumbling march forward.

She had a surgery scheduled for the first day of Christmas break to get fitted with a glass eye. In the meantime, she had to clean the socket and swab it with antibacterial ointment twice a day.

Standing in front of the mirror, pulling her eyelid back with careful fingertips, Gilly thought of that hard, gray morning when she'd glimpsed who she really was. A girl who could steal cops' cars and trap them in elevators. A girl who could make the witch everyone loved fall in love with her. A girl who once had the world in her grasp and let it go to snatch a friend's hand. Now, staring at the red-raw hole in her face, Gilly knew she wasn't pretty, but she was beautiful, and Meek had paid his debt in full.

And in the bargain, he'd even gotten Sam home, far away from the cramped, angry house she'd shared with her mom and stepdad. He'd gotten her somewhere Samantha Grace truly belonged.

December came. One day, Gilly got a postcard in the mail. It was from Varanasi, India, a photo of the Ganges River at dusk. Temple steps led down into the earth-brown water. The city skyline rose in the background, an ancient palace nestled among miles of modern apartment blocks. On the back, Sam had written, *Thanks, G.*

Gilly took the postcard to her room and stared at it. Flipping it around, she traced her fingers across Sam's pen strokes. She tried to envision Sam set loose in India, and every scenario she imagined made her laugh. She wondered how the Carnival had wound up there, if they were still there or if they'd already moved on. Whatever city the Witches' Carnival filled with music tonight, for Gilly they'd returned to the province of daydream.

Gilly became so lost in the postcard, she jumped when her phone rang. It was Keith. He was going Christmas shopping and asked if she wanted to come along. Gilly said she'd meet him at the mall. Tucking the postcard into the bottom drawer of her dresser, beneath summer clothes, Gilly pulled on her coat and headed out.

Shoppers filled the Galleria with a bright, slightly haggard cheeriness. Gilly and Keith went from store to store on the hunt for the perfect watch for Keith's dad.

Keith didn't cuss unless he actually meant it, and Gilly started watching her own language around him. He didn't smoke, either, and while he sort of knew who PMS and Needles were, he couldn't name any of their songs. Gilly started thinking of him as the anti-Sam.

Still, he was fun to waste the evening with. As they window-shopped, he told snarky stories that didn't really go anywhere and bought a giant pretzel for them to share.

"Seriously, Gilly, I got it for both of us," he said after she'd had one bite and wouldn't take anymore.

"Seriously?"

"Yes. I love these things, but I can't eat all of it. The only reason I invited you was so you'd eat half."

Gilly laughed and tore off another piece of pretzel. She imagined Sam would've liked Keith if they'd ever hung out together.

They bumped into a boy and a girl Keith knew; he seemed to know everybody. All four of them continued on together. The conversation veered toward the politics of the Folsom High Marching Band and events Gilly hadn't been part of. She fell quiet, laughing at the jokes without really getting them, but glad for a chance to get out of the house, anyway.

They decided to leave the mall and head for the Waffle House. Stepping outside, the cold cut through their jackets sharp as a knife. Following her friends, a familiar voice made Gilly turn.

"Merry Christmas. God bless you. Merry Christmas."

Calling out against the hard wind, Meek rattled change in a Styrofoam cup, panhandling from the people coming in and out of the mall.

Gilly stopped. Keith and the others walked on without noticing. Meek's crow, perched on his shoulder, saw her first. Then Meek looked over. "Oh. Hello there."

Gilly kept her distance, letting Christmas shoppers pass between them. She didn't know anymore if Meek was a demon, an angel, or something Sunday school never prepared her to face. "You knew if I called Sam, I'd go back, didn't you?"

"You needed a nudge in the right direction, but I had faith." As a woman dropped a dollar into his cup, Meek turned. "Thank you, ma'am. God bless you. Have a merry Christmas."

She disappeared through the sliding-glass doors, and Meek looked back at Gilly. "Also, don't sweat that Rhode Island thing too much. I suspect your luck with the authorities will hold out a little longer."

He'd done something, but Gilly couldn't imagine what. She nodded. "Thanks."

"So? A little dented and dinged, but otherwise all right?"

"Yeah." Gilly shrugged, kicking at the icy pavement with the toe of her sneaker. "I think about them a lot. Think about Sam a whole lot."

Wondering about the Carnival filled Gilly with vague sadness, the loss of what might have been. But losing Sam felt like losing her eye, painful and certain.

Part of her brain refused to accept that Sam was gone. Passing one of their regular meet-up points in school, Gilly would start searching the crowd for her face. Sometimes she thought about calling Sam to see if she wanted to do anything. Once she'd had the phone in her hand before she remembered.

"Gilly, every flower has to risk leaving the safety of its seed to blossom. Christ knows, you're a late bloomer, but you're doing great so far."

"Yeah, I know," Gilly whispered. "It's just, I was Sam's tagalong for, like, two years, you know? And I wasn't even that happy being that, but after two years, I'm really not sure how to be anything else."

Meek chuckled at her. "Be seventeen, Gilly. Nobody expects you to have all the answers right away. But pretty soon you'll think of somewhere you want to go, somewhere even better than the Witches' Carnival. And when you do? You're gonna know they don't have much left to throw at you."

"Yeah, you're right."

"How about you start small? That Ashley Brown still pick on you?"

"No," Gilly snorted. "She's kind of afraid of me now."

"Good. Tomorrow, figure out who's the new person she picks on. The person she does everything she can to convince they're worthless. But this time you swoop in out of nowhere. This time you be the beautiful one."

An unclouded smile spread across Gilly's face. "Thanks, Meek."

"Sometimes you have to raise a little hell to see what you're made of, Gilly. Sometimes it takes a scrape or two." He motioned to his own blind eye. Gilly touched the patch covering her empty socket. "Just never forget what you saw. You'll burn the world down yet."

He started walking away. Gilly watched him shuffle down

the sidewalk, rattling his change cup. "Merry Christmas. Merry Christmas. God bless you, sir. Merry Christmas to you, too."

Turning to leave, Gilly almost smacked into Keith.

"Hey, where'd you go?"

"Sorry." Gilly glanced back at Meek. "I was just talking to somebody."

"Oh. You still want to come eat with us?"

"Yeah. I'm starving."

"Me too." They started walking between the rows of cars. Keith went on. "I won't eat in this food court, though. Once I saw a huge cockroach in there."

"When I was in jail there was—"

"Oh God, don't gross me out right before I eat."

Gilly laughed. Craning her neck, she watched snow dance past the security lights. She wondered where she'd go.

ABOUT THE AUTHOR

Kristopher Reisz lives in Athens, Alabama. After working as a short-order cook and paramedic, he began studying English at Calhoun College. This is his first novel.

A new novel inspired by the explosion of prescription drug abuse among teens

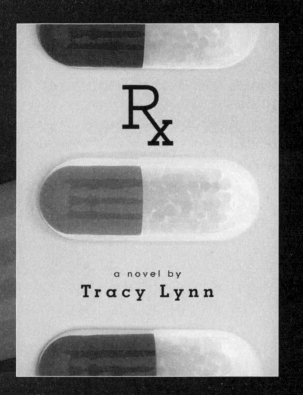

a novel by
Tracy Lynn

GPA, SATs, student council . . .
class superstar Thyme Gilcrest is
dealing with the stress—**by dealing.**

From Simon Pulse
Published by Simon & Schuster